D0031424

From the reviews of *Strange Energy*:

'A wonderful second novel in this magical and dystopian fantasy. The themes and characters develop fully and the narrative is tense and pacey. It's both challenging and exciting, and it's highly recommended by Bookbag'
www.thebookbag.co.uk

'A brisk event-filled fantasy'
www.sci-fi-online.com

'Fast paced inventive writing with original plot involving strange creatures and weird science, it's guarenteed to satisfy the hunger of voracious readers everywhere'
www.lovereading.co.uk

'Older readers will be gripped by this gritty, urban, fantasy adventure'
TBK

'A fast-moving, inventive story'
www.totalscifionline.com

'This is turning out to be a fascinating series. The world created in this novel feels very real and it's easy to visualise all the scenes'
Flipside

Also in this series . . .

1: *Twisted Symmetry*

Look out for . . .

3: *Blood Alchemy*

Visit . . .

www.thebadtuesdays.co.uk

THE BAD TUESDAYS:

STRANGE ENERGY

Benjamin J. Myers

N'APPARTIENT PLUS
À LA BIBLIOTHÈQUE
MUNICIPALE DE GATINEAU

Orion
Children's Books

First published in Great Britain in 2009
by Orion Children's Books
Reissued 2010 by Orion Children's Books
a division of the Orion Publishing Group Ltd
Orion House
5 Upper St Martin's Lane
London WC2H 9EA
An Hachette UK company

3 5 7 9 10 8 6 4 2

Copyright © Benjamin J. Myers 2009

The right of Benjamin J. Myers to be identified as the
author of this work has been asserted.

All rights reserved. No part of this publication may be
reproduced, stored in a retrieval system, or transmitted, in
any form or by any means, electronic, mechanical,
photocopying, recording or otherwise, without the prior
permission of Orion Children's Books.

A catalogue record for this book
is available from the British Library.

ISBN 978 1 84255 640 5

Typeset by Input Data Services Ltd
Bridgwater, Somerset

Printed in Great Britain by
Clays Ltd, St Ives plc

The Orion Publishing Group's policy is to use papers that
are natural, renewable and recyclable products made from
wood grown in sustainable forests. The logging and
manufacturing processes are expected to conform to
the environmental regulations of the country of origin.

www.orionbooks.co.uk

For Eleanor, Rosamond and Rebecca

CHAPTER 1

The razor wire gleamed along the top of the fence. Splinter's eyes narrowed in the darkness as the cold air whipped his face. They would have only seconds to leap from the freight train to the flat roof on the other side of the jagged mesh.

'When I say "Go",' he shouted, 'we jump.'

He crouched on the top of the container, his tatty trousers and long-tailed morning coat blacker than the night, white hair spiky and hanging down to his shoulders.

Chess Tuesday crouched beside him, tugging coils of her thick, chestnut hair away from her face. Next to her squatted Box, knuckles resting against the rusty top of the container, a crowbar in his hands.

'You're sure the codes will work?' he yelled.

'No,' replied Splinter, steadying himself as the train picked up speed and the container rocked slightly.

'What's the point of breaking in if the codes don't work?' shouted Box.

They were nearly at the wire. Splinter switched his ice blue eyes from the razors to Box. 'It's called an "opportunity", fly head.'

Box shook his head. 'An opportunity to end up in the . . .'

'Go,' screamed Splinter and he sprang from the train.

Chess drove her thighs up and dived. She did so without thinking, acting only on her brother's command. She arched her belly and swung her heels backwards so that she tumbled through the air, feeling the razors graze her baggy, purple pullover. She landed on the roof with a roll, finishing neatly on her bare feet. She brushed dry grit from her grime-encrusted, torn jeans and picked a tiny stone out of the palm of her hand.

Chess thought nothing of what might have happened if she had floundered onto the sharp, steel blades. She was a street rat. Climbing, jumping, hiding and stealing were all she had ever done. That was how things were: Splinter was always telling her that, telling her to forget about everything else; forget about Ethel, forget about the Committee, forget about the Twisted Symmetry. She was a street rat, she was his little sister, she was eleven and her brothers were fourteen and he, Splinter, was in charge. That was all that mattered.

Box collided with her back and she crashed forwards into Splinter, knocking his legs away so that they fell on top of each other. She tried to avoid landing on him by turning on her side and hitting the roof shoulder first. A bolt of pain jarred her arm.

The crowbar clattered on the roof but the ringing metal was lost beneath the clanking of the freight train.

'Fly head, you moron,' hissed Splinter.

But Chess's large brown eyes turned on Splinter. They didn't have to be here, like this. They didn't have to be thieving and robbing, taking greater and greater risks as Splinter proved how clever he was, how much better off they were with him in charge. They could have stayed with Ethel. They could have had normal food and somewhere safe to sleep and clothes that weren't filthy and shredded. And they could have helped Ethel, if that was what she wanted. Chess didn't mind helping Ethel. She wanted to be on the same side as the Committee because it was the right side to be on and because she knew that the Twisted Symmetry wouldn't stop hunting her just because Splinter had made them run away.

'What?' snapped Splinter. 'What's up with you?'

'Nothing,' muttered Chess. There was no point arguing with Splinter. He was cleverer than she was; he always told her that and anyway, he had won the argument a month ago when he had left Committee HQ, a week after their return with the slice of the Symmetry's computer brain, and she and Box had followed him.

'Good,' said Splinter.

He wouldn't let them stay at the wharf either. He had said that it was the obvious place for the Committee to come looking. So they'd moved to a derelict block of flats, leaving behind Hex and Pacer, the only remaining members of their gang, and Gemma, Chess's only friend. Splinter hadn't even allowed her that.

He patted his coat and felt inside the pockets. Splinter's inside pockets were full of useful items: string, marbles, a torch, lock picks, tape, matches and his switchblade. He pulled out a piece of notepaper and unfolded it.

'Stupid fat jack, not seeing what I was doing,' muttered

Splinter, sitting cross-legged and studying the writing on the paper.

Chess sniffed to show that she didn't agree with Splinter. He always talked about city people like that, even though they weren't all as bad as he said. But she knelt beside him anyway and looked at the numbers by the glow of the nearby security lights.

'It was a good lift,' said Box in admiration. Splinter had told them how the man had sat at a bench to eat a sandwich only metres from where Splinter was loitering by one of the city's metro stations. It was evening. Probably, the man was on his way home from work. He was leaning forwards, bald head sweating as he devoured the sandwich with hungry grunts. His jacket had ridden up revealing a loose shirt tail, a bulging roll of flesh and, protruding from his back trouser pocket, a fat wallet. Splinter's clever fingers danced and the wallet was his. The man failed even to register the thin, pale boy who drifted into the busyness of the city.

'UNIT 3 VIGO INDUSTRIAL' was written in biro across the top of the paper and below that were three strings of numbers. At the end of the first string was written 'RECEPTION', at the end of the second was written 'ATRIUM'. 'VAULT' was written after the third. When he had pulled the paper from the wallet, Splinter realized immediately that these were security codes for a warehouse. He took the bank notes and the piece of notepaper and threw the wallet and the rest of its contents down a drain. Then he ran to the gutted tower block where his twin brother and his sister were waiting for him.

That was only two hours ago and they had moved fast to

take advantage of what had come into his hands before the loss of the codes was realized. Splinter didn't know what would be in the vault but it was bound to be valuable. The street knowledge was that contraband gems passed through VIGO; too valuable for normal storage but too tricky for the banks. That was why they were smuggled through secure warehouses.

This could be big.

Each of them had taken a rough sack, tied it across their back, and then they had run to where the freight trains passed beneath an old stone bridge on their way out of the city. Splinter knew where the warehouses were and he knew that they were surrounded by high fences. Cutting their way out after stealing would be all right, even if that set the alarms off. Cutting their way in was too risky. That was why he had decided they should jump the fence as the train took them past it.

Now, here they were. No alarm raised, dark as shadows on the rooftop and armed with the codes to disable the security and open the vault. His plan was working. He tucked the paper into a pocket and smiled out of the darkness. Then he tapped the roof.

'Open her up, Box,' he said.

'My pleasure,' said Box and he stepped on the curved tip of the crowbar so that it sprang up to his hand. He spun it in the air and caught it cleanly.

Splinter winced. 'You're such a nobwit, fly head.'

Box dug his fingers into his thick, frizzy black hair and scratched, straightened one of the braces that held up his ragged woollen trousers and loped over to a wide air vent.

Shoving the end of the bar under the lid of the vent, he pushed down and prized it open. It slid from its housing and Splinter's hand was there to catch it before it hit the roof. He put a finger to his lips and frowned at Box. Box knelt and tugged the exposed pipe of the vent.

Chess stayed low and scanned the other warehouses inside the compound; the long, low roofs mottled by security lights that succeeded in bathing some areas in pools of yellow but leaving the rest in impenetrable darkness. There was no movement and no sound save for the dwindling clank of the train. There would be security guards but Chess knew they posed no risk. Security guards never did. They only found you if you let them know you were there. And nobody knew that they were there.

The Tuesdays hugged the darkness and worked fast but silently.

The pipe was loosened. Box rotated it and pulled. Splinter helped him lift it free of its mount. Now there was an opening into the space beneath the roof. Box was in first, then Splinter and then Chess, making no more noise than a rustle of leaves.

They were sitting in the roof joists. Splinter listened until he was sure nothing was moving below. Then he felt for his pencil torch and clicked it on.

'Over there,' he whispered after the feeble beam had picked out the emptiness beneath them. He directed it at a keypad set in the wall. Next to it was a door with a small iron wheel in its centre. 'That's the door to the vault. Just on the other side of this room.'

'Do we jump down?' asked Box. 'It's not far.'

'It's far enough to break an ankle,' warned Splinter. 'And look.' He pointed the torch at the floor below and then switched it off. The darkness welled in Chess's eyes and then she saw the pin-point red of a floor sensor.

'Could be loads of them down there,' said Splinter. 'Tread on one and we've had it; alarms, security guards, the crashers, more gaol.' He flicked the torch back on and it wobbled at the place where the joist met the wall. 'Water pipes, see? Shin down there and follow the edge of the room round to the vault door.'

It was as he switched the torch off that he felt Box slip from the joist. Aware of a shape toppling to his left, Splinter clawed out and gripped his brother's braces, throwing himself rightwards. His hands closed on elastic and his own body jolted to a stop and swung in the dark. Box hung with his braces looping the joist whilst Splinter was suspended on the other side, the end of the braces that had torn free gripped in his left hand. Box's face was inches from his own. He knew it was there because he could feel the hot breath of his brother's laughter on his skin.

'I've dropped the torch.' Splinter spoke through bared teeth. 'What the hell do you think you're doing?'

'Just hanging around,' gasped Box.

'You idiot.'

'You're the one who switched the torch off as I was putting my hand down and I missed the metal,' bridled Box.

Splinter gulped air. His arm was burning. 'You better lose weight fast, fly head. Not even you could miss the floor.'

'We're not far from the wall. Can't you swing along this bar?' suggested Chess. From the grunts below, she guessed that her brothers were doing as she said. She heard the scrape of the braces as they were dragged along the joist and then a thump and yelp followed by a sharp crack as her brothers swung into the wall at the same time that the braces snapped.

There was a groan and then Splinter swearing and then Box complaining loudly: 'My trousers won't stay up.'

Chess felt for the pipe with her toes, slipped across to it and slid to the floor. 'Come on,' she said. 'Stop messing about.' She felt long, hard fingers dig into the nape of her neck, pulling her back.

'After me,' Splinter whispered in her ear, and he pushed past her.

When they had felt their way round the walls to the vault entrance, Chess heard the scrape of a match. Splinter's face flared orange and he handed the match to Box.

'Hold this.' He scanned the sheet of notepaper and then lifted his hand to the keypad.

'I can't,' squealed Box and darkness flooded in as the match went out. Chess heard him sucking his burnt fingers.

'Idiot,' hissed Splinter. There was a rattle as he pushed the matchbox at his brother's chest. 'Take them and make sure it stays light. If I press the wrong number we're in trouble.'

A rasping strike and there was light again. Splinter thrust his narrow face up to the pad and pushed the buttons, checking what he was doing against what was written on the paper.

Chess listened to the space around them but heard only the slow hiss and crackle of the flame and the rise and fall of their breathing. There was a tang of smoke.

The match flickered out as Splinter pushed the final key.

He crumpled the paper and shoved it in a pocket and groped for the matchbox which he snatched out of Box's hand. Then he grasped the metal wheel that was set in the vault door.

'Now,' he whispered, 'you will see why I am the King of Cunning.' He turned the wheel and pushed. Smoothly, the vault door swung inwards. One after the other, the Tuesdays entered.

The floor was made of steel and it was cold. From the way their bare feet slapped loudly against it, Chess could tell that this was a large chamber, at least the size of the one they had just come from. But it wasn't the size of the vault that mattered. It was what it contained. Or what it didn't.

'Empty!' gasped Box, as Splinter struck another match and lifted it above his head.

The door slammed shut behind them. The flame guttered out.

'Not empty,' growled a voice from the dark.

Chess spun round and grimaced as a bright beam of torch light burst from near to the door. Then the torch was turned off, although her eyes were still flooded with colours, and the vault was illuminated by humming ceiling lights.

As her eyes recovered, she saw a man with one eye and a bristling ginger moustache who sat in a wheelchair next to the door. A large flashlight rested on his lap.

'Professor Breslaw!' she exclaimed. 'What are you doing here?'

Professor Breslaw chuckled with a throat full of phlegm. The web of cables that connected his body to the wheelchair quivered as his body shook. 'Waiting for you, of course. A nice surprise, no?' He nodded towards a large, wooden crate that sat near to him with its mouth open. 'I came by special delivery.'

Splinter realized what had happened, immediately. 'You set us up.' He advanced on the professor, arms rigid by his sides, fists clenched, face white with fury. 'You made me steal the wallet, you put the codes in it, you knew we'd come here.'

Joachim Breslaw stopped laughing and his eye riveted Splinter. 'We made you steal nothing, my boy. You did the stealing. The fact that you are as predictable as you are dishonest is your fault alone.' He rubbed his moustache. 'You know, Splinter, I confess, I thought you were too smart to fall for this. But Mevrad said you would fall for it.' He wagged his finger. 'She said that getting you to come here would be as easy as knowing you.'

Splinter started towards Joachim but Box rested a hand on his brother's forearm, gently but firmly.

'Careful, Professor,' warned Box. 'This is the King of Cunning you're talking to.' He stifled a grin and hitched up his trousers with his free hand.

Splinter glared at his brother, surprised that Box wasn't more disappointed to see the Professor. Box shrugged, released Splinter's arm and began to wind his braces round his waist like a belt.

'You must come with me now,' said Joachim Breslaw. 'The Committee needs you.'

'Forget it,' snarled Splinter. 'We left because we wanted to get away from you and Ethel, or Mevrad, or whatever you call her, and your stupid Committee.' He leant towards the Professor, spittle spraying.

The Professor leant towards Splinter until his bald, pink head was almost touching Splinter's nose. 'You left because we let you leave,' he rumbled. 'It was better that way and, strange to tell, it was safer for you. And now the time has come for you to help us again, we pull you in like so many little, wriggling fishes.' He jabbed a sausage of a finger at Splinter's midriff. 'Tell me, King of Cunning, who is the stupid one?'

Splinter hid his fury behind a mask of a smile and asked, 'Why are we going to come with you?'

Joachim Breslaw nodded. 'A fair question,' and he directed his finger at a console on the wall beside him. 'Here are the light switches, and next to them there is a red button, see? If I press it, the alarm will sound and the police will come and you will go to prison for a very long time. Unless they hand you over to the hunters.' He brushed his thick moustache with the tip of his tongue. 'I think, probably, they will hand you over to the hunters.'

'You don't want the hunters to take Chess,' Splinter fired back, triumphant.

Joachim Breslaw thumped the red button with the back of his fist. The alarm started to scream. 'Let us make our choices,' he said.

CHAPTER 2

The bulldozer burst through the wall with a squeal of metal and a shower of masonry. Professor Breslaw tucked the small radio back inside his motley coat and shouted over the howling alarm and roaring engine.

'Transport is waiting for us. Whoever is coming must leave now.' His wheelchair shot forwards, jolting him back in his seat with a spasm of cables and as the yellow hulk of the bulldozer tore itself free of the vault wall, Professor Breslaw rattled over the rubble and out through the gap.

Box looked at Chess and Chess looked at Splinter and Splinter glowered at the rent wall where night leaked in. Above the alarm came the distant wail of police sirens.

'Crashers!' warned Box. 'Time to give it long legs,' and he turned and sprinted after the Professor.

'Splinter?' said Chess. 'We've got to go. There's no point staying here,' and then she added, 'We can't hide from the Twisted Symmetry forever.'

Splinter gritted his teeth. 'This isn't a choice,' he said.

Chess turned to leave but Splinter grabbed her wrist.

'When the time comes,' he said, cool as frost, 'I'll show them what making a choice means.'

Then they ran.

The delivery van was parked on the other side of the breach in the security fence. Its engine was running and the side panel was open. A thin man in a baggy jacket and trousers was pushing a ramp into the back of the van as Chess and Splinter clattered across the flattened wire. The bulldozer was already trundling away from the warehouse, down a neon-orange backstreet, but the sirens were much louder now. Chess saw the warehouse walls flashing blue and white as police vehicles screeched into the end of the street.

'In you get,' said the wiry man in the baggy clothes. 'Can't 'ang about all flamin' night.'

Splinter noticed the lettering on the side of the van: ETHEL'S VEGETABLES. 'Very funny,' he muttered.

'Yeah, well, shift it,' croaked the man, 'before you start growin' roots.'

Chess and Splinter scrambled inside, the panel slid shut behind them, the driver's door slammed and with its lights off and a gentle roll of tyres on tarmac, the delivery van ghosted into an alleyway.

'What now?' enquired Box, brightly, as they jostled onto the wooden bench that ran down the van wall. The back of Joachim Breslaw's chair was against the driver's compartment.

'Now, we go to meet Mevrad,' he explained, his guttural accent thick in the darkness.

'Good,' said Box.

It seemed a strange thing to say but Chess knew what he

meant. The thought that they were going to see Ethel lifted a gloom that had hung heavy on her since they had run away. And it was better to go back; to face what would come looking for them however hard they ran. Fighting beats hiding, was what Box would say.

Splinter snorted with disgust. 'Whose side are you on, fly head?' he carped.

'We're all on the same side, remember?' replied Box, shoving his stout body backwards and barging Splinter's bony shoulder into a metal strut. Splinter swore at him.

'It will be a long journey,' interrupted Joachim. 'Maybe you will sleep?'

'Not much chance of that,' grumbled Splinter, 'seeing as how elephant butt is hogging the seat.'

But, eventually, they all slept: Chess with her head against the rear window, oblivious to the way it juddered on the glass, Splinter swaying beside her and next to him, Box, snoring extravagantly. Only Joachim Breslaw remained awake, his eye glinting in the sheen of the street lights.

Chess's head banged on the glass and she heard a loud splash as the van ploughed through a deep puddle. She opened her eyes and saw that the city with its gridline streets and vaunting skyscrapers had disappeared. It was day and the van was plunging down a deep lane, enclosed by hedges and overhung by trees that drooped with the weight of all the rain that had fallen.

'We're in the countryside,' she said.

'I know,' said Splinter, as if she was talking about a disease rather than a place.

Everything looked so green and so brown, slashed by the

dark, wet trunks of the trees. The last time that Chess had been out of the city and into the country was when she and her brothers had gone to the Eastern Airfield to see the Fat Gobster swallow the children that the Twisted Symmetry had stolen. There were thousands of children and amongst them were the street rats from her brothers' gang. The memory of the screams stabbed her chest and she shut her eyes. They opened as the van hammered over another pothole.

Before that trip, Chess had been to the countryside on a couple of bus rides, but only when she had taken the wrong bus. And before that? Before that, there was a vague snapshot in her mind of sunlight and leaves and the smell of cut grass and a voice singing. Her mother's voice. She smiled and began to hum.

'All you ever do is sing that stupid song,' complained Splinter.

'It's not all I ever do,' retorted Chess, 'and anyway, I was humming, not singing.' She paused. 'And anyway, Mum sang it so you should like it.'

'Our mum sang nothing.' Splinter stretched out his thin, black-trousered legs and looked at his filthy toes. 'Our mum just dumped us.'

'You just don't remember it,' said Chess and then she gasped as Splinter's elbow found her ribs. Her eyes smarted and she looked out of the rear window so Splinter wouldn't see them.

The delivery van scattered stones as it swerved noisily past a lichen-speckled sign and into a small village.

'Low . . . Low . . . something,' mumbled Chess, struggling

to read what was on the sign. She wasn't very good at reading. She blamed it on never having being taught how, but Splinter said it was because she was naturally stupid.

'Low Looming,' said Joachim Breslaw. 'The camp is on the other side of the village.'

'What kind of camp?' asked Box, staggering to the rear doors where the only windows were. The van swung off the road and through an open gate. It jolted into a field. Box's head struck the roof and he rubbed it with a groan.

'A scout camp!' sneered Splinter, face pressed to the glass. He surveyed the lines of small, orange ridge tents and the figures in khaki trousers and neat shirts, sitting inside tent flaps and gathered around small fires drinking mugs of tea. He turned and smirked at Joachim Breslaw. 'Scouts! The Committee must really mean business this time, Professor.'

The van slammed to a halt and Splinter lurched towards the Professor who stopped him from falling with an outstretched leg. 'Be careful, my boy,' he said, moustache bristling. 'Now, please, help Eric with my ramp.'

The panel slid open and Box and Splinter jumped out, sinking up to their ankles in boggy turf.

'It's cold,' gasped Chess when she joined them, but it felt good to wiggle her toes in the mud.

When the ramp was in position, Professor Breslaw rolled out of the van, but before he reached the bottom, he halted and pressed a button on the armrest of his wheelchair. With a shudder of the chassis and a clunk, a set of caterpillar tracks extended from either side of the body of the chair. The Professor proceeded down the ramp and stopped at the bottom only to look at where the Tuesdays' feet had sunk in the mire. He shook his head sympathetically before coasting onto the grass. 'Follow me.'

Chess looked about, blinking. The sky was flat with white cloud but it was bright. On one side of the camp was a hedgerow with the road behind it. On the other side the field climbed steeply until it became a hill. On the crest of the hill was a ring of trees, leafless and spindly like black skeletons. Chess shielded her eyes to look up at them and shuddered.

They walked past the rows of orange tents towards a larger, muddy-white pavilion a little distance from the rest of the camp. A wooden flagpole had been erected beside it, at the top of which fluttered a pennant displaying a ball of wool over a pair of knitting needles.

Chess sniffed the musty whiff of wet canvas mixed with the scent of muddy grass and the drift of wood smoke from the small camp fires. She sensed the scouts watching her and she looked down. Box, however, was peering about keenly.

'These are funny looking scouts,' he declared. 'That one's smoking a cigarette.' He stopped to point out a figure by the gate where they had come in.

Now that Box had said this, Chess noticed how the scouts looked older than scouts usually looked. And leaner. And tougher. And they all had crew cuts. Some of them bore scars on their arms and faces.

'That one,' said Splinter, spotting a woman kneeling in the entrance of a nearby tent, 'is cleaning a machine gun.'

They all stopped to look. The weapon had been stripped and its parts lay on a mat inside the tent flap. The woman was cleaning the firing mechanism with familiar skill. Her forearms were taut with muscle and on one of them was tattooed the grey star in a purple circle of the Charitable Operations Executive. She looked only at Box and nodded at him and he nodded back.

Box said nothing but Splinter sensed his brother's deep satisfaction at being recognized by a COE agent. Word of their successful mission to infiltrate the enemy complex at the Riverside Prison and steal the splice of computer brain must have spread. 'Don't think you're one of them, fly head,' he murmured. 'They're just glad to see someone stupid enough to die in their place.'

But now Box was peering inside a canoe that was one of eight mounted on a trailer behind a jeep. 'This is full of metal.' His voice reverberated inside the plastic casing. Then he shouted, 'It's a rocket.'

'It's a missile system,' explained Joachim Breslaw. 'Every good scout should be prepared.'

'Prepared for what?' gasped Box.

'In this case, air to ground attack. You never know what the enemy might try. We have to expect the unexpected.' Professor Breslaw chuckled and Splinter wasn't sure if the Professor winked at him or blinked at him; it was hard to tell with a man who had only one eye. 'Not ordinary scouts, eh, Splinter. The COE have been here, under cover this past week, to secure the area.'

'Secure it for what?' Splinter didn't move although Professor Breslaw had started towards the white tent again.

'For your departure,' came the reply and then a man dressed as a scout but wearing a shoulder holster and a metal vent in his throat, pulled open the pavilion entrance and the wheelchair entered.

Box led the way to the tent but before he entered he stopped to look at the man's neck.

'It's a gullet-gill,' volunteered the COE agent in a voice that brayed like a knife on wire. 'Got my throat shot out two years ago, but this keeps me breathing and talking.' He tapped the black and silver grid. 'Itches like hell sometimes.'

'Welcome to the team, fly head,' said Splinter, softly, and he shoved Box into the tent.

Inside the pavilion it was hot and the walls glowed green from the grass. There was a low camp bed, a picnic table on which there sat a little brass bell and an open packet of garibaldi biscuits, and on the ground, in front of the panel opposite the entrance, a square sheet of chipboard. On top of the chipboard was a small, wooden jewellery box.

Nobody asked where Ethel was. They just stared at the box. Chess wasn't sure how long they had been standing there but suddenly the lid jolted and she flinched. It jolted again and then it flipped open, hitting the chipboard with a crack. Vapour poured out of the mouth of the box and whorled over the floor and with it came a silver-yellow glare.

Splinter leant forward as the light flickered with bars of shadow. A hand thrust out of the casket and landed with a slap on the chipboard. Chess, Box and Splinter started backwards. The hand was followed by a scrawny wrist which was followed by a saggy-skinned forearm. The forearm extended and out of the box came a shoulder and then a ruffled mop of grey hair and a pair of spectacles, lenses yellow in the glow.

Chess was careful not to do anything that would show Splinter how glad she was to see Ethel.

She thought Ethel looked very strange with her head and neck ballooning from the tiny box at ground level and her body still out of sight. But she had learnt that there was more space in the universe than she could see. Things weren't always as they looked. The box was not a box, it was a portable vortex, and through its compact mouth was the vast nothingness of the vortex itself.

Ethel blinked slowly, her eyes magnified behind the spectacle lenses and she said, 'I always feel like a golf ball when my head pokes out like this.'

'And I feel like swinging the club,' muttered Splinter.

Ethel's spectacles slipped to the end of her small nose. 'The same, wretched clothes. And poor Splinter and Chess, thinner then ever. But I'm glad to see that you are still a strapping lad, Box.'

'Which is a polite way of saying you're still a fat slob, fly head,' explained Splinter.

With an undignified grunt, Ethel hauled herself out of the portable vortex, flicking the lid shut with her plastic, open-toed sandal once she was clear. She staggered to her feet, brushing her pink frock over her knob-knees and spitting on her fingers to wipe a stain from her lapel. Then she adjusted her spectacles, walked to the table, tinkled the little bell and beamed at the Tuesdays.

'Isn't it lovely, my dears, all to be together again.'

'No,' said Splinter.

Ethel rolled a small ball onto the picnic table, set down

the bell and picked up the packet of biscuits. 'Garibaldi anyone?'

'Please,' said Box.

Splinter knew that the small ball was a tesseract, used for navigating the vortex. He recalled how his wrist had been trapped by the mortice-gate when he had reached inside the portable vortex. It was months ago but he rubbed his wrist without thinking. Ethel had released him by speaking a password; a password that controlled the mortice-gate and therefore the way into the vortex. A password that she wouldn't trust him with because she trusted no one.

'What do you want?' he demanded, still nursing his wrist.

'Thank you, Eric,' said Ethel to the van driver, who had brought her a mug of tea. He sat at the picnic table, resting his sub-machine gun across his narrow thighs.

'What do you want?' repeated Splinter.

'The Committee needs you.'

'Why?'

Ethel slurped at her tea. 'Time is running out, my love, literally. This time cycle is entering its final phase, the fifth node.'

'Sounds complicated.' Box scratched his head and then his bottom.

'He's looking for his brain,' explained Splinter.

'Time is a spiral.' Professor Breslaw described a spiral in the air with a fat, pink finger and a minute quiver of cables. 'Always repeating but with little changes. That is why it moves forward. Without the changes it would be stuck in a circle. Each loop of the spiral, each time cycle so to speak, has five nodes; the places where time mutates and change happens. At the fifth node the mutation is greatest. That is when the time spiral is most vulnerable to change.'

Ethel turned her steamed-up lenses on Splinter. 'This is what the Twisted Symmetry have been waiting for. This is what its masters, the Inquisitors, have been preparing for.'

'So?' Splinter appeared unmoved by these epic events.

Ethel bit a garibaldi with a loud snap. 'So, now we need you to conduct a reconnaissance; to gather intelligence, to learn what the enemy is about. Then we can decide how best to fight them.'

She set down the mug of tea and folded her hands behind her back like a miniature general. 'With the slice of cerebral torus that you obtained, Lemuel has built us our own universal quantum computer.'

'Where is Lemuel?' asked Chess.

'Not here, my love. He hasn't been very friendly this past month.'

'Because you thought he was a traitor?' suggested Splinter.

'Yes, dear. The Twisted Symmetry have devised a thousand agonizing deaths for him for defecting to the Committee. By helping us he condemns himself to purgatory, should the enemy ever capture him. He believes I did not repay him kindly.' Ethel pulled a shred of skin from her little finger nail and winced. 'I made a mistake, although it was a necessary mistake in the circumstances.'

'I don't know why you have anything to do with someone who has to drill their brain to make themselves be good,' said Splinter.

'I have a lot to do with people who don't even do that, dear. At least Lemuel Sprazkin is doing all he can to be good.' Ethel hesitated long enough to make everyone feel uneasy before continuing. 'Anyway, with our newly-built computer, we have been able to predict when and where the Fat Gobster will strike. The enemy have continued to use the suck worm to transport the children they steal from this world to goodness knows where and they have been doing so in ever greater numbers.' Ethel licked her wrinkled lips. 'We need you to travel down the Fat Gobster, find out what happens to the children at the other end and come back and tell us.'

'No, no, no, no and no,' announced Splinter.

'That's an awful lot of "no"s dear, and there are only three of you.'

'What if we don't want to help?'

Ethel indicated the tent opening. 'You can go, my love. We didn't stop you from leaving last time. We won't stop you this time. I only wanted to give you an opportunity.'

'An opportunity to what?'

'To help, Splinter. An opportunity to help.'

'You're always going on about opportunities, Splinter,' volunteered Box. 'It's not like we've got anything else to do.'

Splinter exploded. 'This isn't a game. The Committee are pathetic. The Twisted Symmetry will destroy them. Can't you see that, you moron? This is her problem. We should keep out of it.'

'Your ability to get it wrong is terrifying, my love,' said Ethel.

'The only thing that's terrifying is travelling down a cosmic drainpipe into the hands of someone you keep calling "the enemy",' retorted Splinter.

'So,' said Ethel, 'this is all about you being frightened, is it?'

'No.' Splinter swallowed hard, containing his fury. 'This has nothing to do with fear. I just don't like playing for the losing side.'

Nobody spoke. Chess fidgeted with the frayed cuff of her pullover. Whatever Splinter said, she was relieved to be with Ethel; to hear her voice, to feel her nearby. But for that very reason, she didn't want to go away from her. She didn't want to come close to the Twisted Symmetry again. The name 'Inquisitors' made her stomach feel weak, even though she didn't know really what they were.

'Do we have to do this?' she asked.

Ethel smiled. 'Do you want the truth?'

'I hate it when she says that,' whispered Box.

'Yes,' said Chess. 'The truth.'

'The truth is, you have to do this: have to do it if we are to prevent a cataclysm so vast that none of you can imagine it.' Ethel returned to her mug of tea.

'So we don't have a choice after all,' stated Splinter.

Ethel screwed up her nose at the cold tea. 'Wrong, Splinter. You *always* have a choice. But the right choice isn't always the nice choice. I'm asking you to make the *right* choice. To be on the right side.' She poked a nubbly finger into the tepid brew.

'We might be able to help the others,' suggested Box.

'What others.'

'From the gang, Splinter. Our gang, from the wharf. The one's that were taken by the Fat Gobster. Remember?'

Splinter grunted. 'Don't try to bribe me with loyalty, fly head.'

Ethel pierced Splinter with her bloodshot eyes. 'It would be very easy to bribe you, Splinter, but loyalty will never be your weakness.'

Chess knew that she had less choice in this than anyone. The Twisted Symmetry wanted her and being her meant that she was part of what was happening. She didn't know why they wanted her, she didn't know why anyone would want her; she was a street rat, worthless, even nameless apart from what they had called her at the orphanage. But helping the Committee meant that she was doing something right. And, maybe, being part of this was what she was; what she was meant to be. There was only one way to find out.

'I'll do it,' she announced.

'Here we go,' muttered Splinter.

'So will I,' declared Box, and then, 'can I have another biscuit?'

'Be my guest,' said Ethel. Then she asked Eric, 'Has Plan B arrived yet?'

'Not when I last looked.' He sighed wearily. 'I'll check again if you like.' He rose from the picnic table as if he'd been asked to climb a mountain and left the tent, sub-machine gun swinging by his side.

'Splinter?'

Splinter's mouth was clenched shut and his jaw muscles worked as he felt Ethel's cool gaze. When he spoke it was slowly and carefully. 'I have no choice so don't pretend I have. And these two won't survive without me.' He glowered back at Ethel. 'This has nothing to do with being on the right side.'

Ethel clapped her hands together. 'Good. We're in business.'

'So what happens next?' asked Box, through a mouthful of garibaldi.

'There are some items you will need,' replied Ethel. She noticed how Splinter was looking about the tent. He saw her watching him and he smiled, took out his matchbox and began to toss it in the air and catch it. Ethel nodded knowingly and said, 'The VAP please, Professor.'

Joachim Breslaw pulled a brown paper bag from the side of his wheelchair. Ethel took it from him, upended it and caught a watch. She grasped Chess's right arm and fastened it around her wrist. 'This looks like a wrist watch, dear, but it isn't. It's called a VAP.'

'A VAP?' repeated Chess.

'A Vortical Alarm Pulse.' Ethel pointed to two tiny metal buttons on either side of the watch face. 'Press both those buttons at the same time and it sends out an emergency beacon from wherever you are in the universes. As soon as you do that, you will be snatched from wherever it is you are and taken to the nearest safe Committee HQ. The snatching is done by a snatch squad. The Committee always has VAP snatch squads on standby and they can be sent anywhere, instantly. As soon as an alarm beacon is detected, its source location is calculated and the squad dispatched. The snatch squad will be very fast and heavily armed and its members will probably not be human so don't be surprised by their appearance, my loves.

'Only use the VAP when you want to come back and remember, whoever is touching you will be rescued at the same time. So make sure the three of you are in contact when the buttons are pressed. You'll only have one chance.'

'So when we have found out whatever is going on at the other end of the Fat Gobster, Chess presses that and we can come home?' asked Box.

'Yes,' said Ethel.

There was a slap of tent flap and Eric stuck his head inside the pavilion. 'Plan B's arrived, Efel.' Outside, an engine was running.

'Come on,' said Ethel. 'There's no time to waste.' She marched over the grass and out of the tent, followed by the Tuesdays, with Joachim Breslaw at the rear.

A taxi had drawn up outside the tent, its wheel arches spattered with mud. Splinter slapped the front of his morning coat before saying, 'My matchbox. I dropped my matchbox.'

'Well, you better go and get it,' said Ethel. Splinter slipped back inside the tent but he was not gone for long. When he emerged he had the matchbox in his hand and a shy smile on his face. 'Sorry.'

Eric went to the back of the cab and pulled open the boot. Chess, Box and Splinter followed him and looked. Inside, there was a large, stone-coloured suitcase. It had 'PLAN B' stamped on its side in bold, black, old-fashioned letters.

'Box, you take the suitcase,' ordered Ethel. 'Dynamite, lots of it and detonators. Right up your street, my love. Something special for an emergency, if an emergency happens. Just follow the instructions inside the case.'

Box approached the rear of the cab with awe and said to Ethel, 'You really trust us, don't you?'

'Not exactly, dear. I wouldn't trust you as far as I can spit, but I have great faith in your ability to wreak havoc.' She patted the case. 'I always say, it's not where you go, it's what you pack that matters.'

'What do I get?' asked Splinter.

'You already have something, dear.'

Splinter blushed and said no more.

'Where do we go?' asked Chess. 'And when?'

With a weight on her chest, Chess guessed where they would be going before Ethel turned to look up at the hill with the ring of black trees. 'Up there is where you must go, my loves. The Fat Gobster is coming, hungry for children.'

Chess wasn't sure if she was imagining it, but already the plain blanket of sky seemed to be rippling and darkening over the trees, just as it had done before the suck worm struck at the Eastern Airfield. Screaming mayhem: children's bodies hurtling into the air; she shut her eyes and it vanished.

There was a crash of tent poles from nearby and a billow of canvas. 'The troops are striking camp.' Ethel rubbed her pink, wrinkled hands together. 'No good having all these tents up when it starts to blow. We have twenty minutes, my loves.'

'So soon?' Chess was surprised. A chill wind brushed over the wet grass and her skin prickled.

Professor Breslaw tugged a gold pocket watch from the region of his bulging belly and said, 'Nineteen minutes, in fact, Mevrad.'

Chess caught the questioning glance he threw at Ethel and heard Ethel say, 'This is the way it has to be, Joachim. This is the next move. There is no alternative.'

The Professor pursed his lips but said nothing.

'Do the Twisted Symmetry know about *this* plan?' Splinter looked from Ethel to Joachim.

'No, dear. They won't know we have been able to predict the worm strikes and they won't know we will be using this one. They have no idea you're coming.'

'Really,' sneered Splinter. 'Like last time?'

'Last time was completely unforeseeable.'

'Exactly,' insisted Splinter. 'That's what worries me.'

'Come on,' said Box. 'Let's get this done.' He heaved the suitcase from the back of the taxi and began to walk towards the hill with Splinter by his side. But Ethel told them to stop. They turned round, Splinter frowning impatiently, Box with his curly-haired head on one side.

'Remember,' said Ethel, 'the Twisted Symmetry have many servants and many schemes.' Her voice was urgent and her fists were clenched. 'Trust no one. No one.' Box and Splinter nodded and continued to walk towards the hill.

Chess felt the weight of Ethel's hand on the back of her head, brushing her hair softly. There was a tenderness, but she knew it was a tenderness that was prepared to send her into the jaws of the enemy: an enemy who wanted her because they believed she could control a weapon called the Eternal. That much, Ethel had told her.

'When you first found us,' said Chess, 'you said that all of this has happened before.'

'Yes dear, but I thought you were sleeping,' muttered Ethel.

'Has it?' Chess turned her head to look at the old lady. 'Has *this* happened before?'

'In a way, yes.'

'Did I come back?'

Ethel sighed and blinked. 'Sometimes you did and sometimes you didn't.'

'I don't know how that makes any sense,' stated Chess. Ethel seemed always to speak in riddles about the most important things.

'That's because you don't know how many different worlds there are.'

Chess thought about this as the wind slapped her misshapen pullover and flicked her hair. 'Do the same things keep happening in all of them?'

'Yes, but differently.'

'Come on, Chess.' Box's call was swallowed by the mud, the hill, the trees, the wind.

'Does anything stay the same?' asked Chess.

'Trust no one, my love. That stays the same. Trust no one.'

'Except you.'

Ethel smiled and patted Chess's arm. 'That's right, dear. Except me.'

Chess started to walk away and as she did so, she realized how strong that made her.

'Good luck,' cried Ethel.

'Thanks,' replied Chess, without looking back.

It took a while to slog up the hill, squelching barefoot over mud and grass. Box had dumped the suitcase at the edge of the tress and was sitting on it with Splinter. Chess sat on it too when she joined them.

Below them stretched fields and woods, criss-crossed by narrow lanes. One by one, the canvas patches of the camp were vanishing, thrown into trailers as stick figures climbed into the jeeps. The COE were pulling out. Only the tent with the flagpole remained but Chess couldn't see Ethel.

Behind them stood the trees, creaking in the building wind. Chess looked up and saw the sky brooding, streaks of iron-grey cloud rolling in from every direction. She hunched her shoulders.

'What do we do now?' asked Box.

'Wait to be stolen by the Fat Gobster, I suppose,' said Splinter.

'We're usually the ones nicking stuff,' observed Box. 'Funny for us to be stolen.'

'Hilarious,' said Splinter with a scowl. He yanked the lapels of his long-tailed morning coat over his rake of a chest as the wind moaned loudly through the branches.

Abruptly, Box stood up and shouted, 'Hello! Fat Gobster! Where are you?' His voice was muffled by the gale. 'Hello! Fatty fatty Gobster. Nice juicy children. Come and get them.'

'Sit down, fly head, and keep your mash shut,' muttered Splinter. His white hair danced round his sharp-boned face. The wind boomed over the hill.

'Do you think it will hurt?' Chess asked Splinter. A mouthful of air made her choke on her words.

'You saw what happened last time.'

Last time. Chess tried to stop thinking about last time: the children screaming and the sky ripping open to devour the earth. But she couldn't block it out because it was happening now. The cyclone was hammering her face, clutching at her hair, buffeting her backwards. She tried to hold on to the case but with an ocean rumble the wind blasted in and slammed her to the ground.

Twigs and leaves rushed through her clawing fingers as

Chess was sucked into the trees. Twisting like a corkscrew, she skidded over rough earth, fingernails breaking on grit, soil crusting her nose and eyes. She couldn't breathe. She was drowning in air.

Chess wheeled into a sapling and clung to it. Box hurtled past her, still clutching onto the suitcase by a handle. She couldn't see where Splinter was; she could barely open her eyes. But she saw enough to make her scream.

She saw the sky collapsing, saw a mouth of boiling black cloud plunge towards her, saw it smash the tree tops and at its centre, saw a disc of brilliant white. Then she saw no more but she felt the sapling tear from her hands, felt the earth fall away from her body, felt her lungs bursting and felt her throat burn with screams that she couldn't hear.

CHAPTER 3

Chess was spinning. Her stomach was in her throat one moment and under her knees the next. Her ears were bursting. She could see nothing. She couldn't tell if her eyes were wide open or screwed tight shut. Even with her arms flailing there was nothing she could touch. She was moving but whether she was travelling forwards or backwards she didn't know.

Then her body crashed onto something hard, or something hard crashed into her. She shook her head and opened one eye a fraction but the light was so bright she opened it no more and kept the other firmly shut. Even through her closed eyelids there was an orange-pink glow. She tried to work out where she was.

Her cheek rested against wood. She was lying on a wooden board. Her fingers explored the rough texture and she realized it was covered with many fine particles. Sand.

The air was hot, she could feel that now. The heat came in waves, seeping through her clammy clothes and drying her skin and bones. Her body was jolted at intervals and rocked from side to side and she could sense forward movement. But this was not the nauseating chaos of the suck worm. It was more like being carried on something.

Chess tried to make sense of the different noises; the rumbling of wheels, the rattle of couplings, the creaking of wood.

She was on a train.

She opened her eyes and sat up, blinking in the glare of the sun. She had to put out a hand to steady herself and with the other she shaded her eyes. Her vision was blurred at first. She was sitting on the floor of a cart and it was one of a line of carts, coupled together and stretching forwards and backwards as far as she could see.

There were iron bars all around the edge of the wooden floor of the cart and overhead so that she was sitting in a cage. There were bars like this on every cart in the line. Through the bars, Chess could see a rust-coloured plain stretching endlessly in all directions, as flat and hard as a plate.

'The desert,' said Splinter who was sitting behind her, leaning against the iron bars. 'We're in the desert.'

The carts were travelling swiftly over a track like a train would. Chess shuffled on her bottom to the edge of the platform and propped herself against the bars as Splinter had done. Box was lying on the floor, eyes closed and breathing slowly. Next to him lay the suitcase.

'He must have banged his head,' explained Splinter. 'He's been out cold since we landed.'

The sound of sobbing distracted Chess. She looked at the cage behind her and saw that it was full of children in school uniform. Their faces were powdered with dirt and their eyes were looking at her, wide and frightened. As the carts rattled over the track, the children swayed but their eyes didn't move. Squashed against the bars and sitting on the floor was a girl much younger than Chess. The sobbing came from her.

'Jacks,' spat Splinter, loud enough for them to hear. 'Think they're great until things don't go their way and then they start squealing. Pathetic.'

'She's only a kid, Splinter,' said Chess.

'Look at the rest of them.' Splinter nodded one way and then the other. 'Like I said; pathetic.'

In every cage that Chess could see, there were children, thousands of children; in school uniform, in jeans, in pyjamas, scruffy, tidy, sitting, lying, silent, crying. There were children who looked like they might have come from the city and children who looked like they came from other countries. Some were solitary on carts, some were in small groups and some were in groups so large that they were jammed against the iron bars.

Chess looked for faces she recognized but she couldn't see any of the street rats who had lived at the wharf before the hunters had come; before they had been swallowed by the Fat Gobster at the Eastern Airfield. But she knew that not long ago their bones would have been shaken by the same rough train that she was on, that they would have been sitting, or standing, or lying where she was sitting, that they would have been taken to the place where she was going.

The heat and the glare and the way the bars striped the wooden floor of the cart were making her feel sick. She closed her eyes and attempted to swallow but her tongue was thick and her mouth was dry.

Box groaned and rolled onto his back. There was a cut with fresh blood on his right cheek and all around his right eye the skin was puffed up and blotched purple with bruise. Chess leant forwards to inspect the gash and wiped away blood and sand with the sleeve of her pullover.

'You must have hit it on the floor when you landed,' she said. 'It looks painful.'

'It is painful,' groaned Box. 'What a trip!' He lay back against the iron bars and when he had finished rubbing his head he said, 'So, this is where the Fat Gobster goes? At least it's hot here.'

'It's boiling,' agreed Chess, yanking off her pullover and tying it round her waist.

'Nice to see we're not alone,' observed Box, once he had taken stock of the children who were so close to them but so distant. 'What are you staring at?' he barked at the faces pressed against the bars in the cage behind. Then, looking the other way, 'And you lot. What's so interesting? Can't believe you're stuck in it with rubbish like us?' He eyeballed the jacks one way and then the other but their moon-eyed faces didn't move and the little girl in the cage behind continued to cry.

'Leave it, Box,' said Splinter. 'Don't waste your energy. This lot are lambs for slaughter. We're not.'

Chess stared at Splinter, wanting to tell him how she hated it when he said things like that.

'What?' Splinter stared back, coldly.

With a lurch, Box sat forwards, looking over Chess's shoulder. 'What's that?' he exclaimed.

Even over the rattling of the wheels, Chess heard a

thumping gallop. When she looked round she saw a riding figure erupt from a swirl of sand and dust. It travelled faster than the train and charged past them and up the line, kicking up more sand and dust in its wake.

Although it travelled swiftly, Chess saw that the rider was not human and the beast carrying it was not a horse. The rider was a blur of fluttering rags, a long spear and a big bony head with wild, black hair. The mount looked like a camel without any humps. It was yellow with broad paws and a long straggly beard that streamed by its side as it galloped and ragged ears that flapped by its head like loose bunting. Both rider and mount wore goggles.

Although Chess had never seen anything like the mount before, she knew what the rider was.

'Trader!' she gasped.

'Traders,' said Splinter as two more came careering by.

'What are they doing here?' asked Box.

'Same as they were doing when we last saw them,' guessed Splinter, 'stealing children and looking ugly.'

'They're dressed differently.' Box scratched his head and wiped sweat from his face.

'That's because this is a desert.' Splinter spat a nugget of grit.

Box peered after the cloud of dust that marked the point reached by the riders, already far up the line of cages. 'Weird camels,' he decided.

'A camel with a beard and long, floppy ears and no hump,' said Splinter. 'So not a camel at all. And camels don't wear goggles.'

'I could do with some goggles,' moaned Box. 'My head is

splitting and this bright light is killing me. And I feel sick.' He rolled his eyes at Splinter. 'I can't believe you're keeping that jacket on,' he said. 'You must be roasting.'

'I'll do what I want with my jacket,' snapped Splinter.

'OK, OK. Boil alive if you want.' Box squinted as he surveyed the flat, ochre rubble that stretched as far as the horizon in all directions. 'Funny,' he pondered, 'being on a train again, so soon after last night.'

Splinter stared at him.

'OK,' sighed Box. 'It's not funny.' Then he cast a bleary eye over the iron bars and spotted a lock that secured the cage door. 'Pick that and we're out, Splinter,' he suggested.

'Brilliant, fly head. Where do we go then? We're in the middle of nowhere at the far end of a suck worm. We might as well stay put for the time being.'

Then Splinter noticed Chess who was looking up at the sky with a hand over her eyes, turning her head one way and then the other. 'What's up with you?' he asked.

'Two suns,' she replied. 'There are two suns.'

Even Box pushed himself up and, wincing, looked at the mercilessly blue sky.

Directly overhead was the blinding white glare that he recognized as the sun. But when he looked to where Chess was pointing he saw a ruby circle low in the sky to the left of the train. Around the circle was a distinct amber glow, smudged by distant bars of grey cloud. Putting out his arm, Box measured the second sun to be a palm's width above the line between desert and sky.

Box turned his head one way and then the other just as

Chess had done. 'Weird,' he murmured. 'It's as if someone has just stuck it there. It doesn't look real.'

'Like a perfectly round drop of blood,' mused Chess.

Splinter snorted. 'There's no need to get poetic just because there are two suns.' But he looked at the second sun for a long time before he said anything else.

With the heat and the rocking, Chess must have fallen asleep. She didn't know whether it was the sudden coolness or the blunt clatter of iron that roused her but she woke feeling chilly so she pulled her jumper back on. It wasn't dark but the brighter sun had sunk and the desert glowed mauve in the dusk. The sky was shot with smoky streaks of cloud that trailed to the horizon where there remained a band of pale light.

On the other side of the train the horizon was darker but the second sun had climbed a little higher. It smouldered like a hot ember but did not shine brightly enough to lighten the falling night.

Box was lying motionless on the floor of the carriage and was snoring gently. Splinter sat with his back to the red sun, thin legs drawn up to his chest and eyes glinting.

'What's happening, Splinter?' asked Chess.

'We stopped about an hour ago,' he replied. 'Traders have been galloping up and down the train. There's loads of them. Checking we're secure for the night, I suppose.' Splinter paused to nod his head one way and then the other. 'And the cannon fodder are still snivelling. They're frightened.' He snorted with contempt.

Chess listened to the disembodied voices that drifted through the gloom.

Splinter continued. 'There's jacks dishing out water.' Chess realized how sore her lips were and how her tongue felt as if it had swollen inside her mouth. She was desperate for a drink. Splinter was still talking. 'They must have been given special jobs because they're older and bigger. They're cocky, even for jacks. They think they're in charge. They're making something to eat now. See the little fires?'

Chess could see the nests of yellow light flickering a few yards out at intervals along the length of the train.

Night fell. The desert musk was seasoned with wood smoke from the fires. Chess felt cold so she shuffled until she was sitting next to Splinter and she leant against him. For once, he didn't shrug her away. He remained huddled, leaning against the iron bars and watching the fires burning. The light glimmered on his pale face.

'What do you think Gemma and the others are doing?' asked Chess. Her friend felt a very long way from this desert with two suns.

'They'll be at the wharf. Still. Gemma will be fine.' Splinter sighed. 'We had to leave them, Chess. It would have been too easy for anyone to catch us at the wharf.'

'The Committee found us anyway,' said Chess and then wished she hadn't because she felt Splinter stiffen and draw away from her.

'They did, but we didn't have to do what they wanted. Whatever happens now, Chess, it's your fault.'

A boy carrying a bucket and ladle appeared out of the shadows and next to the cage. He was wearing a pair of cut-off trousers and a jumper and although he was shorter than Splinter and not much taller than Box, his broad chest, fat belly and wispy moustache showed that he was a couple of years older.

'Food,' he announced.

Splinter and Chess said nothing. Box was still asleep.

'Food,' he repeated. 'Hand your bowls out.'

'We haven't got any bowls,' said Splinter.

'Can I have some water?' asked Chess.

'You're a scabby lot aren't you,' said the boy. He made a show of sniffing loudly. 'Ugh! Street rats. Disgusting. Just arrived today?' Chess nodded. It seemed to Splinter that the boy was smirking. 'Well, if you haven't got any bowls you can't have any food can you? You can go without. We arrive the day after tomorrow anyway. Some of this lot have been travelling for weeks so count yourselves lucky.' As he spoke he gestured up and down the column of cages with the long wooden ladle he carried.

'Some water, please?' repeated Chess.

'What's wrong with him?' asked the boy, coming closer to the bars. He pushed his face up against them and inspected the lump on the floor that was Box.

Splinter and Chess were silent. The boy reached into the cage and cracked Box hard on the back of his head with the ladle. Box yelped and half rolled, half crawled away from the spot where he had been lying. He swore loudly at the boy and rubbed his head. The boy laughed.

'Why d'you do that?' complained Box.

'Just wanted to let you know you're not getting any food,' said the boy.

'You're very brave for a fat jack,' said Splinter.

The boy paused, thinking of a reply. 'No water either,' he

snapped. He turned his back and walked away, swinging the bucket beside him.

Splinter felt inside one of his jacket pockets and found a large marble, cold and hard. Kneeing, he took aim, and threw it as hard as he could. The boy was not very far away and Chess heard the marble thwack the back of his head. He spun round, dropping the bucket and then he exploded in a torrent of abuse.

Muffled snorts of laughter up and down the adjacent cages indicated that there was an audience and they were enjoying this.

'You think you're a hard man, scarecrow,' the boy shouted at Splinter. He stomped away from them and into the night but came back a couple of minutes later with two more boys, as old as he was but thinner. Both boys were carrying rough wooden sticks.

The fat boy had a key which he used to unlock the cage door. The two other boys climbed in. Box and Splinter simultaneously reached into their pockets to seize their knives but before they had whipped them out, the fat boy had grabbed Chess by her hair and dragged her out of the cage. She was so surprised that she didn't realize what was happening until she was face down and spread-eagled on the grit and stones. The cage door was slammed shut and locked.

Now all three boys surrounded Chess.

'I wouldn't trust scarecrow to fight fair,' said the fat boy, aware that he was being watched by the wide eyes of every captive who could see what was happening. Firelight danced up and down his silhouette. He spat on the floor. 'Street rats. You can never trust them.' Then he put his foot on Chess's shoulder. 'So you can take his beating for him. After that we'll see who's laughing.'

'Leave it, Jerome,' said a voice from the darkness and another boy, taller than the others, strolled up to the group.

Chess remained face down on the desert floor. The palm of her left hand was hurting.

'This is our problem, Saul,' said the fat boy.

'Well, you've dealt with it, Jerome,' Saul assured him. 'Everyone can see that you're in charge of this section of the train. No doubt about who's boss. Now leave it.'

'They're street rats,' complained Jerome. 'Important to show them what's what.' The other two boys had already sidled away.

Saul knelt down by Chess and put a hand on her shoulder. 'Are you OK?' he asked.

She sat up and nodded. By the shifting light of the fire she could see that he was a lean, square-jawed boy with long black hair and big, dark eyes. His lips looked soft and kind.

'You've cut your hand,' he told her.

Chess looked down and saw a long gash across her left palm. 'I did it when I fell on the floor.'

Saul stood up and standing toe to toe with Jerome he looked down at him and said, 'I think you've made your point. Now give me the key and go. I'll sort this lot out.'

When Jerome had gone, Saul fetched some water in a mug. Then he tore two strips from the bottom of his shirt. He used one to wash Chess's hand, dabbing it in the water. When the cut was clean he bound it with the other strip of cloth.

After that he brought water and three bowls of warm,

lumpy porridge to Chess and her brothers. By this time, Chess was back in the cage and Saul had locked them in. But he made sure that they had had enough to eat and drink before he left them.

The fires had died and the night was cold once Saul had gone. The Tuesdays sat close together for warmth. The red sun had risen and had moved across the front of the train. It threw out an orange halo that was swallowed by the darkness. Above them the dome of sky prickled with stars.

'He's all right,' said Box. 'For a jack.'

'I like him,' agreed Chess.

'You don't know anything about him,' said Splinter. 'He's one of them. He's not on our side.'

'No one's on our side,' observed Chess.

'Well, then,' replied Splinter with an air of finality, 'how do you know you can like him?'

They saw more of Saul the next day. He had taken charge of their section of the train and whenever it stopped, he and two others would dish out the water ration which was gulped down swiftly. Although the night had been cold, by late morning the white sun was high and the heat was ferocious. The red sun hung low on the horizon behind them.

By early afternoon the heat was hammering down from the sky and shimmering up from the rocks. The train had stopped and water had been distributed. It seemed to Chess that as soon as she swallowed it, it reappeared in a thin film of sweat on her skin.

She heard the clop of hooves and looked across from where she sat to where a trader had stopped near to their cage. He pushed the sand goggles over the top of his head and advanced on his mount, spear in hand, whip tucked in his belt. He was dressed in leggings and an open jerkin with a loose scarf that he pulled away from his mouth and down to his chest. The gnarled face and coils of black hair were caked with white sand save for a goggle-shaped patch around his eyes and over his nose. The wide, flat nostrils flared as he sniffed the Tuesdays. When he spoke, Chess could see teeth like yellow pebbles inside his huge mouth.

The words were harsh and guttural. The Tuesdays didn't understand them although the mount cocked its head on one side and uttered a rising bray before shaking its beard with a slap of reins. Then the trader hawked with a drawn-out crackle of mucus and rolled his bone-crunching jaws before ejecting a golf ball chunk at Splinter. Casually, Splinter dipped his head and the gobbet struck Box in the eye.

Box jumped up, cursing and wiping his face. The trader reined his mount back from the cage and snorted at the Tuesdays before clattering away over the rocks.

When Saul came to them shortly afterwards, carrying a beaker and a bucket of water he said, 'Be careful. The traders have been talking about you. They don't like troublemakers on the train.'

'So?' Splinter raised his chin to Saul, challenging him.

'So, they decided you should be left in the desert to die. Three less prisoners would be a small price to maintain discipline.'

'What stopped them?' Splinter sounded like he didn't care what the traders did.

'I stopped them. I told them that if they didn't give you

anything to eat for the rest of the journey you'd be too weak to cause trouble and your suffering would be warning enough for the others. And since they get paid for every prisoner they deliver, they shouldn't waste the money: even for three troublemakers like you.' Saul grinned. His grin made Chess smile.

'I'll probably starve to death now,' wailed Box.

Saul looked him up and down. 'I don't think so. Anyway, there isn't far to go.'

'Oh good,' said Splinter. 'So we don't have to starve before we're killed.'

A trader cantered by, eyes turning on Chess, Box and Splinter like burning coals.

'What are they riding?' asked Chess.

'It's called a jabaloupe,' replied Saul. 'They pull the train as well. And they can talk with the traders.'

'They must be very clever animals.' Usually, Chess didn't like speaking to people she didn't know very well, but she liked speaking with Saul.

'They're not clever. Just because something can talk, doesn't meant it's intelligent.'

'Exactly!' burst Splinter, slapping Box across the back of the head. 'What do I keep telling you, fly head?'

Box tried to think of a smart reply and couldn't, so he resorted to kicking his heel into Splinter's chest.

'You bonehead,' coughed Splinter. He went for Box's neck.

'Where are we going?' asked Chess. Immediately, her brothers stopped grappling. All of them looked at Saul.

'A factory,' he said.

'In the desert?' ridiculed Splinter.

Saul pointed in the direction of the red sun. 'The ocean is on our left, out that way.' Then he pointed beyond the other side of the train. 'Over there the mountains begin. Hills at first but they get bigger until they meet the ocean where it comes round, the way we're going. That's where the factory is. It's built into one of the mountains on the coast; a volcano, I think.'

'What happens there?' asked Splinter

'You're unloaded. Then the train travels back out and picks up more children before travelling back to the factory again.'

'But what actually happens?' persisted Splinter.

'I don't know,' was Saul's reply. 'All I know is this desert, the mountains and the railway.' He hesitated and then added, 'But whatever happens at the factory, there are no return passengers. Nobody leaves after they've gone in.'

'Why doesn't that surprise me?' muttered Box.

'What happens to you?' Chess asked Saul.

Saul leant against the bars and Chess thought he looked tired. 'I keep doing this. Looking after prisoners. As long as I do that I'm all right. Same as the others who do what I do.'

'How long have you been here?' she asked.

'Months. A year. I don't know.'

Saul filled the beaker and it was passed round.

'Why did you help us?' asked Chess. 'Last night.'

'I helped *you*,' Saul corrected her and although Chess was hot already, she felt her cheeks flush. 'There was no need for Jerome to beat you. You hadn't done anything wrong.'

'We don't have to do something wrong to be beaten,' said Splinter. 'We're street rats.'

'Not here. Nobody's a street rat here. We're all as good or as bad as each other,' and then Saul walked up the line of cages offering water as he went.

Chess watched him.

'*He's* talking about what's going on and *you* start chatting him up.' Splinter was disgusted.

'Chess has fallen in love,' taunted Box.

'I don't fall in love,' said Chess. She stopped watching Saul.

'Don't be fooled by his pretty eyes,' warned Splinter. 'We don't know him. "Trust no one," remember. Just like the old lady says.'

The afternoon heat thickened. As the caravan rumbled across the plains, the land changed. Gullies split the crusted earth, spanned by bridges and by the time that the white sun had begun to drop from its zenith the level rock of the plain was shattering into outcrops of boulders and knobbled fingers of stone. To their right a row of smoke-blue hills broke the horizon and seemed to swing in to meet them. Splinter thought that he could see a thick grey haze hiding the tops of distant mountains, behind the hills. But then the train was enclosed by the hills and he lost all sight of what lay in the distance. The hills rose up, rank on rank and grew darker so that by evening they were travelling in the shadows of purple-cragged mountains.

They saw Saul once more during the journey. This was after the train had stopped for the night. He brought them only water. Apart from telling them that the train would arrive at the factory the following day, he didn't stay to make conversation.

Morning came with a sky streaked grey, then lilac, then pink. Although every cage that they could see was provided with a meagre breakfast of porridge and water, the Tuesdays received nothing. When the white sun rose the train lurched forwards.

They were deep in the mountains now. The carts snaked along the bed of a long-dead river before sweeping into a wide pass. The train picked up speed, throwing the occupants of the cages against the bars as it clattered recklessly over the track. Chess counted sixty mounted traders on the flanks and there were more hidden by the bends and the storm of dust. They were yelling to one another and to the jabaloupes who sometimes hollered back.

'Over there,' said Splinter, 'look over there.'

Chess and Box looked. At first it was difficult to see what lay up the pass because of the grit clouds and because the sky ahead had filled with shadow. Sheets of charcoal fog gathered over the mountains, drifting up and down the crags and swirling on their slopes like phantoms. But as the train shook, going ever faster, they caught glimpses of the end of the pass.

Towering cliffs met at a vast mountain of black basalt rock. It filled their view as they sped closer. The slopes were broad and swept down in a series of ridges and concave stone curtains. Rolling up the sides of this huge mountain was a pall of oily, grey smoke. It was this smoke, pouring upwards in dense plumes and unfurling itself into the great fog that clung to the mountains that Splinter had glimpsed the day before.

The white sun was a bright disc that flickered through narrow tears in the sheets of smog. Chess couldn't see the red sun at all but whether it was hidden by mountains or by smoke she couldn't tell. The air was bitter and foul-smelling.

The train swung right, round a sharp bend in the track and the cages tilted perilously from the rails. There were shrieks up and down the line but not from Chess, Box or Splinter.

Chess gripped the iron bars hard, her lips pulled tight, her teeth clenched. Her hair whipped round her face and she squinted to keep it out of her eyes. She wanted to see as much as she could but it wasn't easy.

They were hurtling towards a tall black wall that ran the breadth of the bottom slope of the mountain. Above the wall, she saw pricks of light stab through the gloom: red, yellow and green. These were the sort of stark lights she had seen on aircraft or skyscrapers. All around the lights were pipes, rails and iron rigging, cooling towers, funnels and tall, cylindrical chimneys. This complex geometry of metalwork latticed the mountain as high as she could see. It drifted in and out of view as the curtain of smoke rose upwards. The smoke was spewing out of narrow chimneys in a dense torrent, shrouding the pass in perpetual dusk.

Chess saw a pair of huge, solid gates slide apart in the black wall, revealing a yawning tunnel. The mountain loomed above her, lights flashing, smoke churning. Then the train plunged into the tunnel and into darkness.

CHAPTER 4

The train stopped. Nobody spoke. Everything was still. Chess could hear her own breathing, loud in the darkness. She could also hear Box and Splinter breathing close by. Then, with a thump of power, the area was flooded with stark electric light.

She saw that they were in a tunnel with uneven walls, chiselled out of black rock. The train was flanked by smooth concrete platforms on either side and it curved out of sight in both directions as if it had drawn to a halt in a huge circle or a crescent.

The platforms were level with the floor of the cage. The one on the outer curve of the tunnel was about ten feet wide. There were plain iron doors in sunken arches at irregular intervals along the tunnel wall. The inner platform was a similar width. On its far side, iron bars extending to the ceiling formed the front of a series of cells that followed the curve of the tunnel like a carousel. Opposite every cage on the train was a cell on the inner platform.

'Not more cages,' groaned Box, whose swollen right cheek and black eye looked especially livid in the glare of the tunnel lights. Then he laughed at Splinter. 'You look like a beetroot,' he said.

Splinter's sunburned forehead and cheeks glowed a deep pink and made his hair even whiter by contrast.

'You look as stupid as ever, fly head,' he said. 'At least my sunburn will go.'

Their exchange was cut short by a voice that droned from speakers in the tunnel roof.

'You have arrived at the processing bay. You will be escorted to the holding area. Please co-operate.'

There was a pause and then the same, lifeless voice spoke again but in a different language. As the flow of instructions in different tongues continued, the clamour of thousands of children swelled throughout the tunnel.

The Tuesdays said nothing. They watched and listened. The messages had stopped now but the buzz of children's voices was punctuated by a series of rapid clangs as iron bar doors were being opened and slammed shut along the platform.

Chess saw that there were parties of traders working their way down the train. Each party consisted of three traders, spears in hand. They opened the cages on the train and hauled out the children who they bundled into the cages that were behind the bars on the other side of the platform. They did this efficiently and it was obvious to Chess that this was a well-practised drill.

Whenever the traders encountered a reluctant victim or one who put up a fight they did not hesitate to use their whips or their long legs to kick or spears to jab. It seemed to

Chess that they enjoyed this. It was the only time that she had seen the traders grin.

They stalked up and down the line of cages with thumping wide strides. Their squat bodies bobbed over their legs and their gargoyle heads jerked, but Splinter wasn't watching them. His attention was focused on the solitary figures in black uniform who were marching between the busy bands of traders, observing what was happening as if they were in charge. The nearest one stood a couple of yards from their cage with his back towards them. Chess and Box had been so occupied looking up the tunnel that they hadn't seen him come.

Splinter nudged Chess in the back and pointed. Chess took a long look at the figure's black boots and black uniform and frowned to herself. They were so familiar. Even though the tunic was hidden beneath a black-slabbed vest of body armour and the utility belt carried equipment she didn't recognize and a hood hung down from the back of the tunic and a segmented tube ran from the hood to the belt and there was a weapon that looked like a power drill without a bit slung behind the figure's back, in every other way she might have been looking at a . . .

'Hunter!' exclaimed Box.

But Splinter had seen what they hadn't and he shook his spiky-haired head. 'No, not a hunter.' He paused. 'This is worse than a hunter.'

Chess stepped forwards to take a better look. Now that Splinter had said what he had she noticed how the back of the figure's head was smooth with sleek black hair that ran down his neck until hidden by the collar of his jacket. She noticed how his ears were also black and they followed the sides of his head, rising to sharp points. And as she strained harder she noticed how the thick hairs from the base of the figure's skull and down the nape of its neck began to bristle.

Chess kept staring. The black-haired head cocked to one side and she thought that maybe the left ear twitched.

Whatever he is, thought Chess, he knows I'm watching him.

With explosive agility, the figure turned and sprang at Chess's cage, his black-gloved hands gripping the bars and jolting them hard. Chess shrieked and fell backwards, colliding with Box who was standing behind her, gawping.

She had seen a head like this before; the snarling muzzle, fangs strung with saliva and crazed yellow eyes. But unlike the Inspector's, this face didn't change back into a human one. It remained a grotesque mix of dog and man as if made out of pieces of both. Patches of human skin were exposed where there was no fur on its forehead and the end of the creature's snout was the colour of human flesh and crusted with a line of grey warts.

The creature's dog jaws snapped shut and he turned his head first one way and then the other, studying Chess intently. He breathed in short snorts, waxy nostrils flaring. Then he put his hand close to his silver belt-buckle where there was a small pack with a button that flashed green. He pushed the button and a section of the bars on the platform immediately behind him slid open.

Three traders joined him and he motioned to Chess and her brothers and then to the cell on the other side of the platform. At spear tip they were nudged out of the cage. Box expected the traders to separate him from Plan B, but they seemed interested only in moving him and his brother and sister from the train to the cell. Once they were in the cell the bars slid to, closing the opening.

The figure in the black uniform and the three traders moved to another cage in the train.

'What was that?' asked Box, sitting on his suitcase and scratching his curly-haired head with both hands.

'It was like the Inspector,' said Chess, quietly. The sound and the smell of the gun battle at the wharf was in her head and so was the sight of the Inspector holding Gemma at knifepoint. She felt a surge of adrenalin that squeezed her heart and left her legs weak and she clutched the cell bars to hold herself up.

'What's the matter with you?' Splinter looked at Chess with interest.

'Nothing.' She took a deep breath and let go of the bars. 'Just wish I knew what was happening.'

'There's four that I can see,' said Box. 'Like hunters but with dog heads.'

'With bits of dog heads,' Splinter corrected him. He leant his tall, lanky body against the bars they had come through and stared at Chess as if his eyes could peel away skin and bone and see the thoughts within.

'Their badges are different from the hunters',' observed Chess, steady now. 'Did you see? Instead of a skull and cross bones there is a number 8, but on its side. On the sides of their shoulders.'

'Their stuff is weird,' Box said. 'Different weapons.'

'What have you done, Chess?' Splinter tossed the question

as if it was nothing more than a pleasantry, but Chess saw the flint chill in his eye and knew there would be trouble.

'I haven't done anything, Splinter,' she protested.

He shouldered himself away from the bars. 'Why have you brought us here, Chess? What have you got going with the old lady? Has she told you secrets? Things she won't tell us?'

'No, Splinter. Honest. Nothing.'

'You're the one that everybody's after. You're the one the Twisted Symmetry want, Chess. You're the one who's meant to be special.'

'Please, Splinter, don't start all that again.'

'You wanted us to come here and now we're prisoners, guarded by traders and dog-men. Well done.' He thrust his face up to Chess's. 'But why? What's this all about?'

'Don't pick on her, Splinter,' said Box. 'Just because you're frightened.'

'I'm not frightened,' Splinter growled. 'But she's going to tell me what's going on.' He snatched at Chess's pullover but she pulled her arm away before he could grip it.

'You want to know what's going on?' Box barged in front of Splinter, blocking the way to Chess. 'Really? Do you? Well, don't ask *her*; ask *him*,' and he pointed at the nearest trader. 'You, with the stupid face and bad hair,' hollered Box.

The trader looked over to Box, dark eyes smouldering.

'Don't be an idiot, fly head,' warned Splinter.

'Yeah, you, you steaming heap of dung,' continued Box.

'Don't Box,' implored Chess.

The trader hesitated, clearly astonished that one of the prisoners was shouting at him.

'That's right. You with the good looks and the breath like road kill.'

The trader marched over and roared at Box, 'Jelabi swaf bi jander!'

Box stood his ground. 'OK,' he said, slowly, 'I'm sorry. I lied about the good looks.'

'Jander bi,' spat the trader.

'You're welcome, you rancid lump of nose hair,' replied Box with a slight bow. The trader shook his head and walked away. Box turned round. 'Gosh, Splinter, they're not very helpful, are they?'

Splinter shook his head. 'You are the most stupid creature alive. Carry on like that and we're going to end up as trader kebab.'

'Well, she doesn't know what's happening,' snapped Box, pointing at Chess, 'and he's not going to tell us. You're the one who's meant to be a genius. Let's hear how you plan to find out what's going on?'

Splinter turned on the spot, studying the cell. It was almost square with bars on three sides and an iron wall with a door-sized panel at the back, opposite the entrance. There were cells on either side, separated by the bars. All the children had been unloaded from the train and they filled the cells that curved out of sight up and down the tunnel.

The dog-men had gone and the trader that Box had shouted at was standing on the platform four cells up from them. The cell nearest to him contained two girls, both younger than Chess. They were sitting on the floor in silence. Splinter noticed the trader move his hand to a small pack clipped to his belt, like the one the dog-man had used to open the entrance to their cell. The panel at the back of the girls' cell slid open and two dog-men entered. One carried a metal rod with large C-shaped brackets at either end. Before the girls could shuffle away they were gripped by the dog-men and the brackets clasped shut around their necks.

The dog-men worked swiftly and silently but the girls screamed and kept screaming until they had been hauled out of the cell, yoked to one another and choking. When they had gone the panel slid back into place but the screams echoed from the other side, gradually receding until all that remained was a heavy silence.

'Any ideas, Splinter?' asked Box, subdued now.

'If they get us like that it's too late,' said Splinter, more to himself than to Box. 'But no locks to pick so how do we get out?'

He stood in the centre of the cell and closed his eyes, hands in his trouser pockets, thinking. Chess closed her eyes too but that was because she didn't want to see what was happening three cells away where the back panel had opened and more children were being extracted by dog-men.

'Five minutes,' said Splinter when the scuffling and shouting was over. 'They're taking about five minutes between each cell.'

'So we have a quarter of an hour before they come for us?' observed Box. 'What are we meant to do, Splinter? Start digging?'

'No,' answered Splinter. 'You have to shout at the trader. Get him over here again. Right up to the bars. Close enough to touch you.'

'But you've just said how stupid that is.'

'It was stupid then, but it isn't stupid now,' replied Splinter, cryptically. 'I'll do the thinking. You do the shouting.'

Box pushed his lips between the bars and shouted, 'Oi! Pig mash.' The trader glanced over and then ignored him. Box shouted again, sticking his hand through the bars and gesticulating as offensively as he could. There was no response from the trader.

'It's like shouting at a brick,' complained Box

'Keep trying,' urged Splinter.

Chess retreated to the wall opposite the bars.

Box considered the available insults. Then inspiration struck. '*Jander bi!*' he yelled. '*Jander bi! Jander bi!*'

The reaction was more dramatic than he had expected. The trader unleashed a blast of furious gibberish and marched towards the cell.

'Yeah,' shouted Box, '*Jander bi* you great chunk of . . .' His T-shirt was gripped by a hand the size of a baseball glove and as he banged face first into the bars, the trader opened wide his stump-toothed mouth and breathed over him. The stench silenced Box and then he felt a hammer blow to his guts as the trader punched him in the stomach. Box staggered back, retching and the trader spat at him before walking away.

Chess ran to her brother, but he told her to get off when she rested a hand on his shoulder.

Splinter stepped back from where he had been standing, close to Box by the bars.

Bent double and coughing, Box managed to gasp, 'What was that meant to achieve?'

'This,' said Splinter, surreptitiously revealing a small cube in the palm of his hand. A tiny green light was flashing on it. 'Jacks couldn't do that,' he boasted. 'We've got to move fast, Box, before he realizes I've whipped it from his belt. We're going to have seconds, maybe a minute at most.'

'Come on then,' groaned Box, belly aching.

Splinter pointed the flashing green light towards the panel at the back of the cell. He pressed the light and the panel slid open. They darted through the opening. Then Splinter pressed the light again and the panel closed behind them.

They were standing in a corridor that was well lit and stretched to their left and right. Immediately in front of them was a pair of doors. Splinter hesitated long enough to throw the cube down the corridor where it bumped and skidded before stopping thirty metres away. Then he ran through the double doors. Chess and Box followed, Chess pulling the suitcase.

'We have to put some distance between us and the cells,' panted Splinter as they ran down another corridor, bare feet slapping the floor. 'Then we hide.'

They dashed through doors and down stairs and along corridors. They had no idea where they were going.

Chess couldn't believe that they hadn't run into someone by now. They had just clattered down an iron staircase and come to a corridor whose walls and ceilings were lined with thick iron pipes. She stopped running and scanned the corridor anxiously for somewhere to hide.

She was panting loudly because she had been running with the suitcase and because she was frightened. Chess noticed that her breathing always seemed to get louder the more frightened she was.

One day it will give you away, she had thought before now. But right now it seemed that there was no one to see her or hear her. However, as she listened to her own breathing she thought she heard something else, something that was just at the edge of her hearing, something that was so faint that she wondered whether she was only imagining it.

It sounded like voices. Lots of voices. Children's voices, all talking at once. They started like a distant murmur but grew louder like a wave coming in on the sea. The volume increased, rushing at her. She tried to hear what the voices were saying but the words were a jumble. She couldn't see where they came from. Then she heard a scream and a bright flash filled her mind and in the flash she thought she saw a door with a small round window at its top.

Then another voice interrupted the others. 'Chess, come on.' It was Box, shouting as quietly as he could from further up the corridor.

Chess stopped listening to the voices. Or maybe they faded away. She was left with an uncomfortable feeling as if she was upset and angry at the same time although she wasn't sure why. Then she heard only her gasps for breath as she ran after her brothers, holding the suitcase which was swaying out of pace and banging against her legs.

She caught up with Box and Splinter. Splinter glowered at her. 'What do you think you're doing?' he spluttered, trying not to raise his voice. It was obvious to her that neither Splinter nor Box had heard the voices or experienced the image that had flashed through her mind.

Chess thrust the suitcase into Box's hands but she didn't

have time to reply because the crump of boots approaching from a corner up ahead sent them scrambling through the nearest door.

The room they entered was hot and dark and it smelt of steam and oil. An orange glow enabled Chess to pick out shapes but there was not enough light to see clearly. The room was filled with metal pipes that ran along the walls, the floor and up towards the ceiling where they disappeared in darkness. Everywhere, the cylindrical hulks of boilers hummed and rumbled gently. Chess could not see where the room ended because it was so dark and the room was so big.

Box seemed to have recovered from the blow to his stomach. Suitcase in hand he was following Splinter who was edging his way around the machinery. With a backwards glance at the door, Chess followed her brothers, rubbing her palm where the suitcase handle had dug into the cut.

The light glowed more brightly and it became hotter as they crept further into the room.

Box asked Splinter where they were going.

'As far away from that door as we can,' came the reply.

'What kind of room is this?' asked Chess from the back.

'Some kind of generator or power house,' said Splinter. 'You can tell from all the boilers and engines and pipes. It's massive. Probably provides power for the whole of this dump. And it's hot.' He wiped sweat from his forehead, smearing grime across his face from where his fingers had touched oily pipes. He went on to explain how they might be approaching a central furnace or something like that but Chess had stopped listening to him.

She had been shuffling forwards and looking up. All she

saw was vaulted darkness from which were suspended chains and tubes, hanging motionless. But she knew that whilst she had been staring into the soaring gloom, she was being watched.

Chess knew what it felt like to be watched; how everything seemed to go quiet, how her skin tingled, how her mouth went dry. Now, her skin prickled all over and the back of her head and the small of her back felt exposed. She noticed how acrid the oily smell had become and she noticed again how loudly she was breathing. She turned on the spot, looking all around her and all around were the looming shoulders of boilers and the pipes, running out of the darkness and back into it. Between the boilers and the pipes there were dark spaces. She looked for movement across these spaces but saw nothing.

But something was watching her. Coming closer. Chess knew this even though her eyes saw only darkness and silhouettes splashed orange in the glow of the room.

Maybe it's above me, she thought and she looked up. She saw nothing. But one long, loose chain was swinging slowly.

They were not alone.

She could hear her own breathing. It was louder than ever. She could tell that the louder she breathed, the closer the thing was coming.

Stop breathing so loud, she told herself. Hide.

But all she did was to turn her head like a bird, wide eyes straining. She could even hear her heart thumping as if it was inside her head.

'Chess,' hissed Splinter. His voice came from a short distance away. 'Get over here.'

As surely as she had known that the thing had come close to her, now Chess knew that she was alone again. She exhaled slowly and looked up. Above her the chain had stopped swinging. Catching her foot on a U-bolt on the floor and tripping forwards, she followed Splinter's voice.

She found him crouching next to Box, behind a low, mesh gate. On the other side steps zigzagged down to a hall. Although the hall was below them and mostly out of sight they had a view, through the stairwell, of a massive cylinder that seemed to come through the metal floor of the hall as if it started from somewhere beneath.

The cylinder was luminous with reds and oranges that rolled up it in swirling rings like liquid bands of flame. As each band of flame spiralled up the cylinder a blast of heat surged over Splinter, Box and Chess and a fierce glow bathed the boiler room.

They could only see a section of the cylinder from their position behind the mesh gate, just as they had a limited view into the hall below. The bands of flame surged up and disappeared where their view was cut by the edge of the stairwell.

Chess didn't tell Splinter what had happened because he was whispering urgently when she reached him. 'Be quiet. Someone's talking down there. I can't see anyone but they're coming closer.'

'Shouldn't we get away?' suggested Box.

Splinter turned towards Box, and Chess noticed how the flame-licked half-light painted his grinning face demonic red. 'No way, Box. This is what we're here for. To find out what's happening, yeah? We must be in the heart of this place so maybe we'll find out something important.'

They were silenced by a steady, jarring thud. It sounded like metal on metal and Chess tried to see where it came from. The thud grew louder and then a dog-man came into view. He was taller than the others she had seen and broad-shouldered and he wore a long cloak of sleek brown fur. He walked slowly, the steel-shod soles of his boots hammering against the metal floor of the lower hall. His lean body was encased by an ill-matched jigsaw of broken black armour that was strung together by chains. The thud of his boots was accompanied by the clink of the chains.

The dog-man's jackal-snouted face was fixed in a slash of snarl.

At the foot of the stairs he stopped and unclipped a long baton from his belt. Chess had seen similar tools carried on the belts of other dog-men. It was black and about two feet long. Lumps at either end resembled thick, hexagonal bolts. He pressed a button on the top of the baton with his thumb. Instantly, a shining blade shot downwards. Holding the baton with the blade pointing down, the dog-man rammed it so that its tip bashed the floor.

As soon as he did this two other dog-men came into view from the opposite direction. They dragged someone between them, a human, whose wrists were bound behind his back and whose clothes were torn and dirty. Released, he slumped to his knees in front of the cloaked dog-man, who fired a series of short, angry growls at the two escorts. One of them answered back. They were speaking in a language that meant nothing to Box or Chess or Splinter. Whatever the escort said didn't satisfy the big dog-man because he shouted, drove the blade against the floor and shook his head.

Then he jabbed the point of the blade under the human's chin. Now Chess could see that it wasn't a blade but a long, thin spike with three edges coming to a sharp point. The dog-man raised the human's head, the point of the blade dimpling the skin under his jaw. The human's face was blotched although whether from dirt or from bruising it was difficult to tell. But in the crazy, orange glow of the cylinder, Chess recognized it immediately.

'Saul!' she gasped

Box elbowed her in the ribs.

The dog-man prodded the stick harder against Saul's skin and spoke in a sequence of questioning grunts. When Saul didn't reply, the dog-man pulled a wire from an iron collar he was wearing. The collar extended in a smooth plate to the top of his chest. One end of the wire remained fixed to the collar. The other he placed inside his pointed ear. He twisted a dial in the same side of the collar as the wire and this time, when he spoke, a grating, soulless voice crackled simultaneously from the collar.

'A boy called Jerome tells us that you spoke with a girl and two boys.' The voice was rough but clear. 'Is this true?'

'I spoke with lots of the prisoners,' said Saul. 'Jerome doesn't like me, General.'

The dog-man he called 'General' paused, listening to Saul's words as they were translated back to him through the ear-piece he was wearing. Then he growled loudly and the collar interpreted calmly, 'I am very busy. I want to know all about the girl. Everything. If you tell me I will return you to your duties. If you don't . . .'

Suddenly the General began to grunt and shake his head. Flecks of spit gathered on his muzzle. He twisted his neck from side to side and Chess thought that for an instant the flesh of his neck bulged in a dark purple ball as if something inside was trying to get out.

The General stamped his steel boot and opened his jaws with his head thrown back and bellowed. The other two dog-men drew away from him. Saul remained kneeling, head bowed.

'He looks like he's in agony,' said Splinter, fascinated.

'He looks like he's going to explode,' said Box.

The General rammed the point of the spike against the floor and bent double.

'What was that?' exclaimed Box, as first the General's back expanded like a giant balloon under his cloak and then a writhing tentacle, thick and brown, uncoiled from his side, thrashed vigorously against the floor and then withdrew back into his torso.

The General heaved himself upright and threw out his left arm so that it was fully extended. On either side of the forearm there was a brass strut and each strut was attached to a brass ring; one around his wrist and another immediately below his elbow. Thin rods inserted between the parallel struts and through his arm held the device in place. Two narrow steel bars ran up the inside of his forearm from the circlet around his wrist to the one below his elbow.

Body shaking, the General clenched tight his leather-gloved left fist. There was a loud click and a small iron bolt shot up the steel bars from his wrist, burying its tip in the crook of his arm. Then a small tube ejected from the bolt.

It hit the floor with a tinkle and rolled to a stop.

Immediately, the General's body relaxed. With his left hand he took a tube like the one that had just fallen to the floor from a box on his belt and using the same hand, adroitly slipped it into the bolt which had returned to his wrist. Then he leant forwards, resting on the baton with the tip of the spike on the floor, like a walking stick.

'As I was saying, boy,' he continued, panting a little. 'If you don't help me you'll be wishing I had sent you to the scream rooms like the other children.'

Saul did not reply.

'The girl is important. The Inquisitor wants her. He has asked me to take you to him if you won't co-operate.' The General dropped his gloved hand to Saul's head where it rested for a moment before clutching his hair. Saul winced. 'But it is a long way from here to the top level and my time is precious. And I prefer to save my energy for more important tasks. So unless you tell me about the girl, I will kill you now.'

Tell them, thought Chess, I don't care. I don't even know why they want me.

But Saul said nothing.

The General roared at him and the voice from the collar said, 'Enough!'

Wrenching Saul's hair, the dog-man yanked him upright. Even though Saul was tall, he was a head shorter than the General. The General pulled back Saul's head, exposing the pale flesh of his throat.

'Human blood,' he grunted, before opening wide his fanged jaws and fastening them to Saul's neck.

Chess stood up. 'No,' she shouted. 'Leave him.'

The General turned his head to look up at her. For a moment it seemed that the ghost of a grin danced at the edge of his sly, dog eyes. Then he growled to the other two dog-men and the voice spoke coldly.

'Get her.'

CHAPTER 5

'Splinter,' urged Box. 'We've got to run.' Already the two
dog-men who had dragged Saul to the General had unslung
their snub-nosed machine guns and were halfway up the
stairs, boots clanging on metal and grunting as they charged.
But Splinter knew that Box and Chess were waiting for him
to say what they should do.

Without me, they are helpless, he thought.

'Not yet,' replied Splinter, calmly. He put his hand into
one of the pockets inside his long-tailed morning coat and
waited until the heads of the dog-men were just below his.
Then he pulled his hand from his pocket and gently released
a fistful of marbles. They clattered noisily as they bounced
down the steps and under the dog-men's boots.

The one who was in front lost his footing immediately.
His foot shot back as it landed on the marbles and he fell
forwards, bashing his shin on the next step. Then he careered
sideways and the second dog-man ran into him and then
lost his footing on the dancing balls of glass. The two of
them crashed down the stairs painfully.

'Now,' ordered Splinter. 'Go!'

He launched himself back into the shadows that they had crept through minutes before. Chess stayed close to him. Box paused, took time to shove PLAN B below a boiler that stood on a low platform and then followed.

We're rats, thought Splinter, so think like rats. His sharp eyes raked the gloom for anything that might help them escape. He noticed a chain dangling from the darkness overhead. It stopped about four feet from the floor. He couldn't see where it went.

'Up there,' he commanded. From somewhere behind and below them there came yells and growls. Then footfalls on the stairs, slow and cautious now. 'Up that chain. It must go somewhere. We're rats, right? We'll find a shaft or pipe we can crawl along. A room like this has to have ventilation. The chain must go somewhere.'

Chess stared at the chain and swallowed hard. It wasn't that she was worried about getting up the chain without falling. She could climb like a cat: or a rat. It was the thought of what might be lurking up there in the darkness that made her hesitate. But she knew that Splinter would not listen to her and she knew that if she stayed where she was the dog-men would get her. So she had no choice. She would have to climb.

Splinter was already climbing the chain and once he was a body length up it, Box jumped, hauled himself up and climbed after him. Chess heaved and began to climb. She locked her ankles against the thick links as soon as she had pulled herself high enough and she pushed up with her legs as she pulled with her hands. Although the surface of the chain was smoother than rope, the width of the links made it easy to climb because she could get her hands inside them. She climbed quickly, even with her brothers above her and the chain swaying.

As she climbed, Chess tried to stop herself thinking about what had been watching her earlier. She did this by concentrating on the physical sensations of the climb; the warm metal against her hands, the smell of oil, the hum of the machinery below. She counted to herself the number of times she pushed with her legs. But she could not stop the thought of an empty chain swinging above her head from creeping back into her mind.

It didn't take long to climb above the tallest of the boiler hulks and now they were moving through a framework of girders and joists that couldn't be seen from floor level. These supported more pipes which interlinked in the air around the chain like scaffolding.

From below there came footsteps and voices; the two dog-men walking and talking quietly to one another.

Splinter and Box had come to a halt above her so Chess stopped, letting her ankles and thighs take the strain so she could ease the pressure where her cut palm was stinging. The chain was swaying only slightly. She and her brothers clung to it, motionless.

The dog-men came into view below, shadows edged with orange. It was only when Chess saw how small they were that she realized how high they had climbed. They walked side by side, weapons ready at their hips and they swivelled left and right as they walked, searching for the Tuesdays.

At the bottom of the chain they stopped and one of them flicked on a torch. The thick, yellow beam penetrated the dark so neatly it might have been a rod of light. It arced left and right before it was swung up to illuminate the shadows above. Chess, Box and Splinter were absolutely still. Chess held her breath. There was a murmur of conversation below. Then the torch light swung back down and the dog-men moved on.

'OK,' whispered Splinter from above. 'We've come to something. A small platform, I think.'

When Box and Chess reached him he was standing on a narrow metal shelf. 'There's a shaft here. It comes down from above and then away from me. I don't know where it goes but it's hollow.' He tapped it gently and it echoed. 'It's bigger than I can feel. There's a bolt and I guess this must be a hatch that leads into it.' It was too dark for Chess to see what he was talking about.

'I'll go in first,' Splinter said. 'There's only room for one at a time on the platform. You two follow.'

Chess heard a bolt slide back and a metallic creak. Then there was shuffling and then the hiss and flare of a match struck by Splinter. Now she could see the head and shoulders of his shadow rear up.

'It's quite big,' he said, voice resonating. 'It must be a service shaft. Easily big enough to walk in. Come on.' The match guttered and went out.

Chess listened to Box climb up and then she let go of the chain, clutched the metal shelf and heaved herself onto it. Kneeling, she felt for the opening above. It was easy to slide inside because the hatch was as wide as the shaft.

Chess could stand inside the shaft. It seemed dark at first but as she walked she realized that at intervals there were dim security lights in the roof. These allowed her to see well enough to pick out Box and Splinter, twenty metres ahead. She noticed that beneath every security light there was a hatch on the floor, secured by a bolt. She didn't notice that there were similar hatches in the ceiling.

'You two are useless,' Splinter was muttering.

'You took us into that room in the first place, remember?' replied Box.

'Only because you were standing in the corridor like a pillock with the words "Catch Me" stamped on your forehead.'

'Only because you nearly got us caught,' said Box.

Splinter stopped walking and turned to face Box. 'Who got us out of the cell? Me. Who got us out of the corridors? Me. Who got us away from the creatures on the stairs? Me. Who lands us in it every time? You or *her*.' Chess had caught up with her brothers but hung back when Splinter said 'her' with particular venom. 'Do you see a pattern?' he asked.

Chess knew that this time, Splinter was right. She had nearly got them caught by sticking up for Saul when he wasn't even a member of their gang. Splinter sensed her guilty silence.

'What the hell did you think you were doing?' he fired at her.

'I wasn't thinking, Splinter,' stuttered Chess. 'I'm sorry. OK?'

'We stick together and help each other. We don't take risks for anyone else. Understand?'

Chess returned his glare without blinking. She did not

regret what she had done. She said, 'It's wrong to watch people die.'

'You just fancy him.' Splinter's words were nails.

'Shut up,' said Chess, hoarsely.

'Don't tell me to shut up when you're the one who can't control yourself.'

'Just shut up, Splinter.'

'Keep the noise down,' urged Box.

Splinter was undeterred. 'You got us into this mess; acting like the old crone's performing monkey.'

'Shut up,' shouted Chess.

'You shut up,' Splinter yelled back.

An abrupt crash of metal behind them as a hatch slammed down and Chess spun round in time to see a dog-man drop through the roof of the shaft.

'Run,' shouted Box.

Chess ran after her brothers, glancing back to see what might be following. But the dog-man remained where he had landed. She saw him pull an object from his belt and throw it after them. She heard it land, bouncing before it stopped. Chess stopped running to see what would happen next.

With a gentle clicking and snapping, a whirling ball of blades unfolded from where the object had stopped. It extended until it filled the whole of the shaft. The light was dim but Chess had no trouble seeing the silver flashes, slashing and slicing in all directions. The blades were mounted on a nest of spindles. Some were the size of swords, others were no bigger than cut-throat razors and they shuffled and hatched across one another at increasing speed but without touching. Then the shaft-wide ball started to roll towards her, silent but for the whirr of riffling blades, picking up speed.

The shaft went in a straight line. It was obvious that before long the spinning, shearing sphere would catch up with Chess and her brothers. The only obstacle in its path would be their bodies.

'What have you done now?' Splinter managed to shout over his shoulder at Chess.

'I haven't done anything,' Chess screamed back, angry as well as frightened and running hard. She was at the back which meant that the first body to be chopped to pieces would be hers. She could tell that the ball was accelerating.

Splinter looked back and shouted at her again. 'You're a total disaster, Chess,' and then he caught his foot on a bolt on the floor and lost his balance, slamming into the shaft wall and landing heavily on his outstretched hand. In moments Chess had caught up with him. He was sitting on the floor and yelping with pain.

'I've broken it,' he whined, holding up his right wrist. The hand hung limply.

'I don't think that's going to matter,' observed Box. 'Not once that thing has chopped it off for you.'

The whirr of razor-edged metal rolled towards them rapidly.

'We have seconds,' said Box.

Chess looked at the blades, looked at the floor of the shaft and then she knew what to do. She stepped to where Splinter had tripped.

'What are you doing now, fool?' Splinter groaned.

Chess kicked the bolt with the heel of her foot. It didn't move. The blades were no more than five metres away.

'Chess,' urged Box, not knowing what she was doing and wondering whether he shouldn't run anyway. He could see the individual blades, sharp and bright. In no time they would be slicing through the place where Chess was kneeling.

Chess yanked the bolt with her hand and felt it give way a fraction. Time for one kick, she thought. All I have is one kick.

She drove her heel across the knob of the bolt to ram it back. A spur of pain jarred up to her groin and she lost her balance and staggered against the shaft wall but the bolt shot free. The section of floor dropped open revealing a broad square of darkness as wide as the shaft. The ball of blades toppled over the lip of the opening and plummeted into the space below.

Box grabbed hold of Chess who was teetering on the edge of the drop. The ring and clash of metal on metal ended with a distant crump as the ball of blades smashed through whatever was in the darkness below until it was stopped by the floor.

They were alone in the shaft.

'What did you do?' asked Splinter, eyes pink and smarting as he held his wrist against his chest with his good arm.

'Nothing,' said Chess. Her voice shook. She was tired of Splinter's constant criticisms and a nauseating ache pulsed from her foot to her belly from kicking the bolt.

'Why didn't you use the VAP?' whined Splinter.

'The what?' asked Chess.

'The VAP. Remember? That thing on your wrist. The thing that's meant to get us out of here.'

'I didn't think of it,' admitted Chess.

'Why not?'

'Because I was thinking of you,' shouted Chess. 'Because you had fallen badly and because you were going to be cut to bits.' Her thick hair clustered round her face which was smeared with oil and her eyes were brimming. 'I was thinking of you, Splinter,' she shouted.

When the echo had died, Splinter said, 'That is what makes you weak.' His voice was slow and deliberate and cold.

'Sometimes you make me sick,' said Chess and she walked along the shaft and away from him, limping slightly.

Box caught up with her as Splinter loped sullenly at the rear. 'He doesn't always mean what he says,' Box reassured Chess, resting an arm on her shoulder.

'Splinter always means what he says,' said Chess, her voice shaking because she was crying now.

'Well, he's stupid then.' Box held both her upper arms and turned her to make her look at him. Chess tried to look away. Sometimes she found it hard to look into people's eyes, particularly when they were staring into hers.

'I think you were brave, Chess, really brave and really clever. OK?' His voice was strong and steady. 'I didn't have a clue what to do. The last thing I'd have thought of was a VAP or whatever it is.' He laughed. 'I couldn't have tied a shoelace. Even if I had a shoe.'

Although Chess was crying she started to laugh. Then, without thinking about it, she grabbed hold of Box and hugged him. Box rubbed the top of her head.

'This place is making both of you ridiculous,' muttered Splinter, walking past them. 'Since when did we play happy families? Anyway, look at what you're standing on.'

Chess let go of Box and looked at what her feet, mottled grey with dirt, were standing on.

'Rock,' said Box

'Correct, genius,' said Splinter, spike-haired head jerking as he looked around. 'The shaft leads into a rock tunnel which gets narrower and then ... well, we can't see because it's pitch.'

'Do we go on?' asked Box.

'We can't go back,' replied Splinter, making the decision. His eyes narrowed. 'My guess is that this is a natural channel, to get air into the factory. So it should take us outside. The only question is, how big is the tunnel.'

'And whether it's one tunnel or a network,' said Chess, wiping her nose with the dangling sleeve of her jumper. 'It would be easy to get lost.'

'Then we follow our noses,' announced Splinter, 'and sniff for fresh air. We're rats, remember?'

'You always say that,' Chess retorted. 'I think it would be nice to be something other than a rat.'

'Ridiculous,' said Splinter. 'Again.'

'But we might get stuck. We might get jammed in a tight place and trapped in total darkness. We might die in there,' complained Box.

'If you get stuck in a tight place you've only yourself to blame, pig boy,' was Splinter's reply. 'And as for dying, that could happen anywhere here. At least you've got two good hands. I've got to make do with one.'

'If we get stuck, we *could* use the VAP,' suggested Chess. 'But we ought to see where the tunnel goes first.'

'Ought we? Says who?' Splinter folded his arms. Chess was silent. Then he said, 'All right. We'll see where it goes. Then we'll have seen everything we need to.'

Chess was not sure how long they spent inching their way through the tunnels and caverns within the volcano. Maybe a whole day; it was hard to tell in a world where it was so dark that she couldn't even see her hand if she touched her nose.

Splinter took the lead as they crawled and scrambled and squeezed their way through the stony darkness. Sometimes they were encased in a coffin of rock, so narrow were the tunnels. At other times they were hit by a waft of cold air and their whispers echoed back and forth as if they were in a church.

But Splinter's nose was as accurate as he had boasted because after what felt to Chess like an eternity of staring wide-eyed at a black blanket, she realized that she could see the shapes of Box and then Splinter edging forward ahead of her. Then she could see that they were worming their way through a narrow, diamond-shaped channel. Then, in front of her was a speck of light that spread into a wide slash before filling the opening ahead so brightly that Chess had to shield her eyes until they had adjusted to it.

What also hit her was the heat: a heavy, damp warmth that flooded into the tunnel entrance like liquid rather than air. With the humid air came musky scents, so sweet that Chess thought she could taste them on her tongue. Mixed with this sweetness was the tang of salt and at first,

Chess had no idea what this could have come from.

She staggered out of the opening to where Box and Splinter were sitting on a slab of cracked rock and there she was hit by the vastness of what lay before them.

They were on the lower slopes of the volcano. Below them was a bowl-shaped valley that was filled with a dense and wild tangle of treetops. To her right, the valley was enclosed by a crescent of cliffs whose shoulders rose up to a high plateau, beyond which there were ridges that merged into the dark blue haze of distant mountains. At the centre of the crescent the cliffs split into a gorge from which a low mist drifted over the trees.

Every ledge, every ridge, every ravine was festooned with rioting vegetation so that from the bottom of the valley to the tops of the heights there was a luxurious and unbroken canopy like green baize.

Out of the canopy below came cries and screeches from birds and animals that Chess couldn't see. Behind these noises there was a constant, rhythmic hiss. It whispered over the trees in the valley from the bay to their left where cream-tipped waves fizzed up a narrow bar of white sand, ripped by black rocks. The forest swept down to the edge of the bay which curved gently.

Never before had Chess seen such a spread of space and colour. She thought she might plummet from the volcano and drown in it. She thrust her palms onto the rock to stop herself falling forwards even though she was perfectly secure.

Opposite them, on the far side of the valley, was another volcano. It reared above the trees, buttresses and ridges of hard black rock scored deep with shadows cast by the sun, sculpting the slopes hard and sharp. The top was plumed white although Chess could not be sure whether this was mist or smoke. Its left face swept down to the sea, like the seaward slopes of the volcano on which she was sitting.

Box was the first to speak. 'How far away is that?' he asked, shielding his eyes from the bright sun and looking at the volcano on the other side of the valley.

'Eight miles, maybe seven,' guessed Splinter. 'How can I tell? I don't spend a lot of time looking at mountains and rainforests.'

'Just wondered,' said Box, lamely.

'Maybe it's a jungle,' volunteered Chess, quietly.

Splinter screwed up his eyes as he tried to penetrate the distant curve of the bay.

'The sea goes on forever,' mused Chess, searching for the place where sea became sky. Out there, everything merged into endless shades of blue.

Splinter shook his head. 'We are stuck on a volcano. To our left is the sea. To our right are cliffs and mountains and below us is a forest, no doubt packed with exotic creatures that eat things like us.'

'There must be water down there,' said Chess, whose throat was parched. Apart from a lick of water that had been running down a crack inside the tunnel, they had not had a drink for at least a day. The bright sun was high and it was very hot. Chess couldn't see the red sun.

'Well, let's go back and we can get a drink,' stated Splinter.

'Back where?' asked Chess, confused.

'Back to Ethel or the Committee or wherever,' said

Splinter. 'Wherever we go back to when you press that thing on your wrist.'

Chess curled her fingers into her palms and said nothing.

'We've done what we were sent to do.' Splinter rubbed his swollen right wrist. 'We know what's at the end of the Fat Gobster.'

'Splinter,' said Chess, coolly, 'that's nothing. We don't know what actually happens to the children.' She wanted to find out about the children. But she realized that wasn't all she wanted to find out.

'OK,' said Splinter. 'We *actually* know they go to scream rooms.'

'That's not enough.' Chess pouted and studied her wrist, darkly. She had the VAP, which meant she decided what they did.

Splinter saw her face harden and recalled how stubborn Chess had been about cutting through the cerebral torus in the Riverside Prison when he and Box were urging her to leave it. She could have died. All of them could have died.

'We should go.' He was agitated, speaking too loudly. 'We know everything we could be expected to know.'

'You must be joking. We know hardly anything.' Chess pushed a stone with her toe.

'We know enough,' argued Splinter.

'We don't,' Chess shot back. 'But you've hurt your wrist and you're fed up and you just want to go back.'

'You're completely wrong,' Splinter screamed at her. 'You're just obsessed with being important because you think this is all to do with *you*.'

Splinter's voice shrieked over the roof of trees below and

for a moment it seemed that the forest noises fell silent and there was only the whispering of the sea.

'No, Splinter,' said Chess, calmly. '*You* are obsessed with this being about me. I wish it had nothing to do with me or any of us. But we're on a side, remember? The right side, for once. So we have to do this properly before we can go back.'

But Chess knew that Splinter was right in a way. She did want to find out about the children but there was something else; something that had started to burn into her like a white hot needle; she wanted to find out about herself; who she really was. Maybe the answer to that was the answer to everything else. If they went home now, there might not be any answers.

Chess said none of this. But she saw Splinter eyeing the VAP so she slid her hand behind her back.

'What's that?' asked Box, looking out at the bay.

'That big, blue thing with little white bits on it,' said Splinter, still looking at Chess, 'is called the sea, fly head.'

'No, what's *that*,' repeated Box, pointing.

Splinter switched his attention from Chess to where Box's thick forefinger was aimed.

'It looks like a pair of giant cartwheels moving through the sea,' said Chess.

'Without rims,' observed Box. 'Just spokes. And each spoke must be a hundred feet long, at least.'

'Two hundred,' said Splinter, quietly. 'It's bigger than it looks; it's still a long way out.'

The calm surface of the sea was churned white as both sets of spokes turned slowly. Each spoke was tipped with blunt spikes that trailed weed like pennants as it soared up and then descended, disappearing into the water in a splash of brine.

Although the wheels had no outer rims they were reinforced by struts that ran between the spokes at irregular positions. A thick axle joined the two central hubs of the wheels. This axle supported a series of decks of different sizes that were connected to one another by ladders and ropes.

'There's people moving on it,' said Chess, spotting tiny figures moving briskly across the decks and up and down the ropes and ladders. 'Not wearing black,' she added as if that might reassure Box and Splinter that this had nothing to do with the dog-men. The figures wore clothes that were light in colour and loose fitting.

Slung from the central axle, on a separate frame, was a long, narrow barrel. There were two platforms beneath it and the rest of the decks were above it. The barrel protruded beyond the spokes and was made of the same russet-coloured metal as the rest of the machine, like beaten copper.

The spokes flashed as they rotated in the sun, propelling the giant structure forwards. A trail of steam issued from a large globe positioned low and to the rear of the central decks.

The carriage was moving ponderously across the bay from where it had been obscured by the side of the volcano on which the Tuesdays were sitting. As it came into view it began to change its course, ploughing its way through the surf in an arc.

'It's turning,' said Box.

'Towards us,' said Splinter.

The carriage advanced to within a hundred metres of the edge of the bay. Then it stopped.

Chess could see that the figures were dark-skinned and that the gowns and scarves they wore covered their heads and bodies. These fluttered as the sashes caught the sea breeze. From amongst the billowing robes there was an occasional glint as the sun was reflected by bright metal.

'Is that armour?' asked Splinter.

Chess shrugged. 'Maybe,' she said.

'What are they doing now?' asked Box.

'One of them is turning a wheel,' observed Chess, watching a figure on the platform immediately above the barrel who was whirring his arm in a circle.

'It's a cannon, isn't it?' said Box.

As the wheel turned, the barrel gradually tilted upwards until it was pointing directly at them.

CHAPTER 6

'Go!' yelled Splinter but he needn't have bothered because Box and Chess were already skidding down the slope in a spray of loose rock.

As Splinter shouted there was a billow of grey smoke and a flash of flame from the cannon's muzzle. After a momentary pause the boom of the explosion rolled over the bay and the tops of the trees.

Chess heard a shrill whistling getting louder. Then all she knew was that somewhere above her the rock had erupted with a whoosh and roar and there was a burst of stone. Even though she was already running down the slope she was thrown forwards by the blast. Pieces of rock clattered to the ground around her and Box was shouting.

'They shot high. Come on!' he bellowed. 'Get down to the trees before they fire again.' The wall of forest was still some way below but it would hide them if they could reach it in time. Spread-eagled on the slope of the volcano they were exposed and vulnerable.

'My leg,' Splinter was shouting. 'I've hurt my leg.'

He was lying on his side a little higher up the slope than

87

Box and Chess and he was holding his right ankle with his left hand, the knee drawn up to his chest. Chess and Box scrambled up to him.

'I think I was hit by a rock,' he winced. Chess pulled up his trouser leg and grimaced at the lump of red and purple beneath the skin of his right ankle. 'A broken wrist and a broken ankle,' gasped Splinter.

'Can you stand?' asked Box, anxiously casting a glance over his shoulder and out to sea. The barrel was moving downwards slowly, re-aligning itself.

Splinter got to his feet but couldn't stand unless supported by one of the others.

'Lean your back against me,' said Box. 'That's it. With your legs in front of you. It's a smooth slope. I'll drag you down.'

'It's going to fire,' said Chess, urgently. She grabbed Splinter's legs and he yelped when her hand closed over his right ankle but she ignored his pain. They had to get down. They moved as fast as they were able and between them, Splinter was wrenched and dropped. Box lost his footing and fell backwards, banging his head. Chess tripped, bashing her knees. Splinter closed his eyes and clenched his teeth and tried not to cry out when pain racked him.

The cannon boomed. Incoming shot screeched through the air. Above them the rocks burst in a shower of flying stone but the shot was high again and Chess and Box kept going, shards of rock pattering down around them.

The bottom of the volcano sloped gently and Box and Chess were able to move more quickly, still carrying Splinter. The rock beneath their feet was suddenly lost beneath a carpet of earth and moss. Low shrubs and tall ferns unfurled from the ground and then Chess and Box were shouldering through damp creepers and they were in the gloom of the forest.

The gun did not fire again.

They pushed forwards until they had lost sight of the place where the open ground ended and the forest began and there, on a mound coated with moss and fungi, they dropped Splinter and collapsed.

Splinter was groaning and Box was laughing.

'This is ... this is ... this is ...' he stuttered, gasping for breath and giggling, 'this is the worst game of knock and run I've ever played.' He couldn't say any more because he was laughing so hard. He kept laughing until his tummy ached and the sides of his chest hurt when he breathed.

'I'm sorry, Splinter,' he managed to say eventually and then burst into spasm of giggles again.

'Very funny,' moaned Splinter. 'Hilarious.'

Chess took stock of where they were. The forest floor was a dense mesh of roots and plants and moss and fern. Trees thrust upward, fighting to reach daylight. Some had narrow trunks and Chess could see where their branches spread flat to form a low canopy. Others had great, thick trunks, gnarled and flanged. They rammed their way past every competing piece of vegetation until their tops were lost from sight.

The trunks were strung with sinewy vines and creepers and coated with sodden moss and patches of lichen. Some vines hung loose in the gloom, their tops hidden in the shadows of trees where leaves the size of dinner plates blotted out the sun.

'I've never seen so many different kinds of green,' said Chess. But there were not only greens. There were trails of scarlet flowers dangling in the spaces between trees and strung over the undergrowth, there were sprays of yellow petals, finely veined with orange and there were orchids which curled, violet and strange, where shafts of sunlight penetrated the deep forest canopy.

The ground was steaming and the air was thick with the smell of vegetation and mould. The cacophony of insects and birds and frogs was relentless and strange cries and howls made Chess stare wide-eyed at the surrounding tangle of greenery which gave up none of its secrets.

'This place is boiling,' complained Box, who had calmed down. He was scratching his head furiously.

'You're infested,' observed Splinter. 'All you ever do is scratch your head.'

'And say you're hungry,' added Chess.

'Well, I am hungry,' said Box, 'and I'm itching all over.'

'We're all hungry,' said Splinter, 'but you're the one who's built for starvation so stop whingeing.'

A trail of minute, orange insects was creeping over the moss and onto Chess's bare feet. 'Maybe this is an ant hill,' she said, trying to brush the insects away but discovering that they clung to her hand as if they had been stuck there with glue.

Splinter drew in his shoulders. 'This place is crawling,' he muttered. 'Everywhere there are things. It's disgusting.'

'There's too many plants and too many animals,' agreed Box.

'I hate animals.' Splinter stabbed the moss with a finger.

'You slept in a zoo once,' Box pointed out.

'I didn't pick to sleep there. I was hiding. And all the animals were in cages.'

'People say it's cruel to keep things in cages,' observed Chess.

Splinter looked up, face pinched. 'This,' he said, with a sweep of his hand, 'is what happens when things aren't kept in cages.'

Chess rubbed her hand on her jeans and winced. The insects had been investigating the cut on her palm and she wanted to get them off it.

'I bet there's leeches,' said Box. 'And snakes and tigers.'

'I'm not sure about tigers,' said Splinter, 'but there are bound to be snakes.' Box looked up, studying the matted creepers in the trellis of branches overhead.

As far as she could see, Chess had succeeded in wiping the insects off her hand. She moved her feet to get them away from the trail of remaining bugs that were moving over the mossy hillock but there were insects everywhere; on the leaves, in the air, marching along vines. There were insects with wings, with pincers, with stings. They came at her whatever she did and soon Chess and Splinter were scratching their heads and arms and ankles as much as Box was.

'Any chance of VAPing us out of this yet?' enquired Splinter, inspecting his ankle and rubbing it lightly, 'or shall we just wait for something to finish the job by eating us?'

'We don't leave until we've found out all we can,' replied Chess, resolute. 'Or unless we really can't do any more.' She didn't want to go yet, and for once, she was in charge.

'I really can't do any more,' grunted Splinter.

The three of them sat on the mound, almost back to back, sweating, picking insects off their skin and thinking silently. All around them the sweltering forest hummed with life. Chess's chin dropped to her chest and she closed her eyes. She fell into a thin, uneasy sleep.

She was at the Eastern Airfield, watching the sky smash into the earth. She was rocking on the train, craggy trader faces leering at her through the bars of the cart. And then, she was back in the factory, walking along corridors.

Children were calling to her. Then there was silence, then there were screams and then her name was called again. She began to run, trying to get out of the corridors but everywhere looked the same. The screams became more desperate. Then she was looking through a small, round window in a door and there was something behind her and she wanted to get away from it because she knew that it was going to hurt her. She pushed her face against the glass to scream for help and as she did so she saw her own face looking in through the window.

Chess opened her eyes. She was lying on the mound and it was evening although the heat was still stifling and she was soaked with sweat. The forest was stained indigo and it was impossible to discern more than the black boughs of the nearest trees and the banana-shaped curve of Box's body; he was still asleep next to her.

She looked for Splinter. It took a little time for her eyes to find him because it was so dark and because he was so quiet. He had moved to the other side of the mound and was sitting with his back towards her.

Chess understood the shapes of Splinter's body, his habits, his mannerisms. She watched him now. He was absolutely still, elbows drawn in, back arched forwards a little, head bowed. He must have been holding something and whatever it was, he was studying it intently.

You've got something you don't want me to see, guessed Chess.

Her first action was to feel her wrist. The VAP was still fastened there. Then she asked, 'What are you doing, Splinter?'

Her brother jerked round, his good hand busy although Chess couldn't see what it was doing. 'What are you sneaking about for?' he snapped.

'I'm not sneaking about,' insisted Chess. 'I only asked what you were doing.'

'You're so nosy,' continued Splinter. 'I never get any privacy.'

'I'm sorry, OK?' Chess held up her hands apologetically although she realized it was a pointless gesture, given how dark it was. 'Sorry, sorry, sorry.'

Splinter grunted and shuffled towards her. 'I was inspecting my injuries, if you must know.'

'You didn't need to go over there to do it.'

'I didn't want to disturb you, or fly head.' He settled himself close to her.

Night had fallen. The yowling and caterwauling that had surrounded them earlier was replaced by the buzz and chirrup of insects and the croaking of frogs that were close by but impossible to see. Chess rubbed her face and shivered.

'You've been having bad dreams,' said Splinter. 'You kept

twitching.' Then he added, 'If you're thirsty, suck the moss.'

Chess followed his advice and tore a lump of moss from the mound. She squeezed it as she sucked and was rewarded with a mouthful of earth-flavoured water. She kept doing this with other strips of moss until her thirst had been satisfied.

Splinter was silent as a needle of rock. Chess thought carefully before deciding to say, 'I keep hearing children's voices.'

'Where?' Splinter spoke quietly, tired, not at all mean. It surprised her.

'When we were in the factory. And when I was asleep.'

'Recognize any of them?'

'No,' said Chess, definitely. 'And there's a room too. I keep seeing it, and I keep thinking I'm in it.' Her voice sounded too loud in the deep murk. 'It's like I'm looking in one moment and looking out the next.'

'Like you're watching yourself watch yourself?'

'Yeah, exactly like that.' Chess blew on her palm. The cut was throbbing in waves that pulsed up to her elbow.

Even in the utter gloom of the forest, Chess could tell that Splinter was weighing up what she said, chewing his lip as he considered it, struggling with his own thoughts. When he sighed loudly, she knew that he would be shaking his head.

'The old lady's got to you, Chess. You're always imagining stuff. Thinking things are following you. Thinking there are secrets. You're so wound up, you don't know what's real any more.'

Chess breathed slowly and deeply and when she felt that

she could speak without losing control of herself, she said. 'You're wrong, Splinter. You're really wrong and you know it.'

Splinter shrugged. 'Suit yourself, Chess. But the truth is you're a street rat, nothing more than a street rat and that's never going to change. Your problem is you can't accept that. You think you're something special.'

'No, I don't. And it's not ridiculous to think things can be better.' She was still rankled by what Splinter had said in the tunnel; that it was ridiculous they could be anything other than street rats.

'You're going to turn into a jack, are you? With a wave of the old crone's wand?' Splinter's words were laced with venom whenever he spoke about jacks. 'What are you going to do? Go to school? Become clever? Learn manners? Wear nice clothes and get a job?' When Chess didn't answer, Splinter said, 'Exactly. None of those things will happen to you. They won't happen because you're a rat and even if you try to change that nobody else will let you. When you're as low as we are, people will kick you off the ladder even if you try to climb it.'

'I'd like nice clothes,' said Chess, digging at the holes in the sleeve of the pullover which hung on her like pastry dough.

'Your clothes are who you are, Chess. You can't change them and you can't change you.'

'I'd like a leather jacket and a pair of trainers.' The words alone seemed extravagant, impossible.

'Well, get stealing then,' said Splinter, bluntly. 'Except you can't because you're in the jungle.'

'I don't want to have to steal them,' insisted Chess.

'No grease, no goods, Chess. It's grease or nicking and for us it's nicking.'

'But I just want to know if things can change, Splinter. If they can be better.'

'You've changed.' Splinter spoke sharply. 'Since all of this has started you've got stroppy and argumentative.'

'You mean I don't agree with absolutely everything you say?'

'There you go again,' said Splinter. 'And it's not for the better.'

'Not better for you, you mean,' muttered Chess.

Box snorted and stirred. 'Can't you two shut up? You're like a pair of old women.'

'You're like a fat prat,' snapped Splinter. 'Oh, sorry, you *are* a fat prat.'

Something moved in the blackout, snapping branches, shuffling through leaves. The Tuesdays listened, eyes wide in the darkness.

'I wonder what's happened to Saul,' mused Chess when the noise had passed.

'Who cares?' sneered Splinter. 'Oh yeah, you care. The single member of the Saul Preservation Society.'

'He was nice to us, Splinter.' Immediately, Chess regretted exposing Saul to Splinter's ridicule.

'I don't trust him,' said Splinter.

'Saul's OK. He's no friend of the dog-men,' mumbled Box from where he lay. 'Any enemy of the dog-men is a friend of mine.'

'Very deep, fly head,' commented Splinter. 'And what

about the people trying to blast us to bits with the cannon? If they aren't friends of the dog-men are they friends of yours?'

Box thought about this and when he had said nothing for several seconds, Splinter said, 'Exactly.' Then he returned to the subject of Saul. 'How come, if he doesn't know what happens at the factory, he knew to call the big dog-man "General"?'

'Maybe he's heard of the General?' volunteered Chess.

'He didn't tell *us* anything about the General,' stated Splinter. 'He knows more than he let on. I don't trust him.'

'So what?' concluded Box. 'It doesn't matter, does it! He's probably dead by now.'

'I didn't hear anyone being killed when we got away.'

'What, you mean he's in on it with them? With the dog-men?' Box was incredulous.

'Trust no one.'

'Well,' said Box, speaking slowly because he was thinking hard, 'if what happened with Saul and the dog-men was done for us to watch, how would they have known that we could see it? For all they knew we could have been anywhere in that factory.'

'Maybe they've got cameras,' was Splinter's reply but Chess thought about the hidden thing that had been watching her before they saw the General.

Perhaps they knew where I was, she thought. Perhaps the Twisted Symmetry know more than Ethel realizes. Ethel had been wrong before.

The air pressed in like a hot, damp blanket. Chess flapped her pullover but didn't take it off because it protected her arms from insects. Splinter shifted his position and groaned.

'My arm and ankle are killing.' His voice was tight with pain. 'Can't we just go?'

Chess pursed her lips and scowled at the dark.

Splinter changed tack. 'The Inquisitor is waiting for you, Chess.' He crooned. 'He *wants* you to stay.'

He let the forest hum fill the silence he had left before grasping Chess's arm. She jolted but said nothing.

'Remember what the old lady said when she first planked us?' continued Splinter, softly. 'That the Inquisitors are at the heart of the Twisted Symmetry. And who did the General say was at the factory?'

Although the heat was suffocating, Chess shivered. Maybe it was the thought of the Inquisitor being so close, or maybe it was the tremor in Splinter's voice when he said the name that set her spine on edge. She rubbed the cut on her palm.

'I wonder,' said Splinter, letting go of his sister's arm, 'what the Inquisitor does to the stolen children.'

The sound of Chess swallowing was followed by a bass rumble of distant thunder.

'I wonder what happens in the scream rooms.'

A small room. A round window. 'Stop it, Splinter,' said Chess.

'I wonder what the Twisted Symmetry do to the children in the scream rooms?' Splinter's lips had found Chess's ear. No louder than skin on silk he whispered, 'Does it hurt?'

'Stop it.' Chess's shout tore through the darkness. Flapping erupted from the vegetation all around them.

'Hell, Chess,' burst Box, rattled, 'grip your mash. Warn me before you start freaking.'

'It's him.' Chess choked back a sob.

'Baby's been having bad dreams.' Splinter was smirking to himself.

'Yeah, well, she'll be having badder dreams if she does that again.'

'Sorry, Box.' Chess felt stupid now.

'It's all right.' Box was settling back down. He laughed. 'Gave me a fright, that's all. I can hear better now, anyway.'

When Splinter next spoke, his voice was hoarse again with the pain of his fractures. 'Listen, sorry, OK? I didn't know you'd be that jumpy. But we can finish this now. No need to be stuck out here, scared. We know enough. Please. Can we just go?'

'It's up to you, Chess,' said Box, 'but Splinter's in a bad way. We can't do a lot whatever happens.'

Chess worked her nails into her palms. The pain helped her focus.

Am I thinking about the children or just thinking about me? Then she thought about a room with a little round window: a place where something horrible happened. 'We stay,' she said.

Suddenly the world was streaked electric white as if a camera flash had momentarily turned off the darkness. Then it was night and the sultry air shook as the sky detonated. Immediately there came rain, whipping over the canopy of trees. There was another lightning flash and a bang of thunder and the rain came harder, pursued by a wind that rushed through the tree tops.

At first the rain dripped through the leaves slowly, ponderously. But as it continued to crash down, driven by the gusting wind it leaked through the canopy more and more quickly until it was descending in a steady curtain through the layers of leaves and branches. Even when the storm had stalked away and the thunder echoed like an old man's grumble, the rain continued to fall.

Chess peeled her pullover away from where it was plastered wet to her chest and felt warm air drift up to her face from her body. Then she shivered, again. The cut on her hand had been itching and now there was a burning sensation. She knew that Splinter was staring at her. She had seen him during the storm, hair flat from the rain, face drawn with pain, dejected.

'Listen,' said Chess, cautious, unused to taking the lead but determined to do so. 'Give it a couple more days. We need to find out what's being made inside the factory and what it's for. So maybe we have to get back in. Or one of us does. But if we don't get any further after a couple of days, we go. OK?'

Box dossed down. 'Two more days, Chess?' The ground squelched as he settled onto it. 'It gives them plenty of time to find us.'

'We're dead,' muttered Splinter and he lay on the moss, groaning.

Chess closed her eyes and wished that none of this had happened. Without thinking about it, she started to hum. She waited for Splinter to tell her to shut up but he didn't. The words came to her and with no one to tell her to stop, she sang to the darkness:

'When I was on horseback, wasn't I pretty?
When I was on horseback, wasn't I gay?

Wasn't I pretty when I entered Cork city
And met with my downfall on the fourteenth of May?

Six jolly soldiers to carry my coffin,
Six jolly soldiers to march by my side
It's six jolly soldiers take a bunch of red roses . . .'

But she couldn't sing in the darkness the way the voice could and her song stumbled into silence. She clasped her hands round her shins and blinked to stop her eyes from stinging and she listened to the sounds of the insects and frogs, punctuated only by the sound of Box snoring.

There were voices on the other side of the door and the captain hesitated because he had been told that the General would be alone. Then he knocked anyway because he had been told to deliver the item immediately.

'Enter,' growled the command from the other side of the door.

The door was surprisingly low and built of iron-studded wood. It opened smoothly. Stooping, the captain entered the chamber. It was cavernous, blasted out of the black basalt of the volcano and it was illuminated by clusters of spotlights. The places where the spotlights glared were brightly lit but the rest of the chamber was deep in shadow.

The furnishing was spartan; on one side an iron bed with a chest at its foot, a locker, a high-backed chair and a large, square table supporting maps and a glass decanter filled with a lustrous, crimson liquor. Two glasses stood on a map by the decanter, both brimming with the same red liquid. On the other side of the room there was a broad, iron chair with arm rests. The chair was bolted to the stone floor. The General sat in this chair, wrists clamped by thick manacles welded to the arm rests. His ankles were secured similarly to bars beneath the chair.

Behind the chair was a brass cylinder. It was not quite as wide as the chair but it was taller than the captain. Two tubes ran from the cylinder to the chest plate forming the lower part of the General's collar. The chest plate displayed three small dials on its front and immediately below these were two holes into which the tubes were fastened.

'Basic, isn't it?' grunted the General in the harsh tongue of the dog-men. He eyeballed the captain who was standing in the middle of the chamber holding a grey, metal case in both hands and gaping. 'What did you expect? Gold plate and feasting? This is the life of a commander on campaign, captain.' The General snorted and pushed his foot against a lever on one of the chair legs. 'Hard work,' the manacles clicked open, 'long hours,' he stood up, 'planning,' he unclipped the tube nozzles from the chest plate, 'and if you're lucky, the chance to spill blood at the end of it all.'

Released, the tubes dangled over the back of the chair. A trickle of dark fluid oozed from one of them and then stopped.

The General was tall and rangy and he looked down at the junior officer. 'My treatment, Captain,' he growled, jerking his head at the cylinder. 'Something the warps knocked up for me.' He stomped over to the locker where his brown fur cloak hung on one side. Refusing the captain's offer to assist, he flipped it from the hook and shuffled it over his rugged shoulders.

'You heard voices?' he asked. The captain nodded his flat-muzzled head in reply. The General took a rug from the end of the bed. 'Don't worry about that, Captain. Just talking to an old friend.' He tossed the rug under the table where it landed in an area of thick shadow. The captain thought he saw something scuttle under the rug and he glimpsed a stick-like black leg, long and with no foot. It darted out of sight.

'You have my delivery?' asked the General.

'It's just arrived, sir. It was late. I waited on the sky terrace for over an hour.'

'Storm still raging, I see,' said the General, observing how wet the captain was and taking the grey metal case from him. 'Not a night to be out in.'

The General put the case on the table, tapped a code into the pad on the top of the lid and opening it, removed a handful of small vials which he dropped into a pouch on his belt. Then he closed the case and put it in his locker.

'More treatment, Captain,' explained the General. 'I have to keep some with me. Just in case.'

He returned to the table, steel-shod boots heavy on the stone floor, the chain fastenings on his body armour clinking as he moved. His back was to the captain.

'The Inquisitor wants the girl.' The General spoke thoughtfully. 'She and the others escaped. Surprising. We underestimated their resourcefulness. They are different from the other children. By now they will be in the forest. I do not imagine they will get very far.

'We have orders to catch the girl, Captain. The Inquisitors need her. She is important to them.'

The captain watched the back of the General's head, cocking one way and then the other as he considered the matter.

'This time cycle is ending; we approach the fifth node.' The General paused. 'Does that mean anything to you, Captain?'

The captain shook his head quickly although the General was still looking the other way.

The General grunted. 'For my part, I couldn't care less about the girl. The only good human is a dead one. And their children,' the General shouted suddenly, 'I hate their children.' Then, more calmly, 'The work here is nearly over. We have spent too long on this rock already and we have spent too much time and squandered too many resources on this girl. But the Inquisitors think otherwise.'

The General rested his hands on the table and shook his head wearily. 'The others you may kill but the Inquisitor wants the girl. Alive. Those are *his* orders.'

'And what are *your* orders, sir?' asked the captain.

The General turned round slowly and regarded the young officer through eyes that were gleaming slits. When he spoke, the words cut the narrow space between them like razors.

'Do you suggest I have an agenda of my own, Captain? Imagine, if you were able to reveal to our masters that I was less than totally loyal, that I had my own ideas and did not follow their orders, that I had my own plans for the girl? You could make your name, Captain. They might reward you by making you a general, Captain. Do you like the thought of that?'

The General's lips tightened, revealing the tips of his fangs. 'The Inquisitors question my allegiance, you know. They have done so for some time. But I have a very high regard for loyalty,' and the General leant down so that his breath was hot on the captain's throat. 'Loyalty to *me*,' he growled. With his teeth brushing the soft fur of the captain's neck he hissed, 'If I thought for one second that your loyalty to me was anything less than total I would rip the pelt from your back and pull your tongue through your nose for the flies to feed on.'

The captain didn't move. He stood stock-still, eyes riveted forwards.

'Well,' continued the General, lifting his head to stare into his subordinate's eyes. 'Are you loyal? To me?'

'Yes sir,' barked the captain, vigorously.

The General snorted and handed him one of the glasses from the table. 'This is fresh. From the latest batch,' he announced and a long string of saliva unspooled from his bottom jaw. 'I had it waiting for you.'

Before the captain put the glass to his dark lips the General said, 'Who's to say I haven't flavoured yours with poison, Captain? I am suspicious by nature. And I haven't had a kill for a while. Sometimes the desire is too strong.' Then the General thumped his fist onto the table and roared, 'Drink!'

The captain drank slowly, the red liquid staining his muzzle, his eyes unwavering from his superior's.

'Good,' said the General when the glass was empty. He put his own glass to his mouth and drained it in one hungry gulp. Drops of red flecked the long hairs under his chin. His tongue lapped at them noisily. Then he ordered, 'Take what troopers you need. Stay near the volcano to start with.'

'What about the stonedrakes?' asked the captain.

'The stonedrakes are nothing. They are a primitive society, level three, tribal, steam powered. My sources inform me that they worship the red sun and that they regard the smoke from the factory as a blasphemy because it blots out their god for part of each night. Not that they know who we are or what we are doing here. So far they have not approached the factory sector. If they do the perimeter wall will be impregnable to them. It will be better for the stonedrakes if they stick to paddling their machines across the bay until we have gone.'

The General set down his glass. Then he took a small, plastic card from his tunic and handed it to the captain. 'If you can't find the girl you will have to use a spook. Here is the authority. But make sure it is well fed first. A hungry spook is a dangerous spook.'

The captain slipped the strip of plastic inside a chest pouch.

'One more thing,' said the General before the captain turned to go. 'When you find the girl and if she is alive, bring her to me first. I am curious.' The captain raised his arm in salute and marched from the chamber. The General looked to the space under the table and then locked the door so he could not be disturbed.

CHAPTER 7

Sunlight punctured the gloom of the rainforest in thick, steaming bars as Chess, Box and Splinter wandered through the mist. The mist had come with the morning, draping itself between the trees in a muggy blanket. The forest had fallen quiet, noise muffled save for their voices which seemed much louder than they wanted them to be.

Soon after sunrise they had set off to find their way back to the volcano. However, although they had not come far into the forest the day before, they had no idea which way to go now because everything looked the same, or equally different. So Splinter had said they should walk whichever way seemed most uphill since that would lead to the slopes of the volcano. Then the mist had come. After two hours of pushing their way through palms and ferns, over roots, round swamps and under creepers, they were still surrounded by vegetation. Splinter's nose, so effective at finding its way through tunnels, was less reliable in the chaos of the rainforest.

The silence was punctuated by slaps as they smacked insects and bugs from their necks, legs, heads and arms. But it was a pointless gesture because the insect assault was incessant. Chess thought that she would go mad. Her skin was itching, the palm of her left hand was on fire and she couldn't stop shivering, which she didn't understand because she felt so hot.

'The worst thing, apart from being constantly hungry, is the ground,' complained Box, squelching on what felt like a huge slug. 'It's slimy and always moving.' He pulled a face as he took a leaf and wiped a sticky smear from the arch of his foot.

'At least you can walk properly,' griped Splinter, leaning on Box who was supporting him.

'The mist is going,' said Chess, looking about the trees. 'That might make it easier. Although it will also make it easier for us to be seen.'

Splinter harrumphed loudly. As far as he was concerned, nothing was going to make getting out of the forest any easier. They were lost and the only thing that would change that would be luck or the VAP.

He watched Chess as she wandered ahead, peering into the mist. This was not the same Chess as the one at the wharf. This was a Chess with ideas of her own; a Chess who disagreed with him.

'She'll never find the way,' Splinter whispered to Box.

'Maybe she's keeping a lookout,' Box suggested.

'For what?'

'She thinks something's following us,' explained Box. 'She was going on about it earlier.'

'Chess always thinks she's being followed,' sneered Splinter. 'She's paranoid.'

'Actually, Splinter, she's been right so far.'

Splinter sniffed dismissively.

'How's your hand?' Box asked Chess when she walked back to them. She looked at the cut on her palm. It was bright red and raised in a weal. The edges of the skin were yellow with pus. When she swallowed her throat felt raw.

'It's sore,' she replied. 'Really sore and throbbing.'

'It's infected, that's why,' said Splinter, knowledgeably. 'You'll probably get blood poisoning.'

'Is that fatal?' enquired Box.

'Not always,' Splinter explained. 'She may just lose the hand.'

'We'll be home before then,' said Chess.

'What a pair,' laughed Box. 'You with a hand about to drop off and a sore heel and you,' to Splinter, 'with bits broken. For once I'm coming out best,' he boasted. 'Just a black eye.'

'It's yellow now,' observed Chess, wiping sweat from her forehead. The morning was getting hotter.

'Natural survivor,' proclaimed Box, 'that's what I am. No situation too difficult. Not as fragile as you two.'

'Just a lot more stupid,' said Splinter who yelped as he accidentally put too much weight on his right foot. 'Anyway, we're all covered in spots and bites. Look at my hands.' He held them out for inspection. Their backs were mottled with dark pink dots. 'They itch like hell,' he complained, scratching the back of one hand and then the other.

'It's so hot,' gasped Chess, wrenching her pullover from her head and throwing it on the floor. 'But I can't stop shaking.'

One eyebrow raised, Splinter looked at where the pullover lay and then at his sister. Her face, shoulders and arms were covered with a sheen of sweat.

'Fever,' he diagnosed, as if passing judgement.

'It is hot,' agreed Box. 'I can't believe you keep that jacket on,' he said to Splinter. They were all moving again, Splinter with an arm round Box's shoulders and Box with an arm around Splinter's waist to support him as he hobbled.

'I like it,' said Splinter and immediately Box detected a defensive tone in his brother's voice.

'Just take it off and carry it then,' suggested Box, immediately.

'No.'

'Come on, Splinter, take it off.'

'No.'

'Why not?'

'Because I don't want to.'

'What have you got in your pockets, Splinter?' wheedled Box.

'The normal stuff,' Splinter replied. 'My stuff.'

Box moved his hand to be able to feel the jacket better.

'Get off,' snapped Splinter.

'There's something in it isn't there?' insisted Box. 'You've been funny with that jacket ever since we came here. You haven't taken it off once, not even in the desert. Why not?' and he let go of Splinter to feel the nearside of the jacket.

'Stop it,' shouted Splinter, almost hysterical, and he shoved Box in the chest. But Box had two good legs and Splinter succeeded only in unbalancing himself. He fell backwards, landing on his bottom. Quick as a flash he pulled his knife from the jacket, blade towards Box.

'Back off, Box,' he hissed, eyes narrow, teeth clenched.

Box took the lock knife from his own pocket and ran his thumb across the back of the blade, as yet, unopened. Then he smiled at Splinter and said, 'I'll let you off this time, Splinter, but don't ever pull a knife on me again.'

They stayed like that, facing one another, until Chess shouted over to them. 'Stop messing about. Come over here. Look at this.' They put away their knives.

'You can crawl,' Box said to Splinter and he walked over to where Chess was looking up at the trees. Splinter limped after him, glowering.

Box looked where Chess was looking and saw a skeleton. It was chalk white and picked clean and was suspended by a nest of creepers high in the tree. The tree trunk was strung with a shaggy mass of the same creepers. At their lower ends the creepers bore white flowers, petals cupped like tulips but as large as marrows and with heads drooping down. The flowers were gathered in a deep pile all around the base of the tree.

'It's an animal,' said Box, peering up at the perfect set of bones.

'Obviously,' muttered Splinter and then, taking more of an interest in the macabre sight added, 'Like a dog but bigger.'

'How did it get there?' asked Box.

'Perhaps it was climbing the tree and got stuck,' suggested Chess, sucking her lower lip and then peering left and right through the maze of trees. It was very gloomy in this part of the forest.

'It doesn't look as if it could have climbed there,' said Splinter. 'It's just stuck halfway up the tree trunk. Maybe it's been trapped and hung there by a tribe as a warning. Or as part of a pagan ritual.'

'It stinks,' announced Box with a sniff, 'the air smells rotten.'

'Like old cabbage,' Splinter agreed.

'Worse,' decided Box.

'We should go,' Chess said. They were exposed; they had to keep moving.

'Something following us?' asked Splinter, sarcastically.

Chess chose to ignore his tone of voice. 'Yes,' she replied. 'It's circling round us but keeping out of sight.' She could tell that Splinter thought she was being stupid. It was as if he thought whatever she said was stupid just because she was saying it. 'I think it's tracking us,' she said, anyway.

They walked in silence. Even Splinter felt his senses sharpen now. It was very quiet and that worried him because it meant that other creatures were staying away from where they were walking. That could be because of where they were. Or because of what was following them.

He noticed that the vegetation in this part of the forest was less dense at floor level but the canopy above his head was so thick with branches and leaves and winding vines that it succeeded in blotting out the sky entirely. This was a place filled with shadows and a static, humming heat and a putrid stench that reminded Splinter of the drains beneath the city abattoir.

More of the tree boles were surrounded by the mounds of

big, white flowers. They populated the empty forest floor, revealed through drifts in the mist.

'It's like a church,' muttered Splinter, looking up to where the canopy arched overhead. These trees also had trunks that were ribbed with thick vines trailing the giant flowers. He saw another skeleton, high in one of the trees and then another. The clean bones were ravelled with creepers. One skull had slipped down to a clutch of creepers below the rest of the bones. It hung there, eye sockets regarding him blankly, lower jaw missing.

He looked back, unsure of the way they had come.

'We mustn't go back,' Chess said, quietly and urgently, 'we have to keep going forwards.'

'Don't tell me,' said Splinter, 'it's right behind us now?' But he was more worried than he sounded.

'It is, Splinter,' insisted Chess, brown eyes imploring him to believe her, 'it really is. I'm sure.'

He sighed. 'What difference does it make? All right, we'll go your way.' He didn't like the way the skull was staring at him from within the knot of vines. 'Come on, Box.'

Box had taken his lock knife out again. 'Let's just leave a mark,' he said, walking over to the nearest tree, a tree that stood close to those bearing the skeletons. 'Just to show whoever's been putting skeletons in trees that they don't own the place.'

'Don't be ridiculous,' grumbled Splinter, resting on one leg like a stork.

'Not now, Box,' implored Chess. 'We have to get away from here.'

'Your wrist?' suggested Splinter, indicating the VAP.

'Maybe,' wavered Chess, 'maybe.'

'Just do it,' he urged.

'Hang on,' said Box, pulling aside a strand of vine to reveal a bare patch of bark. He jabbed the blade of the knife into the wood which was unexpectedly hard. 'BOX' he carved with some difficulty.

'Come on, Box,' hissed Chess.

'Just a minute,' said Box, concentrating on producing a legible 'WOZ'. More digging with the knife and then Box stepped back.

'There,' he announced. 'BOX WOZ ERE.'

'Very original,' sighed Splinter.

Chess heard something move, behind the trees, the way they had come. She started to walk on, hoping her brothers would do the same.

'It's the flowers,' said Box and when Chess looked back he was bending down at the foot of the tree next to the one he'd been carving on. The tree was festooned with vines that ended with the large white flowers. They were piled around the base of the trunk like a heap of snow.

'Phew! What a stink,' announced Box.

'Well, stop smelling them and let's go,' Splinter told him. He had just heard a stick crack. Something was coming closer, very carefully.

Unlike the other flowers they had seen, these ones had their heads up with petals half open. Box studied the thick, fleshy petals at arm's length, noticing the thin indigo filigree ribbing the centre of each one from its fat base to its pointed tip like a vein. They looked like snake heads, jaws open wide to reveal their narrow tongues. The stink was so foul it made him gag. He shuddered and stepped back from the lily-white mound.

As he did so he heard a deep growl rumble behind him and at the same time his brother saying in a voice that sounded like it was trying to stay calm, 'Box, turn round slowly. Very slowly.'

Box turned round as slowly as he could. Facing him and not more than fifteen feet away was a huge, black cat, shoulder muscles bulging, green eyes flecked with gold, muzzle wrinkled, ears flat back against its sleek head. Its back was arched downwards so that its hindquarters were higher than its shoulders, coiled, ready to spring.

The growl erupted into a wild snarl that raked the silence. Box was close enough to see every detail of the cat's long, gleaming teeth and its black claws, extended and sharp.

'I said there would be tigers.' Box spoke slowly and quietly.

'It's not a tiger, fly head,' whispered Splinter. He was standing further away from the cat than Box and was trying very hard not to wobble, unsteady on his feet as he was. 'Tigers have stripes. I think this is a panther.'

'OK,' said Box, as if the information was helpful in some way. He swallowed hard and gripped the handle of the lock knife in his clammy palm. One blade against however many teeth and talons. He felt very soft as he tried not to look at the sharp points. One of those claws would go through him like a scalpel through liver.

He looked at the creature's eyes. That was what he had heard; when a cat stares at you, stare back and don't stop. It was all about showing who was in charge. Just like squaring up to someone for a fight. Except that this wasn't someone, it was some thing. Some thing that was about twice his size and could cut him to ribbons like a lawn mower.

The rumble was building in the cat's throat and its head dropped lower to the ground.

It's going to jump, thought Box. He got ready to thrust upwards with his knife. He might manage one stab into the animal's throat before he was mauled.

The roar built from a rasping growl into a lung-shaking blast. The cat sprang. Box set his legs and arms to take the impact he expected. But the impact didn't come. Instead, as soon as the cat's forelegs left the ground, creepers swept up from the forest floor like tentacles. They coiled round the animal's body, swift and tight and bundled it up the tree from which they had been hanging limply just before.

The cat snarled and tried to break free but it couldn't get a purchase on the vines which gripped its body closely. Its raging cries became howls of panic as it was drawn further up the tree by the creepers. More of the arm-thick tendrils curled up to bind the struggling creature against the upper reaches of the tree trunk until only minute patches of black fur could be seen beneath the heaving cocoon of vines.

A rustling, shuffling noise came from the foot of the same tree. Box saw that where the white flowers had been dormant at the end of their creepers, now their heads were up and they were jostling against one another as if vying for the best position. Their stalks entwined, white heads thrusting one another aside with petals wide open as if hungry and eager to be fed. They writhed at the foot of the tree like a bed of serpents.

Then every tendril stopped wriggling and the indigo-streaked petals closed tight until every flower resembled a spear head, broad and white and quivering as if straining to be free. The spears all pointed upwards.

As if a signal had been given, every flower-bearing tendril hurtled up and plunged its head into the cocoon. Flower after flower buried itself in the vine-bound lump until there were no flowers left to be seen.

Slowly and in absolute silence, dark red blood seeped out of the knot of plant and cat until the whole tree trunk was streaked with gore.

Box looked down at where he was standing, at the creepers lying dormant under his feet, at the nest of flowers heaped beneath the tree beside him.

'Get away from the tree, Box,' urged Splinter as Box realized the same thing.

He had been standing very still. The question was, did he dive away from the tree or did he edge away as gradually as possible? He thought of how the cat had been caught even as it sprang at him. He doubted that he could move any more quickly. So the thing to do would be to inch away, barely moving at all.

Chess was standing several trees away. There were no white flowers near to her. Splinter was closer to Box, but not too close.

'Easy does it,' Box whispered to himself as he breathed out, sliding one foot forwards, taking care not to make contact with anything beneath it before he put it down again, very gently.

He looked across to Splinter and risked a grin. 'So far so good,' he mouthed.

It was as he slid his other foot forwards that something gripped his bare ankle like a vice. A slim, green tendril twitched up from the tangle of the forest floor and took hold.

'Oh, no,' despaired Box before a throng of creepers lassoed up from the ground and out from the tree. He flung his body forwards but was held fast by the vines that whipped round his legs, coiling thicker and thicker.

With his legs bound tight, Box was dragged face down towards the tree. His nose was filled with dirt and the stench of the flowers that were waiting for him to be hoisted up.

Chess sprinted across to Splinter but there was nothing that she could do. Already Box was being pulled up the tree trunk, feet first. The bed of white flowers beneath him began to squirm into life.

Box was grunting and struggling. Creepers twined themselves around his legs and along his body up to his shoulders. This made it impossible for him to stab at the tough, thick vegetation with his knife because his upper arms were bound fast beside his head. He could see the huge flowers waving beneath him, mouths open. He wriggled harder but felt weaker and weaker as the vines squeezed him more tightly.

'Help,' he cried, weakly at first but then, taking as much of a lungful as he could, 'Help me.' He tried to stick his knife into the tree to stop the vines from pulling him any higher. The flower heads were shutting, pointing upwards.

'No,' screeched Box, the knife slipping out of his fingers and spinning down to the flowers that were ready to strike.

Chess wanted to run to Box and pull him back but he was hanging out of reach, lashed high by the twisting vines. She heard his frightened cries for help and it sounded as if they were coming from further and further away as he vanished beneath the vegetation. She thought she would go crazy; she was desperate to help her brother but there was nothing that she could do.

Then a light exploded inside her head and for an instant she wasn't looking at Box. She was looking back at herself. She was hanging upside down, drowning in the coils of the creepers that were plastering themselves across her face and into her terror-wide eyes. Then the last of the light was shut out.

And she was looking up at Box again.

Another flash and the seething darkness and helplessness and fear filled her.

It was as if she was switching between her own mind and her brother's. When she was inside his head she felt his searing terror and his pain. She didn't understand what was happening and she couldn't control it.

With each jolt of emotion, Chess felt energy burst through her body; burst after burst until the surging energy made every fibre feel like it was expanding, rushing outwards. She no longer knew who she was or what she was doing because the energy roaring through her had driven out every other feeling.

Then, from far away she heard Box cry out. It was like a switch had been pressed inside her. The power had to escape. Her body jerked back, her arms were flung wide apart and her head was filled with a blaze of light.

CHAPTER 8

Flames.

Magnesium-bright flames burst from every flower beneath Box. Splinter staggered backwards to be met by a blast of heat from behind as another mound of flowers erupted. He turned on the spot, looking all around as mound after mound of flowers ignited and burnt with rapid fury. The forest was filled with balls of flame. The air was thick with crackling embers and smoke that drifted through the trees.

The flames burnt fiercely, eating their way up the thick arms of the creepers which twisted and shrivelled in the heat, a heat so intense that it stung Splinter's eyeballs. In seconds only smouldering stacks of cinder-brush remained where the heaps of white flowers had been.

Through the haze that shimmered up from the embers an olive-skinned man came walking. Splinter saw him between the trees, bare-chested and holding a stout quarterstaff. He wore a pair of leather leggings and walked barefoot. His hair was jet black, gathered tight from his face and bound in a plait down his back. His moustache was as black as his hair and it swept extravagantly either side of his mouth. His eyes were bright and bulging and when he spoke it was with a voice so deep that it resonated from his barrel chest.

'Hold this.' He towered over Splinter and thrust his staff into Splinter's hands. 'The bloodsuckers can't harm him now but the stranglers will finish their work if we don't get him down.'

He drew a long, broad-bladed chopping knife from the sheath on his hip. 'Pull him away from the fire when he falls.'

As he strode to the tree from which Box hung upside down, one arm still sticking out of the ball of vines, Splinter asked, 'How did you do that?'

'Do what?' The man's back was towards Splinter as he marched to the tree.

'Do that,' shouted Splinter. The man wasn't paying any attention to him. He was looking down at the charred remains of the flowers. 'Set the flowers on fire?' Splinter clarified.

'I didn't do that,' the man said. 'She did,' and he turned round and pointed at where Chess lay on her side on the forest floor.

'She did!' Splinter's voice cracked and he looked at his sister as if she was a stranger. 'Chess did that?' Then he shouted, 'She couldn't have done. She couldn't,' and there were tears in his eyes.

Even though the man was solidly built he scaled the tree easily, shuffling up the vines using his thighs and his free hand. When he was level with the entwined lump that was Box, he swung the machete into the vines that suspended him. The vines were severed and they recoiled in clumps, releasing Box in a series of jerks so that he jolted one way and then the other, falling and then halting. The man kept hacking the vines and by the time the last of them had been chopped away, Box didn't have far to fall. He thudded onto the remains of the flowers in a plume of sparks. He rolled away from the foot of the tree without any help from Splinter who was still standing where the man had left him, holding the staff.

The man slid part of the way down the tree and then leapt from it with surprising agility. Sheathing the machete he strode to Chess who lay motionless. He put a hand on her glistening forehead and frowned.

Box was coughing and spluttering and then he began to groan and rub his ribs as he sat on the floor. 'Who are you?' he managed to ask.

The man stood up and inclined his head towards Box. 'My name is Balthazar Broom,' he announced in ringing tones, 'mathematician, philosopher and pugilist.'

'My name is Box,' wheezed Box. 'That is my brother, Splinter. That is my sister. Her name is Chess.' Then he added, 'Thanks, for doing whatever you did.'

'I did nothing. It was her,' said Balthazar.

'How do you know she did it?' whined Splinter.

'You didn't do it. I didn't do it. He didn't do it. So she did. It is called logic, Splinter.' Balthazar squatted on his heels by Chess. 'And I was watching. I saw what happened. And I saw what happened to her.' He bent forwards and studied Chess's face. Then he lifted one of her arms and inspected the wound on her palm.

'But I don't know how she did it,' complained Splinter.

'It is enough that she did it. Your ignorance is no part of

the equation,' said Balthazar, dismissively. 'You are a very strange young man. Your sister saved your brother from certain death and you appear to be upset about it.'

'I'm upset because you keep asking questions,' snapped Splinter.

'I'm not asking you questions, I'm helping you,' Balthazar replied.

'Well, we don't need your help,' spluttered Splinter.

Balthazar regarded him coolly with his big, bulging eyes. 'And what aspect of your self-sufficiency are you proudest about? Your broken bones, his near death or her raging fever?'

'He's just upset,' explained Box, who was on all fours, rooting with a stick amongst the embers at the foot of the tree. 'Aha!' He held up his lock knife. The handle was charred but it still opened and the blade gleamed.

Balthazar lifted Chess in his broad arms, her body pale and limp against his dark skin.

Splinter looked to Box, who looked at the bare steel of his knife and then back at Splinter. Then he stood and faced Balthazar.

'Where d'you think you're going with her?' Box asked. The man seemed OK but that didn't mean he *was* OK. Sometimes the crashers seemed OK; and then you got crashed.

'There are Dog Troopers on the edge of the forest. When they smell the smoke they will come. We must put some distance between us and them.'

The brothers stood still.

'What do you know about Dog Troopers?' Splinter's blue eyes narrowed, shards of ice in the forest heat.

'I know they are searching for you,' replied Balthazar. 'Perhaps you will tell me why they want you?'

His bulging eyes flicked down to Chess who looked very small in his brawny arms. Then he nodded at Splinter, knowingly. 'Or maybe they want your sister?'

Splinter's fingers twitched, preparing to reach for the sharp reassurance of his knife. 'What do you want?'

'What does it look like, Splinter.' Balthazar smiled. 'I want to help you. I want to help your sister.'

Box was sure he could hear sounds; smashing vegetation and rasping shouts. They were distant but he knew they were coming towards them. He flipped shut his knife.

'My house is a day's walk,' said Balthazar. 'The troopers will never find it. You may borrow my staff, Splinter. I will carry Chess.' He returned Splinter's ice glare. 'Unless you *want* the Symmetry to find her.'

It was early evening when they stopped in a small clearing. The sky was yellow through the trees. Balthazar lay Chess down on a bed of moss.

'We are deep in the forest. The troopers will not track us here. We can rest for the night.' He took his staff from Splinter. 'I will not be long.' Then he strode into the trees. Box watched his broad back and ebony ponytail disappear.

'He knows about the Twisted Symmetry,' hissed Splinter.

Box clawed his scalp. 'But he seems all right, in a crazy way. A bit slash-dot, but what can we do?'

'Not slash-dot: not random. He's proper mad. Dangerous. We've got to be careful.'

'There's two of us,' said Box, as if that guaranteed their survival. 'And anyway, so far, he's only taken us *away* from the enemy.'

'Big deal. Even if he's harmless, which I doubt, the Twisted Symmetry know where we are. They'll come for us, you'll see.'

Box looked about as if something was approaching right now. Then he said, 'Look, when he gets back, I'll ask him what he knows about the Twisted Symmetry.'

'No, not yet.' Splinter was definite about this. 'That might get too lively. Wait until we get out of this jungle, get clear of the troopers, get to Mr. Weirdo's house.' He considered the possibilities. 'We can have a look at what he's got. It might be worth our while.'

'Nice one,' agreed Box. He scratched his head, recalling how Balthazar had introduced himself. 'What's a pugilist?'

'How should I know?' replied Splinter.

'Is it someone who collects stamps?'

'That's a philatelist, you idiot,' snapped Splinter. He uncurled his leg and groaned. 'My ankle is killing me.' He prodded the sleeping Chess with his toe. 'She could get us out of this.'

The brothers looked at each other and sniggered. Splinter wriggled towards Chess's arm on his belly. 'Remember to keep hold of me,' he said to Box, reaching for the VAP.

'Splinter!' boomed Balthazar.

Splinter jerked away from Chess, gasping as he rolled over his broken wrist by accident.

'Forgive me,' said Balthazar, looming up to them. 'I lost sight of you in the twilight. I thought you had gone.'

'I wish,' muttered Splinter.

Balthazar was carrying an armful of peach-coloured fruit. He watched Box scratching his arms and neck and said, 'You itch because you are food. To the creatures that live here you are nothing but a lump of meat.'

'A lump of meat,' considered Splinter. 'I like that.'

'You like to eat?' said Balthazar. 'Well, so do they.'

'Yeah, even the plants,' grumbled Box.

'Do not blame them. Nature is clever, Box. In that part of the forest where the sun does not penetrate, the vines must seek sustenance from an alternative source. The strangler vines and the bloodsucker vines work together to survive. In that way they are successful.' He paused and smiled to himself. 'We should learn from them. Even where there is darkness we can survive if we adapt and work together.'

'Philosopher,' hissed Splinter into Box's ear as if it were a deadly insult.

Balthazar set down the fruit and went to Chess. Box helped himself. The fruit was mushy and very sweet and he guzzled until his chin and neck dribbled sticky with juice. He saw Splinter observing him and eating nothing.

'What?' he asked, looking up, teeth poised above his fourth piece.

'Just waiting.'

'For what?'

'To see if it's poisonous,' whispered Splinter.

'Thanks a lot.'

Chess stirred. Balthazar used his machete to sever a vine. He took a long drink of water from it and then, moistening his finger, wetted Chess's lips. Then, he rubbed the oil of a delicate, cream flower on her forehead. He washed her hand, took a strip of bark from the pocket of his leggings, chewed on it and smeared the pulpy tip over the livid cut in her palm.

'Here.' He handed the bark to Splinter. 'Chew on this. Its medicinal qualities will counteract infection from the insect bites.'

'Thanks,' said Splinter, handing it to Box. 'Fly head the poison taster will test it for me.'

'My stomach aches,' complained Box. It made a long gurgling noise.

'Too much fruit, too quickly,' explained Balthazar, regretfully, before he strolled into the trees. They could see his silhouette, hunting about the forest floor.

'Gemma!' Chess tried to sit up. In the dusk her sunken eyes were bright.

'Gemma's not here, Chess.' Box moved to sit by his sister.

Her eyes closed and she laughed, feebly. 'I'm getting mixed up. What happened?'

'You tell us,' answered Splinter, accusingly.

Chess's voice shook. 'I thought you were going to die, Box.' Then she said, 'Something happened to me. I didn't feel like I was me. I felt bigger, all pulled apart. It's strange; it felt like when I was at the wharf and the Inspector had Gemma. Everything got really bad inside me. Really angry. But at the wharf, I fainted, didn't I? But here?' Chess rocked her head. 'It's like my body was exploding and I couldn't stop it but at the same time, I wanted it to explode, as if that would stop what was happening to you.' She opened her eyes and looked at her brother. 'What happened, Box?'

Box rubbed her shoulder. 'Don't think about it now. Just rest.'

'Yes, rest,' came the deep voice of Balthazar Broom, soft in the dusk.

Box felt Chess stiffen. 'It's OK,' he assured her. 'This is Balthazar Broom. He's helped us.'

Splinter grunted to indicate that he wasn't so sure.

Balthazar knelt in front of Chess, and pressed something into her hand, closing her fingers over it. 'This flower is good for you. Rub it on your head, here.'

Chess felt how light his touch was on her temple. 'Thank you,' she said. She sat up, propped against Box. 'Why are we with you?' she asked.

Splinter's voice grated the calm. 'He just *happened* to turn up. As usual, fly head had to tag along.'

'You could have waited for the Dog Troopers, or you could have come with me,' Balthazar reminded him.

'Planked,' muttered Splinter. 'Again.'

'Planked?' queried Balthazar.

'As in being made to walk the plank,' explained Box. 'Having no choice.'

'You always have a choice.' Balthazar smiled.

'Don't you start,' grumbled Splinter.

'Dog Troopers?' Chess glanced about as if the dog-men might be anywhere.

'They are hunting you,' warned Balthazar. 'That is why we have moved deep into the forest. That is why we must go to my house, although I need to splint your ankle,' he said to Splinter, taking hold of a short, straight piece of wood he had brought from the trees.

'Why are you here?' asked Chess. Her thoughts were clear although her head hurt.

Balthazar Broom paused, stick in hand. 'Do you know where you are?' he asked. When nobody replied he said, 'I thought not. You have about you the desperate look of the hopelessly lost.'

'Thanks,' muttered Splinter.

'You are on a planet called Surapoor,' continued Balthazar. 'It lies in the Myriad Sea off the Beltine Archipelago and it is one of the loneliest places in this universe.' He sighed. 'This is a very remote planet, almost at the end of the Myriad Sea. Almost at the end of everywhere.'

Then, changing his mood, he continued stridently. 'So why am I here?' Three faces looked back, mute in the twilight. 'I am here because this is my punishment.' His eyes were bright and wide in his dark face and his luxurious moustache framed his white teeth starkly. 'The punishment for my crime.'

'What did you do?' asked Box, voice hoarse with anticipation.

'I killed a man,' said Balthazar.

Box's jaw dropped and he tried not to catch Splinter's eye but he saw Splinter mouth the words, 'We are going to die.'

'I was tricked but that only shows what a fool I was. He died because of me.' Balthazar closed his eyes. 'I interfered in things I should have left alone. So I am on Surapoor, exiled to contemplate my crime for a thousand years.'

'A thousand years!' blurted Box.

'That's impossible,' stated Splinter.

Balthazar's goggle-eyes opened. 'Only if you believe time travels in a straight line.'

'Here we go,' muttered Splinter with a weary sigh. 'More universal fruit cake.'

'Cake.' Box smiled, dreamily.

'There are so many ways to understand time.' Balthazar spoke as if this was a very beautiful thing.

'I'd settle for one simple way,' said Splinter.

'If all the times that have ever been and ever will be were cards in an infinitely large deck, all existing at once, then your experience of time is merely a matter of where you have been put in the pack. Every future exists at the same time as every past. Take me from one place in the deck and put me in another and I am moved forwards or backwards in my experience of time.'

'So you've been shuffled back from where you were?' asked Chess.

'Exactly. I was born five hundred years from now in a place called New Phoenicia.' He chuckled deeply. 'My life was colourful. Full of adventure, full of danger. I was wealthy, sometimes. I fought battles, I consorted with princes, I travelled to many times and places. And I became involved in games that are played for power. I thought I was very clever indeed. But I knew too much, I saw too much, I did too much. As a result, a man died.

'For this crime I was sent one thousand years back from my time to this place. Sent here because it is a very isolated place. Sent here to contemplate my folly.' Balthazar coughed apologetically. 'I haven't spoken to another being for five hundred years so you must excuse me if I talk so much now.'

It was dark; too dark to see anything more than the hard blackness that was their bodies.

'A thousand years is a very long time,' said Chess, as kindly as she could.

'It is a just punishment,' stated Balthazar. A band of fireflies speckled the night.

'What happens at the end of it all?' asked Chess. 'After ... well, after ...'

'After the next five hundred years? So long as I have done nothing, I may return to where I came from. I can start again and not make the mistakes I did. But should I involve myself in the affairs of this world before a thousand years have passed, that changes everything. From that point, the life I had is lost and time catches up with me.'

'It sounds a very complicated punishment,' said Box, scratching his head and wondering how doing nothing could be a form of punishment at all.

'But how have you survived here for five hundred years?' asked Chess.

'I am a clever man as well as a foolish one. I am good with my hands. I can look after myself. And I was allowed to bring certain items with me: books, tools, clothes and the three objects that assisted me with my crime, to remind me of my folly. And I have had occasion to steal from the stonedrakes.'

'Stonedrakes?' interrupted Splinter, with a sidelong glance at Box.

'A lizard race,' explained Balthazar.

'Lizards?' Splinter arched a thin, white eyebrow. 'You steal things from lizards?'

'They are a highly developed species, Splinter. They

occupy the volcano to the right of the bay as you look out to sea from my house. They fired upon you two days ago. That is what drew my attention to you; what excited my fatal curiosity.'

'They fired the cannon?' asked Box.

'Ah,' said Splinter calmly, 'lizards who fire cannons. I see.'

'That cannon is called a marine culverin. Doubtless the stonedrakes believed you had something to do with the Dog Troopers. It would be an easy mistake to make.'

'But we don't look like dogs,' sniffed Splinter.

'You don't look like stonedrakes,' replied Balthazar, 'that is the point.' He climbed to his feet. 'Sleep. I shall be guarding you.'

Chess's head was thumping but she asked, 'Why are you helping us? I mean, it might be bad for you, getting involved in something.'

'Because you need my help. I have had plenty of time to consider what is right. This is right, whatever the consequences to me.' He padded into the night.

'*Whatever the consequences to me,*' mimicked Splinter in a ridiculous voice. 'What consequences? And as for lizards with cannons and living for thousands of years? He's mad. And dangerous. Just as I said he would be. We should go. Now.'

'No,' insisted Chess. 'I don't think he means to hurt us. All he's done so far is to look after us.' She rubbed her eyes.

'Remember what the old lady said,' Splinter warned her.

'Yes, I know,' yawned Chess, tiredness flooding her now. 'Trust no one.'

'Apart from each other, I suppose,' pondered Box.

Splinter hesitated before saying, 'Yes, well, obviously, apart from each other.'

The Dog Troopers were hunting them. That thought drove Chess on, all through the next day, even though she was exhausted. But it wasn't the fever that had left her so tired; her energy had been drained by what had happened with the bloodsucker vines. Nobody spoke about it but Chess thought about it constantly. It was as if she had soaked up all of Box's terror and this had fused with her own fear and anger before exploding out of her; exploding from her as she had wanted it to, just as she had felt the fury surge when the Inspector had threatened to kill Gemma. Except on that occasion it was Gemma's fear she could feel.

When Chess asked Box if he had seen a bullet wound on the Inspector, he had looked at her as if she was talking rubbish. 'I'm not going mad,' she explained. 'I'm working things out.' Splinter listened but said nothing and all the time, Balthazar stayed close to her, padding with silent strength, ever-watchful.

Late that afternoon, they came to the gorge. It split the centre of the monumental cliffs that curved round the vast bowl of the rainforest and dropped sheer into the valley, buttressing the high plateau above. At the back of the gorge a vast curtain of water crashed into the chasm, filling it with a cloud of drizzle and a rolling rumble. The drizzle soaked the trees and floated over the river that flowed out and into the forest. It was this perpetual mist of spray that the Tuesdays had seen from the slopes of the volcano.

'Up there,' said Balthazar as they stood at the foot of one of the cliffs, close by the churning river. He pointed high with his staff. 'We climb up there.'

Chess squinted up through the spray which drenched her face. She couldn't even see where he was pointing. The way looked impenetrable, a tangle of roots, drunken trees and loose rocks.

Box wiped the moisture from his face. Everything glistened with the spray from the cascading waterfall. 'It must be a thousand feet to the top!' he exclaimed.

'Nine hundred and eighty-four feet,' said Balthazar. 'I have measured it. But it may as well be a thousand feet if you fall so take care to tread only where I tread. Splinter, you must ignore the pain.'

'I'll tell it to go away,' growled Splinter.

Balthazar led them by a path that they would never have found without him. Up narrow clefts in the rock, across half-rotten tree stumps that spanned bowel-churning drops, around spires of stone where shallow-bedded weeds sprouted, loose and treacherous to hold. The roll of the waterfall grew louder, the air wetter with spray and the rocks more slippery as they worked their way into the gorge. Chess focused on the surefooted figure of Balthazar picking his way ahead of her and ignored the boiling waters below.

Before they reached the waterfall they jack-knifed back along the same cliff, still going up. The clamour of the falls died away and the spray now billowed below them. The rocks were not as slippery but the cliff was just as sheer.

Chess listened to the stream of curses that came from Splinter who was struggling behind her. Her attention wandered to the grey-backed gulls floating over the abyss, only an arm's length away, rising and dropping in the thermals. Looking forwards she could see the ocean now, an uncompromising band of deep blue cutting straight across the horizon and over the tops of the trees that filled the valley ahead of her and far below. She stopped, closed her eyes and smelt the air, fresh and with the tang of salt. A breeze soothed her cheeks, whipping the hair from her face.

'Shift your butt,' grumbled Box.

'Sorry,' said Chess and she stretched up for the next handhold.

They did not have much further to climb.

'We are here,' announced Balthazar, portentously. With that he pulled himself over the last wedge of rock and on to the top of the cliff. Chess saw how the muscles bulged beneath the dark-brown skin of his back. His body was bulky but the smooth fat covered powerful blocks of muscle.

When they had crested the ridge, Splinter sat on a rock and scowled at the floor. Box lay on his back and laughed. 'You're like a stroppy old wrinkly,' he told Splinter.

'Yeah, with a broken ankle and a broken wrist and who has nearly fallen to his death a thousand times. Very funny, fly head.' Splinter drilled his eyes into Balthazar's back. 'Just waiting for the weirdo with the ponytail to strike.'

Chess turned, looking in all directions. To her left was the volcano with the factory and the veil of smoke that clung to the mountains and hid the sky. In front of her stretched the valley, filled with forest and then the great sweep of the bay. To her right and further down the coast a chain of volcanoes faded purple into the haze.

She looked inland. Not more than fifty metres from where she stood was the cascading lip of the waterfall which was fed by a wide, lazy river that meandered across the high plateau. Behind the plateau there were more ridges, row upon row and beyond the ridges there were mountains.

Balthazar had left them and had walked to where the top of the cliff jutted over the forest like the pointed end of an anvil. Standing solitary on the very edge of this promontory was an ancient tree whose colossal girth towered, bough over time-knotted bough above the scrub and scrawny trees that matted much of the cliff top.

Chess was astonished to see that the gnarled trunk was encased in smooth walls of toffee-brown wood. These spiralled up the trunk and into the lower boughs. They leant crookedly in all directions and at different heights. This wooden case around the trunk looked big enough to drive a train up. As she approached, Chess saw that between the boughs there were ladders made of weathered vine and planks of wood. Some of the ladders ran between wooden rooms that sat in the boughs and were as large as sheds. The rooms had balconies and windows with shutters. A silver-toned tinkling drifted on the wind from the tree to Chess.

'My house,' announced Balthazar, proudly, big eyes popping out more than usual. He stood at the foot of a wooden ladder that led up to where the wooden walls started, about ten feet above the ground. A set of wind chimes dangled from the top rung and the tinkling came from them as they glanced against one another in the breeze.

Chess bent her head back to see the huge construction corkscrewing up to where the top canopies spread. A scaffold of thick planks and planed tree trunks supported it from the ground and this was strengthened by spars that jutted out from the tree like the spokes of an umbrella.

Then Chess looked down to where the twisting roots on the far side of the tree were as thick as elephant legs and gripped the tip of the ridge like claws.

'Do not worry,' said Balthazar. 'It has stood like this for over four hundred and fifty years. You won't make it fall over.'

'Nice one,' admitted Box when he joined them. 'How did you do it?'

'You can do plenty of carpentry in five hundred years, my curly-haired friend,' laughed Balthazar.

Box considered whether Balthazar might have been laughing at him. He wasn't sure so he let it pass. 'How many rooms does it have?' he asked.

'I haven't counted,' admitted Balthazar. 'Please, let me show it to you.' He turned round to them as he put his foot on the first rung of the ladder and said, 'Don't forget to remind me to warn you about the vine store.'

They followed him up the ladder and into his house. The rooms ran from one to the next up the trunk and along the boughs, each connected to the other by a short, enclosed staircase or open ladders. Chess was amazed by how solid and comfortable it was.

Amongst the many rooms, Chess counted: a workshop containing tools, a bench with vices attached, lumber and piles of animal hides; a long kitchen with a stone oven and shelves stacked with bowls and with herbs and cured meat hanging from the ceiling; a library crammed with books in plum-dyed leather, tooled with gold and in one corner a lectern on which there sat a slim, folio-sized case, made of lead and padlocked.

Then there was a study with a Moroccan-red armchair in one corner and a high desk in the other. Chess sat in the armchair when no one was looking. It was so big her feet dangled. It made her feel sleepy. The top of the desk was hidden beneath a sheaf of papers, a pot decorated with Aztec-style figures and bristling with quills, fountain pens and pencils, a solar-powered calculator and a rack of tobacco-pipes in different styles. There was a bedroom with rugs and a hammock, another library neatly lined with books made of plastic and whose pages were as fine as silicon shavings and utterly transparent, three empty rooms and, at the top of the house, an observatory.

The observatory was equipped with an astrolabe, two telescopes, notebooks on shelves, a collection of prisms on a steel table, a shelf full of mirrors all of which made Chess look strange when she looked into them, a tripod supporting a copper still that was bubbling slowly over a flame and exuding the whiff of strong liquor, star charts, maps and a typewriter. A door from the observatory opened onto a wide balcony that circled the tree so that Chess was able to look out in any direction that she wanted. The view was massive and the valley bottom was dizzyingly far beneath them.

The whole house was thick with the resinous scent of timber and it creaked gently when the wind blew hard. The chimes tinkled from far away.

'I used to live by a river,' said Chess. The sudden thought

of the wharf and Gemma made her chest ache. But nobody was listening.

'Stuffed with loot,' was Box's hushed verdict.

'When the time comes,' responded Splinter, 'we'll need sacks.'

When Box realized Balthazar was interested in their mutterings he asked, 'Does it go higher?'

'It is possible to climb higher but I have not built so high. It is important to give the tree some privacy.'

'Mad,' mouthed Splinter to Chess.

'And there is a shallow cave in the cliff below the tree. That is where I store things that I brought with me but do not need; spare tools, non-perishable supplies, and ...' he hesitated, choosing his words with precision, 'and items I do not wish to see.' He changed the subject. 'It is getting late and we are all very hungry. Let me set your fractures, Splinter, and then I shall prepare some supper.'

Balthazar wrapped Splinter's right ankle and right wrist tightly in cloths impregnated with pungent oils. Then he splinted the right ankle so that Splinter couldn't move it at all and he fetched a length of wood from the workshop that Splinter could use as a crutch. Balthazar described the broken wrist as 'only a crack' and he was satisfied that supporting it in a sling would be sufficient.

He took the Tuesdays up to one of the empty rooms. It had been built on a bough halfway up the main trunk which reached like a gothic arch over the precipice beneath the jutting tip of the cliff.

'You can sleep in here,' said Balthazar who had brought a

stack of animal skins from the workshop for them to lie on. Then he went down to the kitchen.

When Balthazar's footsteps had receded, Splinter turned on Chess. 'How did you do it?' he hissed, anxious for Balthazar not to overhear.

'Do what?' Chess was surprised by her brother's virulence.

'That thing with the flowers.' His narrow face was close to hers.

'I don't know,' said Chess. It wasn't really a lie because she wasn't sure. She knew it was safer not to talk to Splinter about what she'd been thinking. 'I've told you, it just happened.'

Splinter remained full of spleen. 'Have you got something? Something secret? Something that lets you do things?'

'No,' laughed Chess, nervously, astonished at the suggestion.

'Did you take something from the old crone?' he cross-examined her.

'No,' and Chess was getting angry now. 'I didn't take anything. What gave you that idea?'

'It doesn't matter,' responded Splinter, swiftly.

Box was inspecting a sliding door on the far side of the room. He pushed it and as it jolted none too smoothly to one side he saw that there was a small room beyond. A room that was full of coils of rope.

'I want us to go and to go now,' demanded Splinter. 'To go before anything else happens. To go before the latest maniac we've encountered tries to finish us off.'

'We're not going. Not yet,' said Chess, firmly.

'It's been a couple of days.'

'They don't count.'

'Ever since we got here you've acted like you're in charge,' Splinter accused her. 'Acting like you think you're special.'

Box slipped into the room. It had no windows and it smelt of old leaves. There was rope everywhere; coiled in piles, strewn across the floor, looped from the ceiling.

'It's nothing to do with who's special and who isn't,' said Chess, struggling to keep her temper. 'You're my brother, OK? We're doing this together. No one's "in charge".'

'Says who?' Even though he was speaking quietly, Splinter stopped to catch his breath. 'I'm the one who knows what to do. I'm the one who looks after everyone. I'm the one who has the ideas. Me. Splinter. Without me you two would have been dead long ago.' He was ranting at her, pale eyes wild with a blue fire. 'Without me you wouldn't last five minutes, burning flowers or no burning flowers. It's always me that does everything. And now you think you're something special.'

'Well, *you* be special then,' Chess replied, trying not to shout, eyes smarting, 'because I hate it.'

The was a screech from the room into which Box had disappeared. Chess and Splinter hadn't seen him go and the cry startled them. Chess ran, with Splinter shuffling after her. Light was pouring up into the shadows and the swirling dust from a square hole in the floor. Clutching onto the edge of the hole with his body dangling in the empty space below was Box.

'A loose plank,' he gasped. 'I nearly fell right through.' He was looking up at them through the square gap. 'Give us a hand up. This is a bit lively. I could of died.' The valley was a blur of green beneath him. 'I still might,' he grimaced.

Chess knelt down to grasp a wrist and help him up. Splinter stood where he was, just staring down.

'Come on, Splinter,' Chess urged, 'you can lend a hand.'

The only part of Splinter that moved was the corner of his mouth which twisted into a cold sneer.

It was left to Chess to help Box up from the hole. When he was sitting safely on the floor he shouted at Splinter. 'You moron. Why didn't you help? I could of died. Did you want me to die?'

But Chess knew what Splinter had been thinking. 'You wanted it to be me that was hanging there, didn't you?'

'Sometimes, Chess, I could murder you,' replied Splinter and he walked from the room.

CHAPTER 9

'It was my fault,' Balthazar was saying. 'I meant to warn you not to go into the vine room because the floor needed mending.'

They had had a supper of cassowary eggs baked in the stone oven, smoked bush-pig and sweet potato and sago mash.

'Best fodder ever,' Box had grunted, cheeks stuffed.

Chess had been cautious because the food looked so different from the pickings she was used to. And whilst she didn't think it would harm her, she reminded herself that they knew very little about Balthazar. But it smelt good and although it was too full of taste, she ate until her jaws ached. Full bellies made the Tuesdays happier. Splinter's mood lightened but Chess couldn't forget the malevolence in his eyes and what he had said to her in the vine room.

When they had finished eating, Balthazar led them up to the observatory and out onto the balcony. They sat facing the plateau and the mountains from which the river flowed. He had brought rush mats for them to sit on and a long stemmed pipe from his study. He also brought a slender taper that he lit from the flames beneath the still and which he carried onto the balcony, shielded by his hand.

When they were all sitting down he packed the pipe bowl with flakes of brown leaf from a pouch carried in a pocket of his leggings. He put the tip of the stem between his lips and touched the leaf with the flaming taper. It flared red before exuding a swirl of creamy smoke. Balthazar closed his eyes, drew harder and sighed as smoke poured from his nostrils, temporarily veiling his long, black moustache.

The bright sun had set behind the far mountains, rippling the clouds orange and pink so that they looked like unrolled bolts of rough cloth. The oddity of a second sun continued to perplex Chess and she looked at it now, a pale pink disc, obscured by the drifting edge of the smog that belched from the factory on the hidden side of the volcano. As she watched, the disc was swallowed entirely by the pall of smoke that hung over the mountains and blotched the sky.

It was quiet enough to hear the hiss of the leaf burning in Balthazar's pipe. The air under the boughs that arched over their heads grew rich with the aroma of the smoke and the clouds turned purple with the fall of night.

Balthazar spoke and his voice was deep and vibrant and it mixed with the pipe smoke to fill the space where they all sat. 'I have told you about myself but I know very little about you.' He rested his pipe against his broad and naked chest.

'Here we go,' Splinter whispered in Box's ear. 'Weird time.'

Balthazar continued. 'I have chosen to help you, whatever the cost to me. I ask for nothing, but if you were to tell me what your business is here, I may be able to help you further.

144

And, what is more, it would amount to common courtesy, would it not?'

He planted his pipe back in his mouth, brushed some ash off his leggings and puffed contentedly whilst nobody spoke. Then he said, 'Rest assured, my friends, I have had plenty of time to study your behaviour and consider your circumstances. Let me see what I have deduced.' He cleared his throat with a fine, rasping cough and proceeded confidently: 'First, you are criminals. That much is obvious by your clothes, your habits, the way you play with your knives and the way you weighed up the value of every item in my house when you first entered it. I mean no offence. I, too, am a criminal. To that extent we are similar creatures.

'Next, either you came here by accident or somebody sent you. If it was an accident you would have told me by now. You have told me nothing, *ergo*, somebody sent you to do something. Very mysterious!' He blew a large and perfect smoke ring. 'But you have no idea how to do the thing that you were sent to do.' Another smoke ring. 'That is unfortunate.'

Nothing but the hiss of burning tobacco. All eyes on Balthazar. All mouths shut. 'And the Symmetry want you, but they want you *alive*. Believe me, my friends, if the Symmetry wanted you dead, you would be dead by now.'

Nobody spoke. Being with a stranger who talked about the Twisted Symmetry made Chess feel as if she was about to fall off a skyscraper. But although her brothers had warned her that Balthazar knew about the Symmetry, so far, he had done nothing to harm them.

'Your silence tells me that my deductions are correct.'

Balthazar beamed a crescent moon of satisfaction.

'I don't think they'd mind if me and Splinter was dead,' suggested Box. Splinter hit him with his crutch.

Balthazar placed a hand on the crutch to keep it still. 'I am curious to know more. And whatever you are doing on Surapoor, I think that you would benefit from a little help. You will not get very far without it.'

Chess looked at Box who raised his eyebrows and then at Splinter who just stared back. They couldn't sit in silence all night so, trusting her instinct, Chess said, 'We were sent by the Committee to find out why the Twisted Symmetry are stealing children.'

'The *Twisted* Symmetry, is it?' said Balthazar. 'Well, I suppose they are twisted in a manner of speaking.'

'You know about the Twisted Symmetry, don't you?' coaxed Splinter.

'Oh yes,' replied Balthazar, bulging eyes solemn. 'Too much. You could say I have been an authority in my time.'

'Are the Symmetry *very* powerful?' asked Splinter, masking his excitement behind a solemn face.

Balthazar regarded him steadily. 'I thought you called them the "Twisted" Symmetry? Are they "Twisted" no longer, Splinter? Yes, they are very powerful; terrifyingly powerful.'

When Splinter next spoke, Chess could tell by the tremor in his voice and the fake honesty of his eyes that he was luring Balthazar to reveal secrets. 'In the volcano, out there, there's a factory where the Symmetry take children they steal. It's guarded by Dog Troopers ...'

'The troopers came to Surapoor three years ago,' interrupted Balthazar, eager to reveal what he knew. 'That is when the smoke started. But I haven't gone to the volcano. I don't know what the Symmetry are doing. I have wanted to …' he hesitated and then said, 'I have been careful not to get too close.'

Splinter observed the glisten of sweat in the crease between Balthazar's lower lip and chin. He lobbed his next comment like a well-placed grenade. 'And in the factory there is something called an Inquisitor.'

'I knew it!' exclaimed Balthazar, so vigorously that Chess jumped. 'I could feel it. I knew that one of the Five was there. There is a feeling you see! They have such power.' He drew hard on his pipe and said, 'I fear for you. I fear for the children you have told me about.' He heaved a breath; calmed. 'You say a committee sent you?'

'*The* Committee sent us,' clarified Box.

Balthazar shook his head. 'I know of no such committee.'

'Ethel's on it.' Box looked at Balthazar expectantly.

'I know of no such Ethel.'

'Lucky you,' observed Splinter

'Mevrad,' Chess interjected excitedly. 'Her real name is Mevrad.'

Balthazar spluttered. 'Mevrad! Mevrad!'

'She fights the Twisted Symmetry,' explained Box, brightly.

'She does many things, that included.' He shook his head and repeated her name to himself.

'Is she a friend of yours?' asked Splinter.

'No, not a friend.' He hesitated before saying, 'She was one of the judges who sent me to Surapoor.'

'Ethel is a judge!' gasped Box.

'Not the sort of judge you are familiar with, you fuzzy-headed varlet.' Balthazar laughed to himself quietly. 'Oh Mevrad, you are clever. You are very clever.'

Box eyed Balthazar warily. He had no idea what a varlet was but he didn't like being called one.

Balthazar's pipe had gone out. He did not re-light it. 'Who else is on this committee?' he asked.

'A professor called Joachim something,' said Box trying to remember the rest of his name. 'He has a red moustache and one eye.' Balthazar shook his head.

'And somebody called Julius,' added Splinter. 'A man with half a face. Well, half a normal face.'

'And the other half?' enquired Balthazar, frowning.

'Silver.' Splinter shrugged. 'It looked silver.'

'I know who you mean,' said Balthazar with a heavy voice, 'but he is not a happy memory.'

Chess had only met Julius once; when she had first been taken to Committee HQ. But just being close to him had made her believe that she could be more than a piece of rubbish. She recalled his strength and his touch. He's not a bad memory for *me*, she thought.

Balthazar was smiling sadly. He looked up at the night sky and said, 'You are very clever, Mevrad. Have you seen all of this?'

'Are you all right?' Chess asked. Balthazar's turns of emotion didn't seem right in a grown-up.

'Yes,' replied Balthazar. 'A little surprised, maybe. But let me see how wisely Mevrad is playing this game. You are here to investigate the Symmetry?' Chess nodded. 'Very well, have you been taught about them?' Heads were shaken. 'Can you speak Chat?' More shakes. 'Can you fight? I don't mean your silly little knives, I mean fight properly?' He was answered by silence. No one was going to admit that they couldn't fight.

Balthazar continued more loudly. 'Do you know the purpose of the Symmetry? The forces at their disposal? The weapons and tactics of the Dog Troopers?' He shook his head in disbelief. 'Do you know the battle order of the Havoc Legions? The war cries of the Plague Marshals? The perfidious science of the warps?'

'What does "perfidious" mean?' whispered Box in Splinter's ear.

'Double-dealing, I think,' replied Splinter, very quietly.

'Do you have the first idea of how you are going to find out what the Symmetry are actually doing?'

'Go back and have a snoop?' suggested Box, lamely.

'Dear gods,' erupted Balthazar. 'What are you doing here?' Then he looked at Chess and repeated softly, as if pleading, 'Mevrad, what do you think you are doing?'

He rose, resolute. 'Wait for me in the observatory. I want to show you something.'

'Crazy. Like I said,' proclaimed Splinter after they had retreated to the observatory.

'You'd be crazy after having no one to talk to for five hundred years.' Chess sat on a stool.

'I'll go crazy if I have to listen to him for another five minutes,' smouldered Box.

'He's trying to help.' Chess was surprised. 'I thought you said he was all right?'

'He keeps having a poke at me,' complained her brother. 'Treating me like an idiot.'

'So?' said Splinter. 'You can hardly blame him. Everyone else does.' He picked up a pyramidal lens and held it to his eye.

'He called me a varlet.' Box paused and thought. 'What is a varlet?'

'A kind of idiot with curly hair, I imagine.'

Box kicked a cupboard door. 'And all this stuff about armies. Ethel mentioned Havoc Legions and the Plague Breed but she said we wouldn't have to face them.'

'Not yet, was what she said, fly head. But you were too busy volunteering for suicide missions to read the small print. I've told you this is hopeless. The Symmetry are too powerful. Broom the loon is an expert on them and you've heard it from him.'

Splinter's tongue whetted a finger tip and he traced a letter S on a cupboard top. 'Still, it is interesting, hearing what he has to say about the enemy,' and he smiled at Chess.

When Balthazar returned he had under his arm the lead case that had been sitting on the lectern in the study. 'I was looking for the key,' he explained. 'Drop the shutters on the windows. I want no light to escape.' He extinguished the flames under the still.

As Balthazar knelt on the floor and opened the padlock on the case, Chess and Box secured the shutters. Splinter watched everything that Balthazar did, intently. When the room was in total darkness, Balthazar spoke.

'This is an Omnicon, a Book of All Things.' In the blackout there was nothing but the deep buzz of Balthazar's voice and fumes of alcohol mingled with the aroma of wood resin. 'Only two were ever made. One is lost, the other is here. I last gazed at these pages over five hundred years ago. I had hoped never to look at them again.'

Chess heard something being taken out of the lead case. 'There are only two pages in this book,' continued Balthazar, 'the page you are on and the page you want to get to. But you can use these two pages to find out about anything that exists.'

'How?' asked Splinter.

A pale glow appeared on the floor. It emanated from an ivory-coloured page of parchment and it was sufficient to illuminate the page but nothing else. 'You start on the first page,' said Balthazar. 'It is full of general facts. Amongst those facts you must find a reference to something that takes you nearer to what you want to know. This may involve a degree of lateral thinking. Then you turn to the second page. There you find information about what it was you wanted to know about on the first page. You read that and find something else that takes you nearer to what you wanted to know about in the first place. You then turn back to the first page and so you carry on. The contents of the pages change as you move between them and follow the different references. In this way, you use one reference to lead to the next until you find what you seek.'

'Like following a string of clues,' suggested Splinter.

'Indeed,' replied Balthazar.

'And you can find out about anything at all in that book?' queried Splinter.

Balthazar paused before answering. 'It will not reveal

thoughts or schemes, it will not predict the future, but it will tell you any *fact* you wish to know.' Balthazar sensed Splinter's fascination welling in the darkness. 'Knowledge can be dangerous, Splinter. I knew too much, I saw too much, I did too much. It was because of the Omnicon that I knew too much. That is why I keep it locked, even from myself. Now all of you, watch.'

Balthazar had been moving quickly between the two pages of the Omnicon. He stopped. Suddenly a stream of light projected up and into the room from the open page. The light formed an inverted pyramid with its apex at the centre of the page and its flat base just below the ceiling of the observatory. In the body of the pyramid of light there appeared a large figure 8, lying on its side and twisted one hundred and eighty degrees about its axis. It shimmered silver and revolved in the air.

'An 8,' said Box.

'No,' Balthazar corrected him, 'the awlis; the symbol for infinity; the sign of the Symmetry.'

Chess could see how Balthazar's olive-dark face gazed up at the symbol that filled the luminous pyramid. He spoke gently and with a reverence that unnerved her. 'That which is never changing and goes on until it comes back on itself and thereby goes on forever. There is a terrible, raving, mathematical beauty to this. The promise of eternity. This is the purpose of the Symmetry. To remain unchanging, forever.'

'That's the sign we saw on the dog-men's uniforms,' Box whispered to Chess. She nodded.

'Change is natural,' continued Balthazar, 'it drives the

universes. But to stop change and to gain eternity, the Symmetry must stop time. This can be done but to do it they need energy; sufficient energy to collapse time and space into the nothingness from which they came; to pack every dimension back into its original, infinitesimal state; to destroy the time spiral.'

The twisted symbol continued to revolve. Chess was relieved to see that Balthazar's face had relaxed although his forehead was beaded with tiny drops of sweat. Splinter sat with his long legs crossed and his face laid bare by rapt fascination.

Chess recalled how Professor Breslaw had talked about these things. But he had said that the energy required was too great to imagine and she told this to Balthazar.

'Your professor is an optimist, I think. I know more about the Symmetry than he will ever have the misfortune to. Listen. At the head of the Symmetry are the Inquisitors. There are greater, more ancient powers but it is the Inquisitors who created the Symmetry and it is they who control it. They command three armies; the Havoc Legions, the Plague Breed and the Dog Troopers. With these and their other forces they extend their reach through time and place. They seek power endlessly but above all, they seek power over humans.'

'Why?' asked Chess.

'The Inquisitors harvest energy from pain and suffering and fear; from the dark emotions. They call this process extraction. Whether it is a moment of agony or an epoch of misery, the potential energy is vast. It can be released by the wars they wage and by their merciless dominion. But humans are special because their potential for great happiness is matched only by their potential for suffering and misery. The energy to be extracted from humans is boundless. So the Inquisitors desire humans greatly but most of all, they crave human children. To corrupt human children is their greatest source of energy and their special pleasure.'

A room with a small window where children were taken. Chess felt her nails dig into the palms of her hands so sharply that it blotted out the image.

'This corruptibility is the beauty of humans.' Animated, marvelling at what he spoke about, Balthazar continued. 'By lies and temptations, humans can be manipulated to inflict upon themselves the miseries that the Inquisitors desire. Beware their honeyed words. Their aim always is to destroy others so that they can live. Our world is a perfect source of energy for them, rich and self-sustaining.'

'Like a battery?' suggested Splinter. Balthazar nodded slowly.

'Why haven't they done whatever it is they want to do?' asked Box.

'Words are not your strength, Box, are they?'

Box clenched his fists and gritted his teeth as the heat in his head made his eyes mist but Balthazar ignored this. 'It is a mercy that whilst the Symmetry have succeeded in extracting vast quantities of energy, they do not have the capability to deliver it across time and space. Yet.'

'Is that why they need the Eternal?' asked Chess.

'You go on about that,' complained Box.

'Eternally,' groaned Splinter.

'I have said enough about the Inquisitors,' said Balthazar

abruptly. His fingers flicked the pages of the Omnicon, the awlis vanished and Chess was shocked to see a dog-man standing in the pyramid of light, arms by his sides, revolving so that she had a complete view of him. She drew back.

'It's only a hologram,' Balthazar assured her, 'it isn't real although the likeness is perfect.'

The dog-man stood to attention before them, looking straight ahead with his nightmare mix of dog snout and human face impassive. He looked real, from the ebony fur gathered in tufts under his lower jaw to the patch of human skin with dirty pores above his right eye. He wore the black tunic jacket and body armour that Chess had seen in the factory. Now she knew the significance of the silver symbols on his shoulders.

'I expect there will be a battalion of Dog Troopers at the factory so you need to know about them.'

'How many in a battalion?' Box interrupted.

'About four hundred,' answered Balthazar.

'OK,' said Box, doing a quick piece of mental arithmetic, 'so we are only about three hundred and ninety-seven short.'

'The Dog Troopers are raised in colonies,' explained Balthazar. 'They were bred by the warps to be a loyal and aggressive fighting force. Their bodies and minds are a jumble of dog and man but there are some who can shape change. They may assume the body of a human or dog or dog-man at will.'

'The Inspector,' Chess said aloud. 'He must have been a Dog Trooper.'

'Dog Troopers are known to move amongst humans but that is not their principal role. Usually, they are deployed to protect the cross-universal shipping lanes used by the Symmetry to transport raw amarantium.'

'Crystal,' breathed Splinter.

'Yes. Crystal. It is dug from the Alluvial Mines where matter flows out of the Calyx Nebula. It is a most valuable material; valuable enough for there to be perpetual war between the Symmetry and those other powers who desire it.'

'The Crystal Wars?'

'I see you are an authority of the Symmetry already, Splinter.'

Splinter blinked modestly.

'The endless, pan-universal battles over the amarantium deposits are where the many millions of Dog Troopers are deployed. Even as we speak, war is raging as it has been for millennia.'

The tree creaked and there was a shriek from the jungle, hundreds of feet below.

'Why is crystal so important to the Twisted Symmetry?' asked Box.

'For creatures who want to control time and space, something that connects all time and all space is important.' Then Balthazar pointed to the hologram. 'Take a good look at your enemy. He wears standard body armour with a hood and breathing equipment. That is the tube to his respirator on the rear view. See?' and Balthazar pointed to the narrow tube running from the back of the hood to a cylinder at the small of his back. 'So he can breathe in hostile atmospheres.

'Let me tell you about the weapons the troopers use. He carries a firearm on his back. Look.' Chess recognized the weapon with the snub nose like a power drill. 'That is a blaze carbine. It can fire single shots like a rifle or burst fire like a machine gun. Up to five hundred rounds in one minute. Very effective, very destructive. Now, look at the baton on his thigh. Watch this.'

Chess reared back as the hologram freed the long baton and held it in an outstretched fist, crouching. It was the same weapon that the General had held.

'This is a mace-blade, for hand-to-hand combat. Like this it is used as a cosh or club.' Then the three-edged spike flashed from the body of the baton. 'Like this, it is used to slash or stab.'

The blade retracted into the baton and the trooper replaced it on its clip and took from his belt an object that he slipped onto his hand. It looked like a knuckle duster with a protruding spout in the centre of its front edge.

'This is a nerve wrench. It's used to subdue an opponent by plucking his nerves when directed at them. The effect is extraordinarily painful but not usually fatal.'

'What about the thing with all the blades?' asked Box. 'We were in a tunnel ...'

'It was a shaft,' Splinter corrected him.

'OK, a shaft and something came at us. A ball with loads of different blades.'

Balthazar nodded. 'A spider grenade. It can expand or contract to fill small spaces and rolls in the direction it was thrown. The troopers carry different sorts of grenade; tangler grenades, blast grenades, smoke grenades, tenebrous grenades, gas grenades, shatter grenades.'

'What's a tenebrous grenade?' asked Splinter.

'One that spreads darkness when it explodes,' answered Balthazar.

'How do they do that?' Splinter was curious.

'Warp technology,' Balthazar replied.

'What are warps? What's warp technology?' Ethel had been guarded in what she would tell them, but Splinter knew that Balthazar could be pumped for information.

Balthazar sighed but Chess could see that he could not resist. 'Warp technology is the perverse science that the Symmetry rely upon for many of their tools and processes; for systems and contraptions that go against the normal order of the universe. Items that are sometimes beautiful and sometimes monstrous, devised by the most cunning and distorted artifice. And the warps are those who invent and manufacture this technology.'

'Like magic?' suggested Box

'Nothing like magic,' said Balthazar. Box grunted and bit his upper lip. 'It is science but the wrong sort of science.' Balthazar ran his fingers down the page of the Omnicon, delicately tracing their tips over the black script. 'Every piece of warp technology exercises its own attraction and its own treacherous influence.' His fingers toyed with the edge of the page. 'Just to touch it is to be forever changed.' Then he slammed the book shut.

'Open the shutters,' he commanded.

When the shutters were open, Balthazar locked the Omnicon back in its lead case. He tugged the padlock to check it was secure and put the key in his pocket. Unblinking, Splinter watched everything that Balthazar did with the book and the lead case.

'The Omnicon,' enquired Splinter, almost sweetly, 'is that warp technology? Is that how it works?'

'I feel you have a great interest in things of darkness, Splinter. Beware,' warned Balthazar. 'You cannot be interested in the darkness without the darkness becoming interested in you.'

Splinter smiled innocently and said no more.

CHAPTER 10

The Tuesdays left the observatory and followed Balthazar. He led them down to their room. The warm night air was loaded with fragrant musk that had drifted up from the forest. Chess inhaled it, trying to enjoy its fresh delicacy, but her thoughts were pulled back to the factory, to the children, to Saul. As Balthazar was about to leave, she said, 'One of the dog-men has a fur cloak, and a face that's meaner than any of the others and a strange collar round his neck and chest, and the armour he wears is all in bits. He's really tall. He's called . . .'

'The General?' Balthazar said with quiet surprise. 'The General is here? General Saxmun Vane commands the Dog Troopers, many millions of them. Every trooper, every battalion, every division does what he orders them to do. He is answerable only to the Inquisitors although he sees himself as answerable to no one. The Symmetry must have important business on Surapoor for there to be an Inquisitor *and* the General.' Then, with vehemence, Balthazar said, 'You must avoid him at all costs. He is dangerous, extremely dangerous.'

'But what's wrong with him?' Chess asked.

'The General was once a shape changer. His preference was for human form. But as time went by he wanted more than that. He did not want merely to look like a human. He wanted to be a human. There are those who serve the Symmetry who say that the General's desire for human form was a blasphemy and that what happened to him was a punishment; a punishment for trying to become something that he wasn't.

'The General conspired with the Symmetry's primary warp to undergo a total genetic re-definition of his body. It was an unusual request but not an impossible one. The operation should have resulted in his transformation into a human. Unfortunately, for the General, something went wrong and as a consequence of the failed operation his body became prone to spontaneous and unexpected changes of shape. Not into dog or man but into shapes that resembled unnatural creatures, or parts of them.'

With a quickening in her chest, Chess suspected that she knew who was responsible for the failed operation. 'What happened to the warp?'

'This was many centuries ago, by your time.' Balthazar tugged his moustache, evidently surprised that Chess should have asked this question. 'But the General has a Rhadamanthine memory and an unquenchable thirst for vengeance. The primary warp vanished before agonizing torment could be inflicted upon him but the General is waiting to exact his revenge. It will not be a happy existence for the warp; in the end, General Saxmun Vane always gets what he desires.'

'His name?'

'The warp?' asked Balthazar. Chess nodded. 'His name was Sprazkin. Lemuel Sprazkin. But for reasons that are not entirely clear to me, he is forever known to the Symmetry as the Traitor.'

'The Traitor,' echoed Splinter.

'I do not know what the warp, Sprazkin, is doing now,' concluded Balthazar.

Chess did. 'He is trying to be good,' she whispered.

Balthazar chose not to ask her what she meant. 'The General's metamorphoses are random and unexpected. To stop them he must administer regular doses of a serum, manufactured for him by the warps.'

'What about the pieces of armour?' asked Box.

'Would you pack your body into a solid shell of armour if it might change shape at any moment?' Balthazar asked him. 'The General's armour has to allow for sudden and dramatic changes in the shape of his body.' Balthazar stroked his chin as he pondered. 'It is strange that as a consequence of his desire to be human, the General's body became a grotesque confusion. Perhaps that is why, above all things save the Traitor, he hates humans. The Symmetry desire their hearts but the General wishes merely to kill them. He is a cunning soldier, a master tactician and he is very, very dangerous.'

Chess was tired now. Splinter was quiet, his face thoughtful. Box had one thing left to ask. 'What's a pugilist?'

'You'll find out tomorrow,' replied Balthazar Broom with an air of superiority and a big smile. He left the room.

'What's up with him?' complained Box after Balthazar's footfalls had faded.

'He's treating you like a varlet, varlet.'

'Yeah, well it's going to stop. I'm not having some philosopher stamp collector talking to me like that.'

'He's not a stamp collector,' yawned Splinter.

Chess woke to birdsong and a desperate feeling that she had to get back to the factory.

Box and Splinter must have gone for breakfast already because she was alone. She hurried through the wooden rooms and down their short connecting staircases. The timber was warm on the soles of her feet and the wood had a ginger hue in the bright morning light. It was cool now, but as the bright sun climbed the day would become sweltering.

The kitchen was almost at the bottom of the house. After the kitchen there was the workshop and then the ladder to the ground below. Balthazar, Box and Splinter were sitting on the kitchen floor, eating breakfast. Chess joined them and picked at the mangoes and nuts dipped in honey. It was a lot more fibrous to chew than she liked.

After breakfast, Balthazar took them outside, where they sat on a cluster of large boulders that scalloped a bare patch of ground a short distance from his house. Beyond the boulders there lay wiry scrub and low palms, interspersed with short trees. After that the vegetation grew more thickly until it spread along the banks of the river which drifted smoothly to the edge of the ridge and the nine hundred and eighty-four-foot drop.

'You must stay with me, at least until Splinter's bones have healed,' announced Balthazar.

Chess's spirits sank. 'We need to find out about the factory, and then get back to the Committee,' she protested, but was surprised to see Splinter nod in agreement with Balthazar.

'That's a good idea, Balthazar,' he said. No sour face. No demand to go home.

'We can use the time profitably. I can teach you the rudiments of Chat.'

'Chat?' Box wrinkled his nose.

'That's what I said, Box.'

'Is he trying to wind me up?' Box mumbled to Splinter.

'Chat is the name given to a language that is commonly spoken throughout the universes by creatures that are capable of speech and a basic level of thought. It is very useful as a travelling language. It isn't sophisticated. No good for mathematics or philosophy. But it is an effective way of making yourself understood.'

Then he turned directly to Box. 'And you and I have business out here, in this clearing.'

Box was baffled. 'What business?'

'You will find out. Be patient, Box. You can join us, Chess, but it will involve an amount of exertion and perhaps some sore bones. You will not be able to participate in that particular activity at all, Splinter. I am sorry. It will be very boring for you.'

'That's all right,' said Splinter, cheerily. Chess was astonished. 'Maybe I could use that time to read. I like reading and I've never seen so many books before. Would you mind if I was to read in the library?'

Balthazar was impressed. 'So, we have a scholar in our midst. You are welcome to use my library although you will only be able to read the old books. I broke the machinery that is required to read the leaf compendia after I arrived here. They will seem like transparent pieces of plastic and be impossible for you to read.'

'That's fine,' said Splinter. 'Thank you very much, Balthazar.'

'But we can't just hang around,' complained Chess. She looked to Splinter for support. He smiled back, benignly.

'You have no alternative,' said Balthazar.

'But the Twisted Symmetry might find us here.'

'Unlikely. Unless they have a spook on you.'

'A spook?' asked Box. 'What's a spook?'

'A creature that hunts,' explained Balthazar. 'Designed by the warps to enable the Symmetry to find whoever they want to find. Spooks are invisible to us. They listen. Very carefully.'

'Listen to what?' asked Box.

'For the person they are tracking. They listen for breathing and for a beating heart.'

'How?'

'Blood,' said Balthazar. 'If they are given even a tiny amount of someone's blood they are able to listen for the heart that pumped it. They listen across time and space. Sometimes they find the target quickly, sometimes it takes years. But a spook always finds what it looks for. Particularly children. Their blood is so vibrant.'

Into Chess's mind came a memory of the chain swinging in the boiler room and the nakedness of being watched by something she couldn't see.

'Blood from any one of you will lead to the others because you are brothers and sister. But without your blood a spook cannot find you. They don't have any of your blood, do they?'

'No,' said Box.

'No,' said Splinter.

Chess tried to remember everything that had happened. The Committee had her blood, Lemuel had taken it, but that was not what made her hesitate. There was something else; something she couldn't remember and it nagged at her.

'No,' she said after a long pause.

'Good. If the Symmetry have your blood, they will have *you*.'

Flies buzzed. Birds called. A muffled rumble came from where the river pounded into the bottom of the gorge. The sun was getting hotter, beating the land into silent stillness. Chess felt trapped. Box bit his lip and glowered at the floor.

'Can I go now?' asked Splinter, politely.

'You may come and go as you please,' replied Balthazar.

'Well,' said Splinter, lurching to his feet and leaning on the makeshift crutch, 'I'll leave all of you to your exertions. See you,' and he hobbled to the ladder and climbed up it, vanishing from sight.

Balthazar kept his eyes on Box the whole time. Box was sitting close to him and he felt Balthazar's stare as intensely as he felt the sun. It seemed that Balthazar was finding something very funny. Box didn't want to lose his temper but he could feel himself sliding into anger. However nice Balthazar had been, that didn't mean that he could make fun of him.

Don't ever let anyone think they can get away with disrespecting you, Box reminded himself. It didn't matter who they were unless they were Splinter which was different.

Nobody else was allowed to stare at him or laugh at him. People who did that got hit.

And maybe Splinter had been right when he said that Balthazar was a dangerous weirdo. Maybe Balthazar was planning something. Maybe he had got Splinter out of the way and was preparing to strike. Maybe the time had come to sort this out.

'What?' Box snapped. 'What are you staring at?'

'You,' replied Balthazar, vaulting from the rock so that he was standing at the edge of the clear patch of ground.

'Why? What's your problem?' demanded Box.

Chess woke up to what was happening. She didn't want any trouble. She didn't want Box to lose his temper. 'It's OK, Box,' she reassured him. 'Leave it.'

'It's not OK,' Box dismissed her. He jumped from the rock and squared up to Balthazar who was much taller and much broader than he was.

Balthazar goaded Box. 'You're full of fight for a little boy.'

Box's hand slipped to his trouser pocket.

'No, Box. Don't,' pleaded Chess.

'Ah yes, of course, your knife,' jibed Balthazar.

'Yes, my knife,' said Box, displaying the blade. He stood with his right arm forwards, bent slightly so that the tip of the blade was at his chest height and pointing towards the top of Balthazar's belly.

'Now what?' asked Balthazar, hands on hips, legs apart. Box said nothing but glared with rage. 'Are we going to stand like this until one of us faints? Or shall I dance until I collapse with exhaustion and you have half a chance of landing a blow on me.'

Chess was astonished to see Balthazar perform a jig in front of Box, his solid bulk skipping nimbly from toe to toe. It would have been very funny if Box hadn't been standing there with a knife out, waiting to explode. But Chess noticed how calm Balthazar was, despite the knife, how he moved speedily and gracefully even though he was a big man and how his body was poised, apparently relaxed but ready to burst into violent action at any moment.

'Put the knife down, Box,' coaxed Chess.

'No, keep it out,' urged Balthazar. 'That's right. Keep pulling that angry face. I haven't laughed at anything for five hundred years. Now, come at me, Box. Try to cut me. Come on.'

'Don't,' said Chess. 'Please, Box, don't.'

Box was ready to launch himself at Balthazar.

'Come on, Box,' jeered Balthazar. 'Come on, my fat little chicken.'

That was enough. Box attacked. But he didn't lunge, blindly. He sprang forward but at the last instant he sidestepped left and slashed low, at the front of Balthazar's right thigh. He knew it was a quick and clever move. But at the moment that the blade should have severed muscle, Box was aware of Balthazar jumping high and over his arm.

Box turned and drove the knife towards Balthazar's midriff. He hoped to catch his opponent off balance. But as his knife jabbed forwards he glimpsed Balthazar's large, dark body spin backwards full circle, pivoting on his left foot and bringing his right leg up and behind Box. The heel of Balthazar's right foot connected with the back of Box's head.

Dizzy, Box went lolloping forwards. He might have

regained his balance but a firm kick against his backside sent him spread-eagling into the earth. By the time that he had gathered his wits, Balthazar had the knife.

'What are you going to do now?' he asked, helping Box to his feet and handing him back the knife with the blade closed.

Box's head ached. He snatched the knife and propped himself against the rocks, stinging with anger and shame.

'I have watched you closely, Box,' Balthazar said. 'You have courage. When all else has gone, bravery and hope are all we have. Your brother and sister will need your courage. You're not a little chicken. I only said that to see if you are as foolish as you are brave. And you are.' Balthazar smiled kindly but Box did not look at him.

'Listen to me, Box. A big man with a knife is a little man without a knife. Do you understand what I mean? You are a fighter, Box, a fighter from your heart. We need our fighters. But you must learn to fight properly. To fight from your head as well as from your heart. And to fight for the right reasons. I cannot teach you the right reasons but I can teach you to fight. To fight well and to fight wisely.'

Box was still struggling to control his temper.

'That was a spinning hook kick,' explained Balthazar, ignoring Box's smouldering face and stepping closer to him. 'Look,' he commanded and Box raised his head. Balthazar performed the same backwards spinning kick that had sent Box staggering. Chess was fascinated by the way that his huge body could move so quickly and gracefully but with such power.

'I could have used a front leg hook kick.' Balthazar leant

back and drove his left leg high and forwards, curling it out and to the left slightly. 'Useful for beating your opponent's guard and striking the side of his head. Or I could have simply broken your wrist with my elbow. But that would have been my bad temper spoiling my judgement. A good fighter uses judgement, not rage.'

He placed his hand on Box's shoulder. 'Forgive me, Box, but sometimes a hard lesson is the best lesson, if you choose to learn from it.' Box was turning the knife in his hands. 'Are you a fool with a knife or are you a fighter, Box?'

Box studied the knife as if it might answer the question on his behalf. Chess watched him nervously. She knew how quickly he could whip out the blade and Balthazar's belly was well within striking distance. She knew what a temper Box had. But she was surprised by one of her brothers for the second time that morning when she saw Box sigh and slip the knife back into his pocket.

'How come you fight so clever?' asked Box, looking back at the ground.

'There was a time when I made a very good living from my fists and feet,' admitted Balthazar and he smiled so modestly that Chess thought he looked almost shy about it. 'Don't be hard on yourself Box; ours was not a fair fight.'

Box looked up at Balthazar and smiled wryly. 'I think I've worked out what a pugilist is,' he said.

Splinter could hear noises as they drifted up to him through the open library window. There had been raised voices and then the sounds of scuffling. That had been followed by quiet talking and then laughter and then more scuffling and playful shouts. He didn't know what was happening and he wasn't interested. He stood stock still in the centre of the library, closed his eyes and felt the swell of knowledge.

One long wall was lined with shelves. They were full of leather-bound volumes of different sizes. But Splinter had no interest in any of those. When he opened his eyes they alighted on the lectern in the far corner of the room. Resting on the top of the lectern was the lead case, padlocked, just as it had been the day before.

Splinter approached the lectern slowly, eyes never wavering from what lay on it. His skin tingled with the thrill of what was locked inside the lead case. When he reached the wooden stand he leant his crutch against the wall and placed both his hands on the case. He closed his eyes.

Here is knowledge, thought Splinter. Here is power. It was calling to him, wanting to give itself to him.

He stood back and inspected the heavy iron padlock that secured the opposing hooped brackets on the case. It was an ordinary padlock. He dipped spindly fingers into a pocket inside his long-tailed morning coat and reached for the lock picks. Then he set to work.

'Sloppy, Balthazar,' he whispered to himself. 'Very sloppy.'

CHAPTER 11

They will come for me.

Chess knew this and it ate her like a curse; a curse as inescapable as the thousand-metre stare in a dead man's eyes. Food became tasteless, sunlight cold and the nights raw with hours of waking. And when sleep did come, she was back in the factory where the children screamed for her and she searched the corridors for a place she couldn't find.

A steel door. A small, round window.

I want to find them. I have to know what happens to them.

That was why she and her brothers were here. And that was the only way in which she would start to discover the truth about herself. Chess was certain about that.

But as days crawled into weeks, they went nowhere. Box said they couldn't do anything with Splinter recovering and Splinter was maddeningly happy to spend hours alone in Balthazar's library. He hadn't mentioned the VAP since the day they had arrived at the tree house.

In the mornings, Balthazar tried to teach them the rudiments of Chat, but Chess found it impossible to concentrate. And anyway, street rats didn't do school. She could tell it was the language the traders used and she enjoyed learning what *jander* meant; swear words were always good to know. But Chat wouldn't tell them what was happening in the factory and it wouldn't stop the Twisted Symmetry from coming.

Box spent hours with Balthazar in the clearing near to the ancient tree. He learnt to use his fists to jab, hook and deliver an uppercut, how to use his feet to kick forwards, backwards, spinning and jumping and how to bob and weave, to parry and block. Chess stayed with them; it stopped her thinking about other things.

Balthazar drilled Box on the importance of weighing up his opponent to decide what kind of fighter he was, the value of swift and nimble footwork and the necessity to defend himself and then counter-attack. He taught Box that when he launched an attack it should be with a combination of punches and kicks that would exploit his opponent's weaknesses and given him no time to recover.

Chess experimented with her fists and feet. She discovered that she could deliver an uppercut just as swiftly as Box, but whereas her fists seemed to bounce off his face, his pummelled hers like hammers. It seemed a stupid way of getting nose bleeds.

The training and exercise that Box underwent were hard and the sweat streamed from him in the tropical heat. But over the weeks, Chess saw him become faster and more skilful and she saw his body change so that podgy flab began to transform into muscle.

But in the afternoons, when the heat drummed the cliff

top into silent stillness, Chess would sit on the wet, black rocks close to the where the river rolled into the chasm, and stare into the spray below, until the rush of water cleared the bad thoughts from her mind. She would stay there until she felt Balthazar's hand on her shoulder, soft and heavy, and without saying anything, they walked back to his house for supper.

Balthazar watched her a lot. Chess could feel it even when she couldn't see it. She hadn't forgotten the strange expression on his face when he had looked up at the awlis; as if he was fascinated and frightened by the Twisted Symmetry at the same time. This didn't worry her although she knew that it should. Ethel had warned them to trust no one but when it came to people like Lemuel Sprazkin and Balthazar Broom, trusting no one was not as easy as it sounded.

On an evening when the purple clouds had marched towards the distant mountains leaving behind echoes of thunder and the air was damp with the rain that had fallen, the Tuesdays were in the observatory with Balthazar. Splinter was inspecting scientific instruments laid out on a high shelf, Box had his eye to a telescope that was angled towards the bay, and Chess sat on the floor with her knees under her chin, her face collapsed in desperate gloom.

Splinter came to an object that excited his curiosity. Slightly longer and thicker than a penknife, it was made of brass and had a dimpled button on one side. It would be easy to pocket and might be useful. He looked about. Balthazar was bent over a desk in one of the windows, inspecting the horizon through a theodolite and making entries in a fat notebook with minute handwriting.

Splinter caught Box's eye and, saying nothing, told him to keep Balthazar occupied.

'They've got some normal ships and some that are proper mad.' Box observed the activity on the bay through the telescope.

'This will be a holy war,' announced Balthazar, portentously, his pony tail trailing black down his back as he continued working.

'Don't see how you can have one of those.' Box caught Splinter's wink and returned a grin. 'You can't kill anyone with a prayer, Balthazar.'

Balthazar switched his attention to Box, which conveniently, drew it in the opposite direction from Splinter. 'The stonedrakes occupy the volcano on the far side of the bay. They believe the red sun is the eye of their god. Their army and navy returned from war against a rival colony only a few months ago, to discover that night after night, their god is hidden from them by the black smoke from the factory.'

Splinter rubbed the brass body of the tool and placed an inquisitive finger on the button.

Balthazar was in lecturing mode. 'I assume they are reconnoitring the factory as a preliminary to making war upon it.'

'Who's your grease on, then?' asked Box. 'Dogs or lizards?'

Balthazar sighed. 'The stonedrakes do not have the first idea what is inside that volcano. They are fine warriors, but the troops commanded by General Vane will obliterate them.'

Splinter pressed the button.

Glass shattered and wood smashed as a fan of extending metal spokes flashed out of the brass case and whirred in an arc, demolishing the high shelf as they did so. The shelf collapsed, sending lenses and prisms to the floor. The spokes clicked back into the case and with a shriek, Splinter dropped it.

'Oops,' he said as silence fell.

Box snorted back laughter. Chess continued to stare at her toes. Balthazar pushed himself up from his chair and surveyed the mess.

'That is a pity,' was all he said and then he bent down to see what could be salvaged. When he did so, Splinter took the opportunity to pocket a bone-handled magnifying glass and a miniature steel screwdriver that Balthazar used to adjust his instruments.

Box gave him a thumbs-up.

'This is a rock flail, a hand-held mining tool.' Balthazar picked up the brass device. 'Useful for taking samples. You were fortunate not to be decapitated.'

'Lucky is my middle name,' boasted Splinter, before stepping on a sliver of broken glass and gasping. Box sneezed with laughter, messily.

'Tomorrow,' said Chess, 'I'm going.'

Splinter picked at his foot, dabbing a pimple of blood. Balthazar stopped gathering implements.

'Whatever any of you say, I'm going.'

Everybody knew that Chess was talking about the factory.

'*We* might not want to.' Splinter licked his bloody finger. 'Ah!' he sighed. 'Vintage Splinter.'

'I don't care.' Chess stuck out her legs and frowned at her feet.

'We can't just go back to the factory, Chess,' reasoned Box. 'We've talked about it. And if we went back, how would we know where to go?'

'I've dreamt where to go,' said Chess.

Balthazar sighed more loudly and with great mystery in his voice, intoned, 'Dreams.'

'Oh no,' whispered Splinter. 'You've set him off.'

'I have considered this for days, for weeks. But is it safe? Can it be trusted?' Balthazar stared out of the window, at the final rips of day.

Box looked at Splinter and shrugged.

'There are such dangers.' Balthazar pulled at his thick moustache as he continued to wrestle with himself. 'It is not what I would have wanted.'

'Tomorrow,' repeated Chess, with bleak determination, 'I am going.'

'Come with me,' commanded Balthazar.

It was almost night. Balthazar strode through his house and down the tree. The Tuesdays followed, Splinter limping at the rear. They descended the ladder at the bottom. Balthazar used a flint to light a wooden torch that he had taken from the workshop and he hurried over to the stone outcrop where they liked to sit in the mornings.

'Hold this,' ordered Balthazar, thrusting the torch into Box's hand. Box held the torch high so that their shadows flickered over the rocks. 'Lower,' commanded Balthazar. 'Hold it lower. I need the light, the Dog Troopers don't.'

Balthazar found what he was looking for. He stood up,

grasped the top of a small boulder with his hands and with a grunt he pulled backwards. The tendons in his wrists stood out like whipcord as he heaved. The rock rolled back to reveal a crack in the ground, wide enough for a body to slip through.

'We go down there,' said Balthazar. 'Give me the torch.'

'It's very dark.' It wasn't just the darkness though. As the air crept out of the gap in the rocks, Chess had the sense that something was waiting for her.

One after the other they followed him into the crack and underneath the rocks. Chess found herself in a tunnel, a natural passage through the inside of the cliff.

They did not walk far. The tunnel came out at the back of a tall, deep cave. It had the stale, dusty smell of a place long undisturbed. In front of them the mouth of the cave was sealed with wooden boards. The light was not bright and it kept changing as the torch crackled but Chess could see that there were crates, each nearly as tall as she was, stacked upon one another around the sides of the cave. Some were made of wood and some of metal.

The centre of the cave was occupied by an object that was as long as two cars, higher then Balthazar's head and completely covered by a sheet of canvas. Above it was the sloping roof of the cave from which there dangled roots like withered snakes.

'We are underneath the tree,' said Balthazar. 'This is where I keep those things I do not need. Or do not use. The front of the cave was sealed when I and my possessions were first delivered to Surapoor. I haven't been down here for over fifty years.'

'What's that?' asked Splinter, indicating the structure at the centre of the cave, hidden by the canvas.

'That, Splinter, is why we are here,' announced Balthazar. He grasped a piece of the canvas and pulled it hard. With a flap and a crack the whole canvas sheet flipped up into the air and swirled to the floor. Then, as the cloud of dust settled, the Tuesdays saw what was revealed.

It looked like a colossal dentist's chair, mounted on a huge stand. Curving over the top of the chair from its head was a canopy that supported an array of levers, lenses and scopes that were mounted in blocks, one behind the other. At the head end of the canopy was a pair of eyepieces. The canopy extended from these to the foot of the chair, becoming narrower all the way. At the foot end there were concentric sections of scope, like an elephant's trunk, sticking out horizontally. The machine dwarfed them all.

'I knew too much, I saw too much, I did too much,' recited Balthazar. 'This, my friends, is why I saw too much.'

'What is it?' asked Splinter breathlessly, walking around the massive device and admiring it in the light of the torch.

'This is a skulk rack,' said Balthazar. 'For those who dream true it can show them what they look for.'

'Dream true?' asked Splinter.

'Those who dream outside their thoughts,' Balthazar replied. 'Those who walk the world and not just their imaginations when they sleep.' He spoke firmly. 'I have considered the matter very hard. Maybe I should keep this from you, it did me no good. With its help I was misled. It is a useful tool but it can be treacherous.'

'Warp technology?' probed Splinter.

'Yes, Splinter. Warp technology like the Omnicon and as such it is as dangerous as it is helpful. But I think we have no choice. You cannot walk blind into the factory. The skulk rack can let you look inside before you go.'

There were rungs up the body of the machine that led to the long, reclining seat. Splinter planted his weaker foot on one.

'No, Splinter, not you,' objected Balthazar. 'Chess is to use the skulk rack, if she wishes. She has the power, she dreams true, her mind moves in ways that yours does not.'

A shade of the old malice passed over Splinter's face and then, smiling too sweetly, he stepped back from the rungs and with a sweep of his arm said, 'Chess,' inviting her to climb.

Balthazar had taken a crowbar from where it had been propped against a crate and he passed another to Box, handing the torch to Splinter. Then Balthazar and Box worked on the wooden panels that sealed the mouth of the cave, prizing them loose. There was much heaving and grunting and the wrench of timber splitting and nails squeaking free.

Chess stood at the foot of the skulk rack. She felt its pull.

It wants me to use it.

She was frightened by Balthazar's warning but they needed to find out more about the factory and he had said the skulk rack would let her do that. So whatever the dangers, she had to use it.

'Torch out,' shouted Balthazar as the planks of the wooden screen broke open. Splinter stabbed the flames into the floor. After the sparks had stopped spitting, the cave swam inky-black. Then a wide, pale, oval of sky speckled with stars filled the mouth of the cave. Against this was silhouetted the mammoth bulk of the skulk rack.

There was the rattle and clatter of Balthazar searching through a crate. Silence, and then a dull, lime-yellow light appeared and then another. They produced enough illumination to perceive nearby shapes but no more.

'Lowlux lights,' said Balthazar. 'Nuclear powered, low-level radiation. Enough to see by but not bright enough to see clearly. And not bright enough to be seen from any distance away. That is important my friends. This cave looks out over the valley and then to the ocean. Even up here, bright light would be visible to the volcanoes left and right of us.'

Now that her eyes were adjusting to the darkness, Chess could see the dark line below the stars where the ocean reached the sky. Air sharp with salt, freshened the musty odours of the cave.

'What do I do?' asked Chess, meekly.

'Climb up,' instructed Balthazar. Chess followed his instructions, her lime-bathed shape scaling up to the seat that reclined beneath the huge canopy. She sat back on the leather which was cold. It creaked loudly and then sighed as it took her meagre weight. It's greeting me, thought Chess.

'To work it you pull down the part of the canopy nearest to you,' continued Balthazar. 'When the eye pieces are level with your eyes they will extend. Don't be alarmed. They will stop when they touch the skin of your face.'

Chess did exactly as she was told, shuddering as the cold metal pressed itself against the arches of her eye sockets.

'Now,' said Balthazar, 'you must sleep.'

'How's she meant to do that?' interrupted Box.

'There is a lever immediately under the eyepieces,' explained Balthazar.

'Yes,' said Chess, fingers alighting on a metal stick.

'When you push that you will see shapes moving in the eyepieces. Keep looking at them. You will pass into sleep. But you will also be able to see through the skulk rack and go wherever you want as quickly as you want. You can go up or down, see round corners, go through windows. And as soon as you want to come back, that thought alone will bring you back here, awake. Of course, Chess, your body will have been here throughout, it is only your mind that is moving.'

'Well, that sounds simple enough,' said Box, encouragingly.

'It is simple,' agreed Balthazar, 'but there is always the risk that your mind may be deceived, just as your eyes can be. That is the danger.'

'I just want to go to the factory and look,' said Chess. 'To know where things are.' Then she asked, 'Will anyone be able to see me?'

'No,' replied Balthazar, 'although there are some who may sense your presence. We will remain here whilst you use the machine. It is important that a watch is kept over you.'

Chess preferred not to ask why a watch should be kept over her. She felt giddy. The optics pressed against her face and she wanted to sit up. Her heart beat hard, she could feel it pulse in her ears. Sandwiched between the canopy and the body of the skulk rack, it was easy to feel that things could go wrong.

There was no more to be said. Chess pushed the lever. Her hand fell to her side and her body sank back into the seat. Very relaxed. Asleep. She breathed slowly and deeply.

Box studied Chess as carefully as he could in the gloom. He did not like to see her prone beneath the heavy metal but his attention was distracted by a rapid sliding and clicking noise from the body of the canopy in front of the eyepieces. He saw different lenses and tubes slipping into it like slides on a projector but from all angles. As some clicked into place others clicked out. They were supported by thin, rigid wires. There was more movement, further lenses sliding into and out of place down the length of the canopy.

'Chess!' shouted Box, starting as the whole contraption jolted forty-five degrees to the left on its mount. The movement had been sudden and violent but Chess continued sleeping.

'Easy, Box,' reassured Balthazar. 'She has turned to look at the volcano. Her mind drives the machine and the machine lets her see.'

The rapid clicking continued up and down the canopy and now the segmented scope at its end was twisting. It wriggled left and right and up and down as swiftly and erratically as an eyeball might.

'She is inside the volcano and looking,' said Balthazar, gently. 'Now we watch and wait for her to return.'

What Chess saw when she pushed the lever were shapes spinning quickly. It felt as if she was diving through the shapes and then she came out on the other side and was looking over the forest that filled the valley and out to the ocean. She looked left, towards the volcano where the factory was and the whole scene lurched past her. She laughed to herself. I must look more gently, she thought.

Here were the lower slopes of the volcano. Although Chess knew it was night the ground she looked at was lit as if flooded with bright white light. It wasn't like daylight, it was more like a searchlight. The areas that she didn't look at directly were grey and indistinct. She searched for the fissure from which she and Splinter and Box had come out of the volcano. Her eyes scanned much more quickly through the skulk rack than they could do when she was awake. In moments she had seen the whole of the lower slope and she focused on the tall crack with ease.

Chess swam up to the crack. That was how it felt; like swimming up to things very, very fast. When she looked close up the view was distorted, as if it was reflected on the back of a spoon. The shapes nearest to her were magnified whilst other shapes contracted until they were grey and blurred.

She entered the crack and sped down the tunnel and along the service shaft, noticing that there were no trap doors open now. When she came to the bend where she had climbed into the shaft the panel was still open. That way she saw into the room with the boilers and pipes. With the aid of the skulk rack she could see what a vast chamber it was, too big to see in one go and crammed with pipework.

She wanted to find the children. Because her mind moved so fast she was able to check different routes very quickly. In moments, she identified the route from the boiler room, through the corridors, to the row of doors that led to the cages on the platform where they had first arrived. But no children. She searched faster.

The first time that she came upon a squad of Dog Troopers she began to panic. There were eight of them walking out of step and talking, although she couldn't hear their voices through the skulk rack. One walked ahead of the others and his face spread into view in front of her. It was more human than dog, mostly skin with tufts of hair. However, the eyes were like a dog's and his lower jaw jutted forwards bearing long canine teeth that were exposed like tusks.

The troopers moved through where she was standing, the face of each one looming up to her as she looked at them. She felt nothing of them and they saw nothing of her.

She discovered that she was getting better at controlling the machine. Her progress was smoother and her focus more accurate. She had gone down to the lower levels. Here, the walls were rough stone and they were narrow. She was moving very fast.

Suddenly, voices burst inside her head; children's voices like the ones she had heard before. The voices didn't come from anywhere that she could see but a corridor with steel walls veered before her mind's eye. Then she was back in the stone corridor, moving quickly, knowing that she had to find this corridor with steel walls.

Voices. Shouting. Another image of the steel corridor. It was very long and lined with doors that were all closed. In the top of each door there was a small round window.

The children's voices were constant now, an audible background wherever she went. She didn't recognize them but they were calling to her. Frightened. Desperate. Wanting her to help them. She wanted to help them but where were they? Where were the voices coming from?

Chess slowed down, realizing that it was becoming difficult to distinguish where she was from the images of the steel corridor that kept flashing into her mind. She stopped moving, tried not to look at anything in particular and breathed slowly. The babble and cries of the children faded. She was in a stone corridor, deep in the volcano and at the end of it there was a low door that was closed. She dived to the keyhole and she was through, into the room on the other side. She steadied herself as she focused on the scene before her.

Immediately, she recognized General Vane. He had his back to her but the fur cloak draped over the tall, lean figure was unmistakable. His head was bent forwards, his attention riveted on something that was on the table in front of him. Chess moved round the cavernous room to take a better look. The General's body was distorted by the skulk rack so that his middle bowed towards her and looked very wide whilst his head looked very small.

The General was talking, jaws moving, but Chess could hear nothing save for the distant cries of children. What gripped her attention was the thing that was on the table. It looked like a large, flat face from which there sprouted four long black legs that reminded her of spiders' legs. When the General stopped talking the face part of the thing appeared to quiver in reply.

Chess shuddered at the sight of the creature on the table. Unsure of what she was looking at, she backed away from the General and the thing with the spindle legs and she left the chamber through the keyhole by which she had entered.

Outside the room, the discordant voices rushed upon her. She had to find where they were coming from. The relentless cries made her feel trapped and desperate but also angry because she could sense that something very wrong was happening. Up stairs and along corridors, she went the way that the sounds were loudest. Faster and faster, images broke on her mind; children's faces mixed with glimpses of the steel corridor.

Why is this happening to me? wondered Chess. Why are they calling to me? What is happening to them?

What she was seeing and what she was hearing gripped her mind like it had been gripped when Box had been caught by the vines in the forest, like it had been gripped when the Inspector had hold of Gemma.

And then she really was in the steel corridor. The skulk rack made it dip in front of her so that one moment she was looking up it and the next she was looking down it. It seemed to go on forever, lined with doors all of which were shut; doors that each had a small, round window.

Chess had seen these windows before, in her dreams and in the visions that had burst into her mind. Now she was looking at an endless line of them. Each window was glowing a lurid green, each glow flickering with movement. And Chess knew that on the other side of each window there was a child.

The scream rooms, Chess realized. I have come to the scream rooms.

She did not want to see any more. She did not want to hear. But the children were calling to her and she was moving towards the nearest door, with its little glass window. She did not want to look through the window. She did not want to see what was happening in the garish green light. She did not want to see what was making the shadows that flickered ghoulishly on the glass.

'I want to wake up.'

CHAPTER 12

Box wanted Balthazar to wake Chess because he could see how distressed she was. Her body was twitching and she was breathing fitfully. Then the skulk rack returned to its central position slowly and smoothly. The eyepieces retracted from Chess's face and she opened her eyes.

'Are you all right?' Box asked.

'The children.' Chess spoke loudly and quickly as she sat up. 'We have to help the children. It's horrible in there. Really horrible.' She was upset. Box could see her body tremble and her voice was shaking.

'What is horrible?' Splinter was hungry for details. 'What happened? Tell me what you saw.'

'There was screaming and all these rooms and inside the rooms there was a green light.' Chess's big brown eyes were glistening.

'But what happened inside the rooms?' persisted Splinter, excited.

'I don't know.' The words tumbled from Chess passionately. 'But we have to go back. We have to help them. I need to see more. I need to see more to help them.'

'Not now, Chess.' Balthazar spoke calmly as he helped Chess down. 'Now you need to rest.'

Relieved of her slender body, the long leather seat drew in air so that it sounded as if the skulk rack was sighing; satisfied.

As soon as her feet were on the ground, Splinter was pressing her for more information. 'Did you see him?' he asked, fervently.

'See who?' replied Chess.

'The Inquisitor,' insisted Splinter. 'Did you see the Inquisitor?'

Chess shook her head. 'No.'

Splinter gave a sniff of contempt and walked away, no longer interested in Chess or what she had to say.

Box helped Balthazar to fix the canvas sheet across the mouth of the cave so that the entrance was closed. Then Balthazar placed the lowlux lights back in the crate from which he had taken them. Touching one another so that they would know where to go and with Balthazar in the lead they crossed the cave and took the short tunnel that led back up to the rocks.

They returned to Balthazar's house in silence. Chess wanted to empty her head of the pictures she kept seeing and the sound of the children's voices. But every time she closed her eyes she thought of the steel corridor with all its doors and the little windows full of green light.

Box stayed close to his sister as Balthazar prepared her a drink into which he crumbled herbs and added several drops of liquid from a small glass bottle that he had fetched from the observatory. When Chess drank this she felt her muscles go soft and heavy. Suddenly she was very tired. She wanted to sleep and when she settled onto her bed of animal skins she slept solidly and without dreaming, until morning.

As usual, when she awoke, she was alone. She lay absolutely still, wishing that the skulk rack and everything she had seen with it had been a dream. But she knew the skulk rack was under the ground, waiting for her and she knew that now they had to do more than just find out what was happening to the children. They had to help them.

'Have you seen Splinter?' Box asked when she emerged from the bottom of the house. She shook her head. Box was eating strips of cold, baked fish and licking his oily fingers. Balthazar had caught the fish from the river yesterday morning.

'Funny,' said Box, taking time to speak between mouthfuls. 'I saw him when he got up. He said he was going to the library and I haven't seen him since.'

'Well, he can't have gone very far,' ventured Chess. She poked at a piece of earth with a twig. She didn't feel hungry and even if she had done, cold, baked fish was not what she would have chosen to eat. She looked across the ridge, squinting in the morning light.

'Where's Balthazar?' she asked.

Box stopped guzzling fish to say, 'Don't know. Off wandering, I suppose.'

Balthazar had been fishing. He returned with three large fish speared on the barbs of a harpoon. Although he had been paddling in a dug-out canoe on the river he hadn't seen Splinter.

They looked in the library, in the observatory, on the

balconies, even in the vine room. Box checked the cave under the boulders. Splinter was nowhere to be found. It puzzled Chess because Splinter spent all his spare time in the library and his bad leg meant that walking for very long was difficult so he never roamed far from the tree.

They missed their daily Chat lesson and skipped Box's training session without mentioning it. Balthazar seemed very preoccupied by Splinter's disappearance but Chess didn't think that anything bad could have happened to him unless he had fallen off the ridge and into the gorge below. At first she dismissed this, but as the day wore on she became increasingly worried that that was what must have happened. There was nothing else she could think of to account for his vanishing.

It was late in the afternoon when Splinter reappeared. Chess, Box and Balthazar were sitting on the rocks and saying nothing when there was a tinkle of the wind chimes and Splinter was there, climbing down the ladder. His face was flushed but otherwise he looked no different from usual.

'Where have you been?' exclaimed Box. 'We've looked all over for you.'

'I thought you must have fallen into the gorge,' added Chess.

Balthazar regarded Splinter in a calculating way with his bulging eyes and he stroked one end of his thick, black moustache. 'What have you been doing, Splinter?' he asked.

'After breakfast, I was thinking about last night,' explained Splinter, 'and I went for a walk, you know, thinking things over.'

'Where?' interrupted Balthazar.

'Out here, on the ridge, round to the river. Anyway, I got lost.'

'Got lost?' interjected Chess. 'Up here? How?'

'I don't know, I just did,' insisted Splinter.

'I was out on the river, fishing. I didn't see you,' commented Balthazar.

'Of course you didn't,' Splinter was quick to reply. 'I wouldn't have been lost if you had've done.' He continued, 'Anyway, by the time I got back here I couldn't find where all of you had gone.' Splinter laughed. 'I was so tired, what with walking around without my crutch, and my leg was hurting. So I lay down in the room and fell asleep. I've only just woken up.'

Balthazar didn't look convinced but he said no more. Chess thought Splinter's explanation very strange but accepted it because she could think of no other reason for his disappearance. Box suggested that after all that exertion, Splinter would be hungry and they should have an early supper so they all went back into the house to eat. Balthazar climbed up the ladder first and then Chess. When they were alone and still outside, Splinter grabbed hold of Box's elbow.

'*I can do special things now*,' he hissed in his brother's ear.

Box shook him off and turned round. 'What are you talking about?'

'You'll see,' whispered Splinter, mysteriously, and he said no more.

'I have to go back,' said Chess when they were all in Balthazar's kitchen. They had eaten and were waiting for night to come. It had been a disjointed day and there was an awkwardness between Splinter and everybody else.

'I am worried, Chess,' said Balthazar. His deep voice was full of doubt. 'There is an atmosphere. The skulk rack has enjoyed you. It wants you to use it. That is not good. It is not safe.'

'But we have to help the children,' Chess insisted.

'I may have interfered too much already,' mused Balthazar.

'I have to see if there is a way to help them and I don't care if it isn't safe for me,' declared Chess.

'Chess,' said Balthazar. 'You are very brave, but bravery is not always wise.'

'You told Box that when there is nothing else, hope and bravery are left. Well, there is nothing else. We have to help the children.' Chess stared at Balthazar without blinking. 'I need to use the skulk rack again.'

'I'll go with her,' volunteered Splinter, apparently anxious to be helpful. 'I mean, I'll go down to the cave with her. Just to check she's OK.'

Chess thought that it was strange to see a man as big and clever as Balthazar struggling to make up his mind. He frowned, pursed his lips and ran his hand down the back of his long black plait repeatedly.

'Very well,' he said after sufficient thought. 'It is your decision. Splinter will watch over you until I come down. I won't be long.'

Box stayed with Balthazar whilst Chess and Splinter left the house. It was evening. The crack at the foot of the rocks was still open from the previous night, a black vent in the dusk. Down they went, feeling their way until they came to the cave. Splinter advanced cautiously with hands outstretched until his fingers touched the rough weave of canvas. Then he tugged the material and it collapsed from where it had been fastened around a wooden spar.

The dark hulk filled the centre of the cave, waiting for Chess.

'I'll find the lights,' said Splinter. He searched the crate where Balthazar had replaced them. His clever fingers felt cloth sacks and candles and the knurled grips of tools and electric torches before alighting upon a slim wooden box that was the right size and shape. He clicked open the catch and lifted the lid and immediately saw the pale glow. Each light was the size of a biscuit but smooth like glass. He lifted them from the box and put them on the floor as he had seen Balthazar do.

'OK, Chess,' he said. 'You go up, I'll keep an eye on you.'

Splinter was being uncharacteristically friendly but Chess was grateful that he was willing to help her. She mounted the skulk rack with no further thought of why he was so keen to assist. The machine sighed deeply as she settled onto it.

Once the eyepieces were in place, Chess found the lever and pushed. Lines and figures gyrated before her eyes and then she rushed through them and she was looking out at the ocean, bright through the agency of the skulk rack.

Splinter waited for the machine to swivel towards the volcano. It turned with greater control than the night before because Chess was more adept at using it. The motion was smooth and it came to a gentle halt. Chess was breathing in a slow and steady rhythm. She was asleep and looking inside the volcano. Now he was free to snoop through the contents of the cave.

Chess was in the factory. If she could discover a way to stop what took place in the scream rooms or a way to release the children who were imprisoned, then maybe she and her brothers could sneak back in and help. There had to be an operations room, a nerve centre that controlled what happened. She was building up a clear picture of the layout of the factory and she would be able to find the way once she was back inside for real. Now it was a matter of finding where to head for.

She worked her way upwards. She already knew that the lower levels of the factory were where the troopers had their barracks and power was generated. The scream rooms were higher up but she didn't want to go to the steel corridor again so she aimed for the levels above it.

As soon as she had ascended from the lower levels, she heard the voices. The shrill cries tore at her but she tried to ignore them. It wasn't easy. She focused on the route she was taking.

She didn't investigate the many storerooms and laboratories or the vast chambers where long steel tubes ran in concentric rings through hoops of circulating metal, but she did stop to see what was happening in a cavernous docking bay where teams of troopers were unloading cargo from the rear ports of what appeared to be a huge, flat-hulled ship. Chess could see only the rear of the ship and that was at least one hundred metres wide and as tall as an office block. The troopers were miniscule beneath the vented, duct-riddled, pipe encrusted ramparts, wheeling the cargo down ramps and stacking it carefully on fork-lift trucks.

What struck Chess was not the size of the ship but the

way in which she could only see the rear; she couldn't see the front or sides at all; in fact there didn't seem to be enough space in the docking bay for anything other than the rear.

Chess remembered Ethel telling them how cargo was transported through the vortex over huge distances, even between universes. So, maybe the rest of the ship was elsewhere, in another dimension. It was a bizarre thought, but one that came to her naturally now. Chess had been taught that things were not always as they seemed. There was more space in the universes than people could see. But she was not here to admire the scale of the Twisted Symmetry's operations and she began to hunt for a way that would take her upwards.

She reached a steep staircase that was many levels higher than where she had started. Although there had been troopers all around the factory there were none in this area. At the top of the staircase there was a door with writing on it. Chess always felt tense when she was faced with writing but this looked easy to read.

There were two words. The second word was ROOM; that was no problem. Chess worked through the letters of the first word. CONTROL. CONTROL ROOM. The door was ajar. Using the skulk rack, Chess could look through the gap to see what was on the other side.

This was what she wanted. It was a big room and the ceiling was domed and made of glass but because it was night all she could see in the glass were reflections of the room below. All around the room were display monitors like television screens. There were hundreds of them, arranged in banks, and each had a small metal plate fixed to its casing with a number marked on the plate. Chess approached and saw that every screen displayed children. The children were packed in small cells, squalid and miserable, occasionally shuffling but otherwise motionless; broken.

Her chest wrenched when she saw the street rats, too many to count, crammed into a dozen cells. They were more ragged and starved than any she had ever seen. It was impossible to pick out faces because they were so cramped.

Chess pulled herself away from the screens and focused on the centre of the room where there was a desk the size of a table tennis table. It was studded with knobs and dials and switches. Although it looked mind-bogglingly complicated at first, Chess quickly identified that there was a switch for every one of the cells shown on the display monitors because each was numbered. The numbers went up to five hundred. Every switch was up, in a position marked CLOSE. The bottom position was marked OPEN.

It was obvious to Chess that once her body was inside the factory, she could release the children from their cells by turning the switches to OPEN. Chess wasn't sure what would happen after that but she was sure it would be better for the children to be out of the cells than in them; as long as you could run, you had a chance.

She was ready to leave the control room when her eyes were wrenched. Everything shot before her in a blur, like on a merry-go-round, and she was looking at the night sky. She tried to turn back to the factory but when she did so her vision was ripped back to the sky. She struggled against whatever was pulling her to where she didn't want to go.

'I want to wake up,' said Chess. But she couldn't.

Splinter had been up to his elbows in a crate full of weapons when he heard the skulk rack shudder and jolt. He looked back over his shoulder, and was surprised to see that it was pointing towards the ocean. Then it jerked towards the factory but no sooner had it done that than it recoiled, looking out at the ocean again. The whole machine shook on its stand as if it was struggling to move one way and then the other.

Chess was moaning, obviously in distress. With a swift glance to the tunnel to check he was alone, Splinter stole across to the skulk rack. He knew that he was meant to wake his sister or to fetch Balthazar but he wasn't going to do that. It would be more interesting to see what was happening to Chess.

The machine was still gripped by tremors but it did not change position. It pointed out to the ocean. Splinter climbed the rungs so that he could study Chess. Her face was twitching and her head moved from side to side but not enough to break contact with the eyepieces. Her lips moved but no words came out. Sometimes her whole body shook and she cried out, weakly.

Splinter was fascinated. His face was close to Chess's and it bore the peevish expression he wore when he used to torture ants. He was so absorbed in studying Chess's torment that he failed to notice Balthazar enter the cave.

'What are you doing?' roared Balthazar's gravel voice. He stood at the entrance, staff in hand, glowering at Splinter.

'She needs to wake up,' faltered Splinter. 'I didn't know what to do.' He sounded like a whining schoolboy.

Balthazar strode to the foot of the skulk rack and yanked

Splinter away from Chess. Splinter landed awkwardly on his bad foot and howled but Balthazar paid him no more attention. He placed his hand against Chess's cheek which was twitching and he cried aloud, 'Why do I never learn?'

Box, who had followed Balthazar into the cave, glared at Splinter. 'Why?' he mouthed.

Splinter said nothing. He cast his eyes at the stone floor and frowned.

'We wait,' growled Balthazar, stepping away from the machine. Chess's prone body was still. 'It might be dangerous to wake her and her body is relaxing now. We have to wait.'

When Chess opened her eyes she was lying on a rug on the floor of the cave. She smiled up at the faces of Box and Balthazar who were kneeling beside her.

'Such a lovely dream,' she said. 'I heard singing, beautiful singing. I love that voice; Mum's voice.' She began to hum.

Splinter knew better than to tell her to stop.

Balthazar cupped his hand on Chess's temple and brushed a lock of hair away. 'Good. That is good, Chess.' He hesitated before asking, 'But was there anything else before the singing?'

Chess frowned. All she wanted to remember was the singing. But there was something else, before the singing. It was coming back to her now. She had been looking at the desk in the control room and then her eyes had been wrested away and she was looking out at the ocean and she couldn't look away. She remembered now; it was night and the waters were oil dark and in front of her there was . . .

'A man,' Chess said slowly. 'I remember a man. A very old man. Very thin, with long hands and fingers. A narrow man.'

'His eyes?' beseeched Balthazar. 'Did you see his eyes?'

Chess racked her memory. The image was faint. 'I didn't see his eyes.' Then she added as an afterthought, 'I don't think he had any eyes. The eyelids were all wrinkled and shut, like melted wax.'

Balthazar closed his eyes and shook his head.

'The Narrow Man went when my mother sang to me. He just vanished and everything turned white.'

'Her song made the man go,' said Balthazar. 'Your mother must love you very much.'

'My mother's dead,' stated Chess.

'Then she must have loved you very much. Love doesn't stop with time or space. It goes on forever. Great evil can only be defeated by great love; by sacrifice.'

Splinter had been keeping to himself but now he could not stop himself from asking, 'Was that the Inquisitor? The Narrow Man?'

'No, not an Inquisitor,' replied Balthazar. 'I have told you that there are powers in the universes more ancient and mighty than the Inquisitors. The Narrow Man, as you call him, is a great power, greater even than the Inquisitors.' Then he held Chess's hand in his giant hands and asked softly, 'Who are you, Chess? What do they want?'

'Do they know where I am, now?' asked Chess with a start.

Balthazar reassured her. 'I don't think so. If the singing had not driven away the Narrow Man perhaps they would have located you but unless they have a spook on you, you should be safe.'

Chess's spirits sank. They have my blood, I know they have, she thought. But she couldn't work out why she was so sure of this. She didn't want to work it out. Instinctively, she didn't want the answer.

Balthazar stood up suddenly, quarterstaff in both his hands. 'I should never have brought you down here,' he declared. 'But there is one source of harm that will never act so treacherously again.' He spun round, whirling the staff above his head.

Splinter was behind him and he scarpered away, thinking the iron-shod stave was about to descend on him. But he was not Balthazar's target. The staff came down with all his might and with an explosive crash that scattered glass in all directions, it smashed through the optics of the skulk rack.

Two mornings later, they were sitting on the rocks outside the house having a Chat lesson with Balthazar. Splinter had not been to the library since the day he had gone missing and he had tried to be as pleasant as possible after Balthazar's fury at him in the cave. When the Chat lesson was coming to an end he asked Balthazar to tell them about the Inquisitors.

'Why?' was Balthazar's suspicious response.

'We have to know our enemy,' was how Splinter justified his interest. 'My ankle's almost better. Chess has seen what we need to do and by next week we'll have gone back to the factory to help the children. There's an Inquisitor there. Surely we should know something about him?'

'I don't know which one it is.' Balthazar was evasive.

'Then tell us about them all,' suggested Splinter. 'To be on the safe side.'

'There are five Inquisitors,' began Balthazar, unable to

stop himself. Chess decided that when it came to the Twisted Symmetry, Balthazar Broom struggled. There must have been a time when their hooks were deep into him. 'Their names are Azgor, Malbane, Veer, Snargis and Behrens. Their sole purpose is to exist forever. They do not care for happiness or even pleasure. Infinite existence is their aim.'

'What, just hanging around, doing nothing forever?' Box screwed up his face. 'Sounds like hell.'

Balthazar nodded. 'The relentless pursuit of a single idea by a few people can turn the world into a hell for everybody else.' He plucked a blade of wheat-coloured grass. 'There are ways to prolong mortal life but the only way to live forever is to stop time and survive the pan-dimensional crunch that follows, as space and time collapse into infinite nothingness. This is what the Inquisitors seek, whatever the cost.'

Splinter was drawing a large 'S' in the earth. 'If the Inquisitors are so powerful, why don't they just do it?'

'The Inquisitors are powerful enough to have mastered the science of the dimensions; they can prolong life, travel time, unravel space. But to achieve their ultimate purpose they need sufficient energy and a way of using it.'

'Are they human?' asked Chess.

'No,' said Balthazar, 'but they can take human form. That is how they prefer to move amongst us.'

'So they could be anywhere?' Chess tried not to look at ripples in the water, shadows in the thorn bushes, tracks in the dust.

Balthazar fixed her with big, cheerless eyes. 'Anywhere.'

'How does someone get to be an Inquisitor?' asked Splinter

as innocently as if he were asking for an ice cream. Chess noticed that by joining the ends of the 'S' he had drawn in the dirt he had transformed it into an awlis.

'I was once like you, Splinter,' replied Balthazar. 'I thought myself very clever and very wise and I thought that knowledge was power and power was good. But I was tricked and used. After five hundred years of exile I am still as foolish.'

'I'm going for a walk,' announced Chess, who had had enough of Inquisitors.

'I'll come,' said Box.

'Me too,' said Splinter, with less enthusiasm.

They followed a path that they had beaten over the weeks through the palms and succulent shrubs that led to the river. It came out at a cluster of rocks that formed a pool where they could wash and paddle. The water was shallow and refreshingly cold and the air smelt of soil and grass. On the other side of the rocks the river flowed wide and slow and flat as a sheet towards the falls.

They stripped off, leaving their ragged clothes on the rocks and slipped into the cold water. The chill numbed Chess from her belly to her head but after she had shivered for a minute she began to feel warm and she floated on her back, gazing up at the pale blue sky. She had never washed as often as she had since they had been with Balthazar and now she loved the feeling of the water, the way it enclosed and supported her; its safety.

Box and Splinter climbed onto the rocks to dry in the sun and Chess did the same. Her attention was caught by a butterfly the size of a pancake. It had rich purple wings bearing smudged, amber eyes. It fluttered along the river bank, upstream. Pulling on her jeans and T-shirt, which was infuriatingly difficult because she was still wet, Chess followed the butterfly.

Her brothers were not far away. She could hear their voices. But she was soon swallowed by the vegetation so that she could not see them. She lost sight of the beautiful butterfly just as quickly and was about to retrace her steps when her neck began to prickle and her body shivered. This was the feeling she had had in the boiler room. She was not alone. Something was watching her.

She froze where she stood.

There was nothing to see and nothing to hear but everything that Balthazar had told them about spooks rushed back to her.

It's listening for my heart, Chess told herself. Make no noise. If it can't hear me, it can't find me.

But the more she tried to breathe quietly, the louder her breathing seemed to become. Her pulse was thumping. She could hear it. She could feel her heart, spasming so hard inside her chest that it ached.

Be quiet, please be quiet, Chess thought to herself.

Noises in the long grass to her left. A faint rustling. It could be a small animal. But small animals normally moved away from her. This was coming closer.

Breath rasping like sandpaper on wood, heart hammering, Chess slowly turned her head to look left. There was a gap where the shoulder-high blades of grass were bent apart from one another and formed a 'V'. It was a couple of arm lengths away. Chess was not sure whether it was a natural 'V' in the grass or whether something was holding the long blades open to find her more easily.

Her mouth was bone dry but she needed to swallow. She didn't dare to blink. Her breath sounded like a sack dragged on gravel. Her heart thudded louder and louder.

Suddenly the grass rippled towards her and something that she couldn't see rushed past. Chess shrieked and bounded out of the thicket like a panicked gazelle. Her brothers were with her in seconds.

'A snake,' gasped Chess as they escorted her to the rocks. 'It frightened me.' She looked back. There was no sign of the thing that had been watching her.

'You frightened me,' laughed Box.

She didn't tell them what she thought it really was. She hoped she was wrong, that maybe it was a snake. She hoped she was wrong because if she had been found by a spook, it meant that the Twisted Symmetry would know exactly where she was. And it meant she should accept what she hadn't wanted to remember; the one place her blood could have come from.

Saul.

Saul had bandaged her hand when Jerome had pulled her out of the cage on the train. But before bandaging it, he had wiped the blood from the cut on her palm. What had happened to the makeshift bandage Saul had used to wipe the cut?

Splinter had said that Saul was not to be trusted.

But Chess no longer trusted Splinter entirely and she wanted to trust Saul. It was confusing. Maybe Saul was working with the Twisted Symmetry more closely than he had admitted. But Chess didn't want to believe that.

So she mentioned the possibility that she had been tracked by a spook to no one.

That night, Chess went to bed early, leaving Balthazar, Splinter and Box talking in the observatory. But although the night was still and mild, she couldn't sleep. Worry about what might have been watching her at the river gnawed at her. She wondered whether it was wrong of her not to warn the others. But she didn't want Splinter to be right about Saul. If it was Saul.

Trust no one.

She was distracted from her thoughts by the tinkle of the wind chimes. Then silence. Then another gentle glissando.

But there was no wind.

Another tingle from the wind chimes and Chess knew that something was entering Balthazar's house. Entering stealthily. Entering as if it planned to surprise whoever was inside.

Now there were footfalls approaching the bedroom, cautiously. The wood creaked minutely. Chess wriggled out from the skins, squatting, wondering where to go. She thought as swiftly as a trapped rat. She could dash for the door that led up to the observatory but already there was a shadow at the other door. Whatever was about to enter the room would see her and catch her if she ran. She could hide under the animal skins and hope not to be seen.

But there was no more time.

Chess heard an exchange of gruff whispers and then she saw the sharp-toothed muzzle of a Dog Trooper edging round the doorway.

CHAPTER 13

Chess rolled off her bed and into the vine room. She landed on rough coils of creeper and heard footsteps in the bedroom and the sound of muffled growling as the troopers talked quietly. She slithered on her belly. It was very dark. Tentatively, she felt ahead until her hands were touching nothing. This was the hole in the floor where Box had fallen. Chess knew that on the other side there was a nine-hundred-and-eighty-four foot drop to the forest bottom. But much closer a Dog Trooper was hunting for her. She swung her legs over the lip of the hole and then lowered her body so that she was hanging by her hands in the darkness.

The drop was too far for Chess to be able to see the trees below. All she could see was the black square of the gap above her head and the body of the tree where it wasn't enclosed by Balthazar's house.

In less than a minute her shoulders, forearms and fingers were burning with the effort of clinging to the edge of the hole. But years of too little food and too much hiding meant that Chess wasn't heavy yet her grip was strong. She switched off the pain by counting silently and she tried not to think of what would happen if her fingers failed.

The tread of boots on the wooden floor overhead. Chess shut her eyes tight as if that might stop her from being seen. She heard the trooper trip on a length of rope and curse under his breath. She heard him sniff the air. She heard him walk first one way and then the other but he hadn't come far into the room and he didn't flick on his torch. Chess knew that unless he stumbled upon the hole in the floor, he wouldn't see it.

It was only when all the noise of movement above had ceased for a couple of minutes that she guessed it would be safe to pull herself back up to the vine room.

Splinter would be proud of me, she thought. He would say that only a street rat could think of hiding like this. Only a street rat would be able to hang in the darkness like a bat and then have the strength to climb back up.

Then Chess thought angrily, What does it matter what Splinter thinks? And she began to haul herself up.

It hurt. It really hurt. Her shoulders and arms were stiff. It felt as if all her strength had ebbed away. Chess made her arms move even though they were so numb she could hardly feel what they were doing. She knew that she had to keep raising herself because if she paused or dropped down again she would never manage it. She had to do it in one go.

She grunted as the muscles between her shoulder blades felt like they were tearing and her feet swung forwards making it even harder to pull herself up. She swore. Her teeth ground and her face contorted but her head and shoulders were into the room now. With a final groan, Chess pivoted forwards and flung an arm out and across the wooden boards. She used this arm to lever her body onto the floor. Then she rolled away from the hole and lay there, gasping, darkness swirling before her eyes.

It was the sounds from above that made her sit up.

A shout, a cry, a weight thudding to the floor. More shouting. Then silence. Then boots thumping on wood; no attempt to be quiet now. The troopers were coming back down the house, towards the bedroom.

Chess lay on the ropes and pulled the bristly coils over her face so that her skin would not be spotted easily if a trooper looked her way. She counted the shapes; six Dog Troopers passing through the bedroom. In their midst were Splinter and Box whose wrists were bound behind their backs. They were frogmarched roughly. Nobody looked towards the vine room.

The clatter of boots receded and then Chess heard the wind chimes ring as the troopers left the house with their captives. Chess expected that all would be quiet again but to her surprise, moments after the last chimes had faded, there was a burst of activity from outside.

She heard barks and yelps and then the ripping whirr of a machine gun. Then, at last, there was total silence.

It was a long time before Chess felt safe enough to leave the vine room. When she did, she crept through the wooden house, noticing that mixed with the rich scent of resin there was something that smelt like burnt fireworks. When she came to the top of the ladder she waited, holding her breath, listening. Sure that nothing was moving below, she slipped out and gasped at what she saw.

Scattered about the clearing were the six Dog Troopers. Some were lying face down, some lay on their backs. One had his arm stretched above his head, blaze carbine in hand, finger still curled round the trigger. All of them were perfectly still. All of them were dead.

There was no sign of Box or Splinter.

Chess didn't dare shout their names. She didn't stay to investigate how the troopers had died. She scurried back up the ladder and into the house to look for Balthazar. She found him, sprawled on the floor of the top balcony, unconscious but breathing. She shook his shoulder. Her hand looked very small and white, almost dainty, against the broad chunk of dark-skinned muscle. He did not rouse, even when she nudged him harder. He wasn't wounded in any way that she could see so she waited.

When Balthazar did come round he tottered to his knees, unsteady, and was promptly sick over the edge of the balcony.

'Are you all right?' asked Chess, anxiously, and then, 'What happened?'

'Troopers,' he spat, gulping air. 'From nowhere. They knocked me out with a nerve wrench. It felt like my head had been screwed off. It still does. Where are Box and Splinter?' He looked around the balcony, eyes white and bulging.

'I don't know,' answered Chess. 'Troopers had them but now the troopers are dead.'

'Dead? How?'

'I don't know.'

Balthazar rubbed his moustache. 'How did they find my house? The troopers have never been anywhere near here before and it is impossible to see it from the forest below.'

Chess shrugged innocently but she knew that a spook had found her. However, she wasn't going to admit to keeping quiet about it.

'You hid from the troopers?' asked Balthazar.

Chess nodded. 'In the vine room, where the hole in the floor is.'

'Good.' Balthazar seemed very relieved. 'It would have been bad indeed if you had been taken.'

Chess wanted to ask him why it would have been so bad. She thought it was bad enough that Box and Splinter had been captured.

Balthazar headed towards the observatory but before he left the balcony, he stooped to pick up a small, spherical object. He inspected it closely and then tossed it in his palm.

'Curious,' he decided and then, to Chess, 'You know what this is?' He held it out for her to see.

Chess knew exactly what it was but lied automatically. 'No.' It was safest to act ignorant, even with Balthazar. People got suspicious if you seemed to know things.

'It is a tesseract, Chess. A device for navigating the hidden dimensions. Maybe this explains the troopers' unexpected appearance.' He slipped it into the pocket of his leggings and flashed a smile at Chess. 'Most unfortunate for them that they should have dropped it. And, perhaps, most fortunate for me. We must check the troopers, to be sure that they are dead and to see what happened to them.'

He took a short knife from the kitchen on their way

through the house but when they got outside he did not need to use it. Every trooper was dead, just as Chess had told him.

'See this?' said Balthazar, dropping on one knee beside a body. He was pointing to a thin iron rod, a bit shorter than an arrow. It was protruding upright from the back of a trooper's neck. Chess hadn't noticed it when she had first seen the bodies. 'This is a bolt from a stonedrake crossbow, neatly intersecting the trooper's spinal cord. The stonedrakes are deadly accurate.'

Balthazar inspected every trooper to find that each had been felled by a lethally aimed crossbow bolt, save for the trooper who had fired his blaze carbine. He had been hit in the shoulder which had given him time to open fire before a second bolt had entered his throat from the front and silenced him.

'No dead stonedrakes,' was Balthazar's assessment after he had scouted the surrounding area. 'They must have followed the troopers up here, ambushed them and taken Box and Splinter.'

'But what do the stonedrakes want with Box and Splinter?' asked Chess. 'We've got nothing to do with them.'

'They don't know that, Chess,' replied Balthazar. 'The last time they saw you they were firing a marine culverin at you. Who knows what the stonedrakes think?'

'I've got to find my brothers.'

'You won't find them tonight. You must sleep if you can. And I shall think. I have to think.' Balthazar paced beneath the tree. 'Why could I not let the world go about its business, undisturbed by me? Why, Chess, why?' He thrust his large face towards her. 'Why did I not wait so that I could have my time again?'

Chess couldn't answer that so she just looked back, eyes wide, as the big man became more irate.

'What have I done?' he wailed. 'What has my involvement achieved? Your brothers have been taken prisoner, the Symmetry are wise to you, and I have lost everything: five hundred years for nothing.'

Then Balthazar realized how frightened Chess looked. He gritted his teeth, turned away from her and bowed his head. Chess didn't move. She watched the long, black pony tail move slightly as his huge shoulders shook.

'What have I done?' he sobbed.

Not knowing whether she should, Chess approached him and put her small hand against his back.

'You have been trying to help us,' she said.

'Yes,' he said, heaving in a deep breath. 'It is as simple as that. You needed my help.' Then, with a wan smile he added, 'This is a most cunning punishment, Mevrad.'

By morning, the bodies had gone from the clearing. Apart from a strip of earth stained black with blood there was no sign of what had happened the night before.

As soon as Chess blinked her way outside, Balthazar came to her carrying a bowl of sweet potato-bread and fruit. She sniffed it. It made her want to gag but she was very hungry so she spooned it down whilst trying not to taste it.

'I have hidden the bodies in the scrub. And I am sorry that I lost my temper.' He spoke shamefacedly as he watched her eat. 'I was angry with myself, not with you.'

'I know,' said Chess. 'I trust you.'

'The currency of trust is a very fragile one. You are a strange little girl,' pondered Balthazar and he ruffled her long brown hair before fetching his own food.

When he returned, Chess said, 'You have to take me to the stonedrakes.'

'Of course,' said Balthazar, 'but I can do no more than that, Chess.'

'Why not?'

'I have come too close to the darkness again.' Balthazar spoke uncertainly, his bass voice searching for the right words. 'I must be careful.'

'But you could help us,' protested Chess. 'You are strong and clever and you know all about the Twisted Symmetry. We need your help, Balthazar. I don't know what's happened to Box and Splinter and even if they were here, I don't think we could manage the factory. I can't do it all on my own.'

'Let me tell you something, Chess. Many weeks ago you told me that you knew a man with half a face. A man called Julius.'

'You said he was a bad memory for you.'

Balthazar read the accusation in Chess's eyes which had narrowed, darkened. 'I make no excuses for my own folly, Chess,' he explained, 'but you must understand how the darkness works.'

'Tell me then.' Chess was stony. 'Tell me how the darkness works.'

'We need stories to glimpse the deepest truths,' began Balthazar. Chess stared back at him, face blank. Balthazar wetted his lips. 'When gods and angels walked the universes they passed on to their mortal children a spark of brilliance. We record these unblessed children in our histories of heroes, demigods, Nephilim. But the universes are dark and do not favour those who shine too brightly; the extermination of this race of heroes was its blood-fate. Julius was the last of these children.'

'Can he live forever, then?'

'His spirit was immortal,' replied Balthazar.

'Professor Breslaw says that some spirits are stronger than others. That's why they live forever.' It felt good to mention Joachim.

'Your Professor is a wise man. And you have a fine memory.'

'Splinter says my head is empty because I've never been taught.'

'I disagree. Because your head has not been over-stuffed with knowledge, it has space to remember things that are important.' Balthazar might as well have paid the compliment to a brick; Chess's face was flint and he wondered what bond existed between her and Julius. 'Julius was a mighty warrior.'

'*Was* a mighty warrior?' queried Chess.

'Listen to me, Chess. He chose to fight against the Symmetry. He had been battling the darkness from long before I or my fathers had been born. He fought with every weapon he had, even his blood.'

'His blood?' Chess didn't see how blood could be a weapon.

'He shared his blood with humans; certain, rare humans in whom the after-beat of immortality survives. It is a laboratory process called genetic melding. The recipients became a little more like Julius; they inherited some of his power. These are the Blood Sentinels and they fought by his side, but never for long for the fight was merciless. There were twelve alive at any one time, although the search for a new Sentinel sometimes took many years.'

'What did you do to *Julius*?' Right now, Chess wasn't interested in Blood Sentinels.

'I see, now, that I had studied the darkness for too long. I had come too close. But my knowledge was useful to Julius. He relied upon me as a guide, through the shadow-worlds.' Balthazar cleared his throat. 'At that time I had possession of a skulk rack.'

'The one here, under the ground?' asked Chess. Suddenly she hated to think of how the machine had enjoyed her use.

'The same.' Balthazar was solemn. 'I had paid a high price for it.' He shook his head, remembering. 'I spied upon the Inquisitors. I thought that Julius and I might surprise them and destroy them. Of course, I did not tell Julius of my plan because he would have dismissed it as foolhardy and doomed to failure, which it was.'

'So I took Julius to the Inquisitors, but they were not surprised. They were waiting for us, all five of them. It was Julius who was unprepared. They stabbed him with their long knives. They murdered him but they let me live. I don't know why.'

So this is what kills Julius, thought Chess. 'You idiot,' she said.

'I am sorry,' stuttered Balthazar, apologizing for his crime to the young girl sitting opposite. 'But it is the darkness, Chess. You see why I dare not go any further with you. I cannot trust myself.'

'So Julius dies, in five hundred years time?' asked Chess.

'No, no, no,' replied Balthazar, wearily. 'From the moment that I became involved with you and your brothers, my future changed. Helping you means that what *was* my future has gone. I will never be able to return to it. Time will catch me now.'

'So if your future has changed, Julius will not be killed by the Inquisitors? He lives?' If Balthazar expected pity, Chess was not going to give it to him yet.

'Yes. Unless somebody else kills him,' replied Balthazar, 'for which, I trust, you would not hold me responsible.'

'And you knew that this would happen when you decided to help us?'

'It was my choice,' stated Balthazar, 'and I am glad of it. You needed my help. I am happy to have released Julius from that future, whatever I have done to mine.' Then Balthazar smiled his big smile. 'As I have said, Chess, Mevrad is very, very clever.'

Chess twined a finger in her long hair and said, 'A thousand years is a very long punishment. It wasn't even your fault, really.'

'It was my fault,' said Balthazar. 'I may not have wielded the knife but I put his body in its path.' Then he clapped his hands. 'Enough of metaphysics. It will take us two days to reach the stonedrakes' city and before long this lonely cliff top will be overrun by Dog Troopers. We shall go this morning. I will take you to the stonedrakes and there I must leave you. I can do no more. You have my explanation, Chess.'

Chess wanted Balthazar to stay with her despite his explanation. However foolish he had been, he was kind and strong and clever. But she knew that his mind was set, and so was hers. She would find her brothers and then she would help the children inside the factory. This was what she was here for: she had no other purpose.

'I shall get what we need for our journey.' Balthazar walked to the tree.

When he came back down the ladder, he had a small backpack over his shoulder. In one hand he held his quarterstaff and in the other he had a flaming torch. Heat shimmered from it like rippling glass and a thin trail of black smoke swirled up from the tarred brush.

'What's that for?' asked Chess, puzzled because it was day and she could see no need for the torch.

Balthazar stood tall and square beneath his rambling house.

'My time is coming to an end,' he boomed. 'There will be no return to this place.' He stood motionless and closed his eyes, barrel chest rising and falling. Then he turned and held the torch so that the flames could lick the top rungs of the ladder.

Although the flames had been faint in the daylight, they burnt dark-orange as they took hold of the wood. Balthazar swept the torch under the wooden beams that supported the workshop. At first nothing happened. Then there was a snapping, cracking noise and a long tongue of flame curled out from under the floorboards and flicked up the outer wall.

Balthazar walked purposefully to the rocks, past Chess who was standing, mesmerized by the fire that was spreading all around the bottom of the tree. Burning torch still in his hand, he entered the crack that led down to the cave.

Whilst Balthazar was under the ground the fire began to work its way up the lower sections of the house. With an aggressive crackling it threw out a savage heat that made Chess retreat. Flames rushed up the walls, enclosing them in sheets that unfurled as if billowing in a blast of wind. On all sides now the fire ran along spars, up timbers and poured through windows. Wood splintered, glass smashed and soot-black smoke streamed high above the cliff.

When Balthazar staggered out of the rocks, coughing and sweating, his house had been engulfed in a raging cone of flame. He rubbed his eyes which were pink. Chess wondered if he had been crying until she saw the white smoke issuing from the crack behind him.

'All that can be burnt must be burnt,' he said before bending double with a hacking cough. Chess seized his wrist and pulled him away from the rocks.

With a screech and whoosh, a section of the house plummeted like a fireball to the forest far below. The heat was unbearable.

'I have finished,' sighed Balthazar when his lungs had cleared of smoke. 'We must go quickly now. This fire will act like a beacon as far as the eye can see. Others will soon be here.'

'Well, let's get going then.' Chess was more worried about being hit by a burning lump of debris.

Without turning to look back at the inferno that had been

his home for nearly five hundred years, Balthazar walked towards the river with Chess by his side.

They did not return to the valley by the way they had come. That would have risked running into troopers who would even now be setting out to investigate what had happened on the cliff. Instead, Balthazar walked upstream to where he moored his canoe and he used this to paddle himself and Chess across the river. Then he took Chess over the cliff on the other side and down to the valley beyond. By nightfall they were deep in the forest and far from the gorge.

The forest was as sweltering and tangled as Chess remembered it. However, Balthazar knew trails that she could never have found and he tracked a route around swamps, under creepers and through dense knots of vegetation. Where the way was blocked, he used his machete to hack a clear path. Although she was drenched with sweat and plagued with the crawling and biting of the insects, she was glad to be with him.

They trekked through the rainforest in easy silence. But as the second day wore on and evening approached heavy with a coming storm, a gloom stole over them.

Chess had noticed how the earth under her bare feet had become drier and the ground less tangled with strands of vegetation. Now she could feel the gritty texture of sand in the leaf mould.

'We are close to the ocean,' said Balthazar.

'I know,' said Chess, who had smelt the brine mixed with the sweet musk of the forest.

'I must leave you soon.' His voice sounded heavy and hopeless.

'I know,' she repeated, silently wishing that he would stay with her.

Darkness came early, thunderous clouds drawing a veil across the sky. A rumbling murmur drifted to them from the mountains, far inland. Wind brushed the tree tops, bending them towards the sea as if raking its fingers through their canopies. Louder now, the rumbling rolled over the forest.

Behind the rustling of the trees and the drumming approach of thunder, Chess could hear another sound; the steady crash and hiss of breakers pounding the coast.

'We are close to the edge of the forest,' Balthazar told her. He pointed at the trees which were bending with the wind. 'I have brought you to the top of the bay, Chess. Through those trees lie the ocean and the mountains that come down to it. That is where you will find the stonedrakes. Their city is built within the first volcano. Walk up the coast a short distance and you will come to it.'

Rain started to fall, pattering on the leaves above.

'Please, can't you come with me?' begged Chess. Ahead, the trees were thinning and through them she could see the dark backdrop of water and sky. The black expanse of ocean was flecked grey where the waves broke.

'No.' Balthazar was adamant. 'I have come further than I should, Chess. You must believe me when I say that I cannot trust myself. The stonedrakes and the Symmetry are set to collide; I must not come any closer to the Symmetry.'

The sky cracked electric-white and thunder boomed. Chess glimpsed Balthazar's face, taut and sweating, eyes wide before they were plunged back into darkness. The rain began to pound the tree tops and Chess felt more lonely and more miserable than ever.

Balthazar knelt down and unslung the small backpack he had been carrying. 'You can take this now,' he said. 'There is some food here and there is something else.' He loosened the straps that secured the top flap of the pack and flipped it open. 'Something I want you to have.' He pulled out a roll of cloth.

In the next flash of lightning, Chess saw that the cloth was red and that Balthazar's face was twisted with doubt as if he regretted handing the bundle to her even as he passed it.

He repeated the words he had said three times before, 'I knew too much. I saw too much. I did too much.' Then he helped unroll the cloth that Chess was holding and she could feel his hands trembling. 'I did too much and in so doing I killed Julius.'

'The Inquisitors killed Julius,' insisted Chess but Balthazar wasn't listening.

She saw that he was holding a scabbard and from it he half-drew a long, thin, stiletto dagger. In the next rip of electricity, she saw that it had a pale blue handle and a simple, semi-circular hand guard.

'This is a crystal knife,' he said, hoarsely. 'The blade is of pure amarantium. There is no escape from it; a wound from this knife pierces space and time and will never heal. It is a weapon of darkness, warp built.'

The storm battered the roof of the forest and the rain was streaming through the trees. 'Where did you get it?' asked Chess, shivering as rainwater began to run from her hair and down her back.

'This is one of the knives that killed Julius. I pulled it from his chest but it was too late. It and its sisters had done their work. Once they had been plunged into his body there was no sanctuary, even for his immortal spirit.' He held it towards Chess. 'Take it. Sometimes the darkness destroys itself. I want you to have it, but do not touch the blade. Only the sheath can contain it.'

Chess knew that crystal could not harm her. She had dug through the amarantium-rich tissue of the cerebral torus with her own hands. But she didn't know *why* she could do this. She took the knife from Balthazar, held it up and then grasped its blade in her fist. He went to grab her wrist but she snatched it back.

'Who am I, Balthazar?' she demanded, displaying the knife, pommel upwards. 'Who am I?' Her voice was desperate.

'I do not know,' panted Balthazar, shaking his head, eyes bright and fixed on where Chess's pale hand gripped the pure amarantium. Then he saw her eyes and said, 'I am sorry, Chess. I wish I could tell you. I wish I could help.'

She let him take her wrist and pull it down so that he could hold the knife by its handle. He sheathed it before rolling it back in the cloth. He replaced the cloth in the pack which he thrust into Chess's arms.

'There is something else, something that I need to know,' said Chess, wiping rainwater from her face and pushing rat tails out of her eyes. 'It's just that if I don't ask you now ... well ... I don't know when else I can ask you.'

'Ask,' Balthazar invited her. He picked his staff up from where it was lying on the ground.

'The Eternal. What is the Eternal?' asked Chess.

Balthazar was a long time in answering; long enough for lightning to flash and thunder to rumble and lightning to flash again. Chess was wondering how long they would stand like that, facing one another with rain pouring down around them. When, at last, Balthazar spoke it was in a voice deep and grave.

'The Eternal is the end of all things and, maybe, the beginning. It can change worlds; but to wield that power? I do not think it could be controlled.'

'But what is it?' insisted Chess.

'I am not sure what it is,' admitted Balthazar, 'but I know something of where it is to be found. My study of the Histories and the time charts has revealed that to me.' And then, although Chess did not ask him he said, 'Where the twelve suns are one. That is where the Eternal is to be found. That much I know. I could guess more but then I could be wrong and I know too well the perils of ill-judged knowledge. But where the twelve suns are one: that much my researches have taught me.'

They haven't taught me anything, Chess thought to herself.

Balthazar stood with his staff in one hand and with the other he cupped Chess's face. She closed her eyes, drawing as much of the warmth and comfort from him as she could.

'Go now,' urged Balthazar. 'Through the trees and up by the beach.'

Chess stayed where she was and it was Balthazar who stepped away from her.

'Go,' he insisted and thunder rumbled. 'Go now, Chess.'

Feeling sick, Chess turned towards the sea and began to walk. The wind buffeted the treetops and the rain stung her eyes. She looked back at Balthazar to know that she was not completely alone. His tall body was still between the trees, motionless.

When Chess emerged from the forest she was caught between the sea and the sky. She leant forwards because the wind was belting into her and she followed the trees at the fringe of the forest for shelter. Over the ocean the black chasm of sky was split by jagged prongs of lightning and she looked back again, towards Balthazar. It was difficult to see anything in the darkness but when the night next burst white she saw that there was an empty space where he had been standing.

She gripped the straps of the backpack, pulling it tight against her shoulders and turned back into the wind. The rain lashed down. Ahead, the lightning revealed sharp mountain crags. Chess staggered forwards, not sure of where she was going or what would happen to her.

CHAPTER 14

'You're standing on my foot,' complained Splinter.

'Sorry,' said Box. 'I didn't know it was there.' Then the sack was pulled off his head and he looked about, blinking in the smoky torchlight.

They were standing in a low-roofed chamber that had been dug out of solid rock. The black, pitted ceiling was only a metre above his head and was supported by rows of pillars that were part of the original stone. They curved up and down like stalagmites and stalactites, as far as he could see, in every direction.

Rough rope still pinned his wrists together in front of him. Their captors had removed his knife and Splinter's morning coat when they had first taken them prisoner. Splinter's hands were also bound and when the hood was snatched from his head, he shook the long, white hair out of his face, looked left and then right and muttered, 'What kind of freak show is this?'

They were flanked by four guards who had escorted them from the dank cell where they had sat, bound, hooded and hungry, since their arrival two nights before. The guards wore loose white robes and chest plates that glimmered in the flames of the torches that were mounted on the rock pillars. They carried pikes that stopped just short of the ceiling. Their skin was black and smooth but caught the light with a scale-sharp sheen, their narrow eyes were yellow, their hairless faces were finely boned, tapering to an elfin point with tiny nostrils and their tails were muscular and flexed restlessly.

'Balthazar was right,' whispered Box. 'They *are* lizards. Amazing.'

Splinter eyed his brother with contempt. 'Lizards with weapons, fly head. It's not good.'

Box shrugged. 'Maybe they're friendly.'

There was a sharp click from one of the guards and he repeated the noise rapidly, his throat bulging and constricting with each fricative before shoving the butt of his pike into Splinter's ribs.

Splinter cursed and stumbled in the direction he had been prodded. 'Yeah, really friendly.'

'Just keep walking, Splinter.' Box knew that this was a time to be co-operative.

They were ushered towards an area that was flooded by a circle of light. Box surveyed the gloom that stretched elsewhere, sealed in the narrow space between floor and roof. 'They're taking us to someone important.'

Splinter was distracted by a rough scraping sound that accompanied them as they advanced. It took him a moment to realize it was made by the guards' tails brushing over the floor.

'He's lying on a stone altar,' continued Box, 'with loads of cushions. Fancy clothes.' They looked like silk: pale green, very fine. Raising an eyebrow, he whispered, 'Obviously likes his creature comforts.'

'His two friends don't look pleased to see us,' whispered Splinter, referring to the two figures standing on either side of the stone dais.

As the brothers were pushed into the circle of light, Box looked up and saw that here the roof vaulted high and the stone had been polished so that the blaze from the flames which burnt in the hanging lamps was reflected downwards.

The escort slid to a halt several pike lengths from the raised stone. Now Box could see in detail the figure who reclined upon the cushions; the almond-shaped, yellow eyes with their slit pupils and penetrating gaze, the oval face protruding gently to a tip with two tiny nostrils, a mouth neat and small with thin lips, blacker even than the skin which shimmered with a rainbow sheen like oil on water and beneath the gauze of silk, a body that was flawless and smooth.

'Your he is a she,' stated Splinter.

Box gaped. 'She's beautiful.'

'It's a lizard, you sick little fly head.'

The lizard queen reclined on her couch and regarded the two prisoners coolly. Although they had been brought to her chamber by an armed escort she had been polite enough to greet them with a clicking from her throat which meant 'Be at ease.' She tried to question them but they couldn't switch; they did not understand how to speak in thoughts. To her courteous enquiries they responded with clumsy pulses of emotion.

She blinked slowly, flicked the tip of her graceful tail and studied them. One was stocky with dark, curly hair all over his head. The other was taller and pale and spiky, with white hair on his head and ice-blue eyes that made the queen wary. She warned the escort to pay particular attention to him. The queen marvelled at how white their skin was and how soft it appeared; so different from her jet-black scales that looked as sleek as satin but were tough as leather.

'You told me that three had been seen,' she said to Akrish, her vizier, switching. Because they spoke in thoughts, the prisoners would have heard nothing.

He stood by her couch, hands clasped at chest height, yellow eyes unblinking, the purple point of his tongue protruding between his thin black lips. He wore a simple gown that hung from his shoulders to his ankles.

'There were three when we fired at them, majesty,' Akrish replied, 'but when our soldiers ambushed the enemy two nights ago they found only these two. Perhaps the third has perished in the forests.'

On the opposite side of the queen's couch stood another lizard. He wore a silver-bright cuirass under loose white robes, and pantaloons. A sash was bound about his waist and a long scimitar hung at his hip from a belt that looped over his shoulder. Like all the other lizards, he did not wear anything on his feet which were long and wide, with clawed toes.

'What do you think, Firebras?' asked the queen, dancing her long ebony fingers with their sharp nails across the edge of her couch. 'The shorter one does not strike me as a spy.'

Firebras walked over to the prisoners. His sword swung by his hip and his long, thick tail swished across the floor behind him. The escort stood to attention as he approached, banging the hafts of their pikes hard against the stone floor. He waved his hand to indicate that they should stand easy and he circled the prisoners, clicking loudly to warn them not to move.

Splinter didn't like the way the brawny lizard circled him. Although he could not switch, he sensed a presence at the edge of his thoughts and he answered it with a needle of spite. He stifled a shriek and stumbled backwards as the lizard dropped to all fours, ripped back its lips to display teeth like white thorns and stretching its mouth wide, filled the chamber with a savage roar.

'Whatever you did, Splinter,' gasped Box, 'don't do it again.'

Firebras drew himself upright and returned to his place by the stone couch. 'They are strange creatures, majesty. I do not like the pointed one. But they are very different from the soldiers we ambushed.' To Box and Splinter, the only sound was a light click from the lizard's throat.

'We must be careful,' warned Akrish, as withered and ancient as Firebras was muscular and full of vitality. 'It is the business of spies to fool their captors. If they do not look like spies that may go to show that they are very clever spies indeed.'

'The eve of war,' said the queen to Firebras, 'and still we know nothing about our enemy.'

Footfalls and the sound of something being dragged. Splinter saw the yellow eyes of those at the couch focus, unblinking on whatever was approaching behind him. Then he saw two more lizards haul a dripping bundle of rags in front of the queen.

'Chess!' exclaimed Box, starting toward her. He was pulled back immediately by the nearest guard.

'Well done, Chess.' Splinter pursed his lips, bitterly. 'You know, for once you could have actually helped us. But guess what? You got it wrong. You always let us down.'

Chess was pushed in front of Box and Splinter, directly before the lizard queen. Even though she was shivering with a chill from the rainwater, she returned the queen's steady stare. The queen leant forwards, tilting her head to one side. Her movements were languorous and elegant and she reposed upon the heap of cushions as if nothing in the world could ruffle her.

'We found it in the outer harbour,' Chess thought she heard someone say.

'A female,' said another.

'The third spy,' came an anonymous accusation.

Chess couldn't tell who was saying these things. The female stonedrake looking down on her made a slow clicking noise in her throat. The big stonedrake to the left of the couch stood with his brawny arms folded, silent. The thin old stonedrake to the right of the couch played with his fingers and inspected her through hooded eyes.

'Where have you come from?'

'I smell a thief.'

Then Chess realized that these were voices she was hearing *inside* her head. It was like tuning into a vague thought and then concentrating on it.

Realizing what was happening, Chess was able to fasten onto the words that caught her thoughts.

'The colour has been washed from you like an old skin. Your hide is so frail, I wonder you don't spill your guts on the floor.' This came from the brawny stonedrake with the long, curved sword and the bright eyes.

Chess thought back, 'You're not so good looking yourself.'

All around the room, lizards began to switch. The queen held up a hand, fingers loaded with jewelled rings and there was silence.

'My name as Ashadzi,' she said to Chess, 'and I am queen here. This is Firebras, my champion.' The powerfully built lizard bowed deeply towards Chess. 'This is my vizier, Akrish.' The aged lizard blinked and clicked slowly.

'My name is Chess,' replied Chess by thinking. There was no effort; the idea of the message was enough. 'These are my brothers, Box and Splinter.'

'Are you spying on us?' asked Ashadzi, bluntly.

'No. We're not spies. Honest.' Chess realized that they must know she was telling the truth because if she was thinking of lying, they would detect that.

'Where are you from?' asked Ashadzi.

'That's a bit tricky,' answered Chess, 'but we were sent to find out what happens in the volcano that makes the black smoke.'

'And what have you discovered?' The lizard queen sat

upright with a tinkling of bracelets and she crossed her legs. Her tail stretched along the couch and then it curled under her thighs. Chess noticed the sharp, black nails on the ends of her toes.

'There is a factory and there are soldiers in it. They steal human children and they're making something, probably, although we don't know what it is yet . . .' Chess trailed off. There was still so much they didn't know about the factory.

'What are human children?'

'What's going on, Chess?' asked Splinter who could see the queen leaning forwards intently and staring at Chess who was staring back at her. He could sense that something was passing between them but he could not understand what it was.

'*We* are human children,' Chess said to the queen, switching automatically and ignoring Splinter.

'You have been inside this "factory" and seen these soldiers?' questioned Ashadzi.

'Yes.'

'Good. Now, understand this; this "factory" and these soldiers have tried to hide us from the eye of Ventru. Even as you speak to me, my army is preparing to sail to them. We will destroy them. You will tell me all you know about them and their factory.'

Chess nodded and then, seeing that nodding didn't communicate anything she said, 'If you want.' It was no big deal to Chess if a queen wanted assistance from a street rat. Then she shivered and sneezed because she was soaking wet.

'I do want,' said Ashadzi. 'Rest for the night. Tomorrow

we will talk. The day after that we sail. You are our guests now and no longer prisoners.' Then she turned her attention to Firebras and Akrish with whom she switched too intimately for Chess to hear.

All save one of the guards withdrew into the shadows. The one who remained pulled a dagger from his hip and approached Box and Splinter, who retreated because they did not understand what was happening.

'It's all right,' Chess reassured them. 'He's going to free you.'

Nevertheless, Splinter still shuddered with revulsion as the cool, long-nailed hands grasped his own and the blade rasped through the rope.

'How come you're so friendly with the reptiles?' he asked, but Chess discovered that for all his noise, she was finding it easier not to listen to Splinter.

'How come you're so unfriendly with *everything*?' Box muttered to his brother. 'I said they'd be OK and you nearly got us slabbed.'

Splinter sized-up Box before slapping himself on the forehead and groaning. 'You've fallen in love with a girl lizard, haven't you, fly head?'

Box shoved Splinter in the chest. Splinter's hand shot to Box's throat but before his grip could tighten, his wrist was grasped by a powerful, scaly, black hand.

Splinter stepped back and Firebras let go. Then the stonedrake pushed forwards his lips and made a dry sucking noise.

'He wants a kiss,' sniggered Box.

'He's telling you to behave,' Chess warned Splinter.

Splinter's eyes dropped to the gleaming scimitar at Firebras's hip and he smiled at the lizard.

'*We* only fight our enemies,' Firebras switched to Chess, puzzled. 'You are all so meat-soft outside, but so sharp inside,' and Chess felt a pity swell from him that made her look at the floor.

The Tuesdays were conducted from the hall and upwards through a series of stone passageways by a stonedrake in a plain brown robe.

'A servant,' stated Splinter, as if he was used to identifying such things.

They were brought to a room that was furnished with four cloth pallets stuffed with straw, a long, low table and around the table, large cushions that were embroidered lavishly in blue and silver. The stone walls were softened by muslin drapes that hung in swathes and there were rush mats on the flagstone floor. Mullioned windows in the far wall revealed only darkness. Between the windows there was an open doorway that was also dark. Torches burnt on either side of the door by which they had entered. On one of the beds lay Box's knife and Splinter's morning coat. Splinter snatched up the coat and pulled it on.

Box laughed quietly, shook his head and retrieved his knife. 'Mr Possessive,' he said to his brother.

The servant brought a metal jug of water, engraved with ornate whorls and eye-motifs. It was tall and had a broad, curved spout. He placed it on the table and around it he set three small cups and a small bowl full of fine brown wafers.

Before the servant had left the room with a deep bow and

a stream of clicks, Box had sampled the contents of the silver bowl.

'Good,' he chomped. 'Tangy. Like beef crisps.'

Splinter tipped the wafers across the table and held up the bowl for inspection. 'Nice,' he said, turning it in his hands. 'Silver.' Then sliding his eyes over the bowl, towards Chess. 'Spindle rippers, Dog Troopers, armed lizards? It makes the crashers and the occasional hunter easy. I don't want to sound negative, but what's happening, Chess?'

'The stonedrakes are going to war against the Twisted Symmetry.' She picked up a wafer, sniffed it and dropped it back on the table. 'Except that they haven't got a clue what they're up against. They want us to tell them all we know about the factory, tomorrow.'

Splinter nodded. 'Well,' he sighed, looking around the room, 'this beats the dungeons. How did you talk with them?'

'It's like thinking,' Chess replied, licking a finger tip. 'You just think what you mean to say without actually *saying* it.'

'Is it Chat?' crunched Box. Chess shook her head.

'I could pick up bits,' said Splinter, 'but not enough to understand. I just made sure I didn't think anything back.'

'I just found that I could do it,' Chess stated, artlessly. She wasn't trying to boast.

'Another special skill you have, Chess,' sneered Splinter.

'Well, at least we're back together.' Box's jaws had stopped working. 'This may be how we get into the factory. With an army.' He swallowed with an effort and looked at the wafers suspiciously. 'What exactly is this stuff?'

'Mouse scratchings, probably,' said Splinter, discovering that the bowl wouldn't fit into any of his pockets.

Box grunted. 'I've had worse.' He sucked his fingers. 'Anyway, with an army behind us we really *can* help the children at the factory.'

'Yeah,' scorned Splinter. 'We just click loudly and walk straight in. I'm sure the Dog Troopers will be terrified at the sight of a bunch of lizards with swords.'

'The Dog Troopers didn't come off so well when we were captured,' rejoined Box.

'That was surprise. When it comes to sheer power, you watch what happens.' Splinter placed the bowl under a leg of the table and bashed it flat.

'Splinter!' Chess was worried that the noise might attract attention.

'Whose side are you on?' Box wiped greasy fingers on his trouser legs.

'Our side,' Splinter shot back. 'But *she*,' pointing at Chess, 'is doing her own thing now. So I'm thinking about being on *my* side. And I'll tell you this, fly head. I've done a lot of reading and a lot of thinking and sometimes I can see where the Symmetry are coming from.' Box gawped at him. 'In some ways they have a point.'

'Are you mad?' exclaimed Box. 'How can sticking children in scream rooms have a point. How can planning to destroy the world have a point?'

Splinter was unperturbed. Poker-faced he observed, 'You don't understand these things, Box. They are beyond you.'

'I understand the difference between right and wrong,' said Box.

'Really?' A little smile played at the corner of Splinter's mouth. 'Robbery, theft and assault are your specialities, aren't they? Since when did you care about right and wrong?'

Box didn't reply because he had no appetite for the hard work of arguing with Splinter. He sat on one of the beds and Chess lay on another.

'I win,' whispered Splinter in a way that was meant to make Box explode but Box was too tired to react. Splinter tucked the can-flat wedge of silver into a pocket.

Chess was woken by the sound of her name. When she opened her eyes she saw that the torches were out and the room was frozen with the mirror-glow of earliest morning.

'Chess.'

It was Firebras. He was standing in the doorway, arms folded, yellow eyes blinking slowly. When she sat up he clicked at her in a way that she knew was meant to be a cheery, early morning greeting.

Chess rubbed sleep from her eyes.

'We are going for a walk,' switched the brawny lizard.

Chess found that the doorway led to a small stone porch where she was struck by a pungent whiff, like sulphur. It came through the open archway on the other side. Firebras beckoned her to follow him through the arch and into the street beyond.

Chess wasn't sure what she had expected but she hadn't expected this. She was inside a vast crater. Looking up she saw a pearl-grey sky through a cragged ring of rock that was wider than a city park. Walking across the street and looking over a wall, she saw an even broader expanse of water far below. Steam rolled over its surface.

Lining the inside of the crater and built from its black rock were row upon spiralling row of walls: opposite her, above her, below her. The walls were crammed with arched windows and doorways and the balconies of thousands of buildings that had been carved out of the rock and which overlooked streets which wound their way up and down the inside of the crater like a massive helter-skelter. Stone staircases vanished within alcoves and appeared behind parapets. Shallow roofs jutted out from the rock. Ornate stone balustrades enclosed forgotten terraces that lurched over hurtling drops.

Chess looked over the wall to where jetties ran into the smoking water. These created a series of harbours which were lined with cranes and gantries. The harbours were full of sea-craft, some of which looked like ships and some that were different from any vessel Chess had seen. In one harbour she counted at least eight marine culverins.

Although there was no one else in the street where they were standing, it was very busy in the harbours below. Hundreds of stonedrakes were loading the vessels with equipment; ropes, grappling hooks, barrels of tar, provisions, chests of armour, racks of weapons. She saw that on one jetty there were assembled tall wooden towers and catapults the size of buses.

At the end of each harbour the rippling water shimmered with light that entered through huge semi-circular gateways. These were wide enough to accommodate at least two ships sailing side by side and high enough to be cleared safely by the tallest mast. Chess guessed that these must give access from the inside of the crater to the open sea.

Water. Light. Stones. 'I used to live in a place like this, sort of,' mused Chess, thinking of the reflections over the ledge at the wharf; thinking how far away it was now, trying to black out the thought of what Gemma or Pacer or Hex were doing right now.

She concentrated on how proudly Firebras surveyed the harbours, thick, scaled arms outstretched as his hands were spread on the top of the wall, and she felt very sorry for him. Chess knew how easy it was for a place like this to be destroyed.

She noticed that from time to time the surface of the huge lagoon was broken by great, dome-like bubbles that expanded from the water and then burst, releasing thick plumes of white smoke. This smoke drifted upwards, accompanied by the stinging smell of sulphur.

'We are going up there,' switched Firebras, pointing skywards.

There was no reason *not* to go up there. 'OK,' Chess switched back.

The cobbled street was dawn-grey and their footfalls echoed in the emptiness. In some of the doorways, wrinkled stonedrakes, male and female, sat smoking dark cheroots, eyes bleary and glazed. Higher up they encountered a young lizard throwing stones over the wall and watching them plummet down to the lagoon. He was gripped round the waist by a female in a loose red gown who clicked rapidly and shook him. She banged him over the head with her tail and Chess heard her switching furiously.

After more than half an hour of clambering weed-tangled staircases hidden behind the rock dwellings, Chess was hot and still unsure of what this was all about. If it was walking for the sake of walking, it was stupid; just the sort of dumb thing that jacks did in their goofy boots and fat-mash anoraks.

Firebras read her thought. 'I want you to see why we are going to fight.'

Chess glanced sidelong. She had plenty of thoughts that she bargained on no one else listening to. Suddenly, switching didn't seem such a smart way of communicating.

Firebras chuckled with a grating growl. Then he stopped and without warning, pushed his fingers into her thick, chestnut hair. 'This is very strange. Do all human children wear it?'

Chess laughed aloud. 'Usually.'

'We must be as strange to you as you are to us.' He clicked thoughtfully.

Chess nodded and switched, 'I guess so.'

They had begun to pick their way up a crooked fan of steps.

'Ventru is everything,' said Firebras.

Hardly, thought Chess. I've never heard of him. And then she realized that the stonedrake could hear her.

'This is why you are with me,' he switched back.

They were near to the summit now, scuffing up a narrow path that had been scraped along the rock face. The city spiralled below Chess until it stopped at the lagoon which smoked at the bottom of the crater. She liked the feeling of being here, caught between the high places and the low and she knew how much Gemma would have liked it. She couldn't stop that thought and it made her chest ache.

'Gemma is your friend?' switched Firebras.

Chess nodded. She mouthed 'friend' to herself, wondering at how soft and open it sounded. Then she thought of Gemma again and her throat tightened.

Firebras stroked the top of her head. 'You carry your friends wherever you go, Chess. Minds can be together even when bodies cannot. Don't be upset.' He clicked gently. 'Now, we are here.'

They had come to a knife-edge at the top of the crater. Firebras vaulted over the narrow crest, and Chess did the same, unfazed by the slope that plunged away from her feet. She had grown used to the racing vistas of Surapoor and she settled on the rocks, letting the open space wash over her.

The cool air made her cheeks tingle and her eyes water. It was still early morning. Below her a bed of clouds filled the forest valley and hid the coast. Far to her left, the cliffs that buttressed the high plateau towered out of a white sea of fog, a trail of mist still swirling down their tree-tangled faces. Opposite, the black cone of the volcano across the bay thrust through the clouds, dark smoke hooding its peak and the mountains behind it and filling the sky above. And out to her right, yellow lances of sunlight were tilting over the ocean clouds as the bright sun began to rise.

'It's beautiful,' Chess sighed. 'But the black smoke is horrible.'

'It was very beautiful before the black cloud came. You need to know about us, Chess. We were born from these mountains, from out of the fire and rock that lies in their roots. That is why we call this mountain, Varish, which also means "mother".'

At least you know who your mother is, thought Chess, even if she is a lump of rock.

'Stop feeling sorry for yourself and listen to me,' insisted Firebras. 'We were born when there were only mountains in the world. Before we could leave the arms of our mother we had to have food and water and, most important of all, heat. Ventru, who is our father, made plants and fish and animals, gave us rivers and rain and set his burning eye in the sky to keep us warm.' Firebras pointed to the bright sun, now half-clear of the cloud bed.

'We flourished as the world grew older. But there came a darkness, when the rains did not fall and the plants withered, the oceans were empty and the animals died. Why did the darkness come? It was Ventru's brother, Xafal. He had always been jealous of Ventru and Varish and their children and he had sat in his kingdom of night chewing his knuckles and rolling his eyes. He brought darkness, hoping to blot out life. Then there was a great battle and Ventru stabbed Xafal a thousand times. Xafal was defeated and although night still falls at the end of every day, the stars shine where Xafal was wounded. And now, Ventru uses his second eye to watch over his children all day and all night to see that we come to no harm. But it is hard to be ever watchful and his eye is raw and red from the labour.'

The stonedrake extended his arm over the drifting clouds towards the volcano opposite. Chess looked and saw that from the edge of the coal-black pall, a red orb began to emerge over the mist that clung to the ocean.

'Ventru's eye,' said Firebras. 'One eye to keep us warm and another to watch over us. Weak, tired but always watching.'

He slapped his sword. 'But now, though he watches over us all day, the black smoke hides us from his eye at night. At the most dangerous time, we do not have his protection. That is why we are going to fight.'

'You'll lose this war. Lots of your soldiers will be killed,' stated Chess.

'We cannot be defeated. We are too strong.'

Chess considered how best to make her point. 'I didn't know about Ventru, and now I do. Do you know about Dog Troopers? Do you know about the Twisted Symmetry?'

'No.'

You haven't got a chance, thought Chess, and she knew that Firebras was listening.

CHAPTER 15

'We cannot be defeated.'

Chess clawed at one of her forearms but didn't retreat from Ashadzi, even though the lizard queen was losing her temper.

'You can't just march in there,' Chess switched back. 'They've got automatic weapons, high explosive ...'

'Our blades are sharp and our cannon deadly accurate.'

'They've got warp technology,' shouted Chess, her voice resounding. Firebras pulled her back to where he stood with Akrish and Javoz, commander of the army. A little behind them lurked Box and Splinter.

Ashadzi craned her head forwards and switched as sharp as venom, 'Don't tell me what I may do with *my* army.' The slit pupils dilated and the queen spread her claws on the stone with a scrape.

Javoz stepped in front of Chess. He was a stout, battle-scarred lizard, with thin yellow eyes and a short thick tail notched with wounds. No taller than Box, he wore a long coat of shining silver mail and grey, baggy leggings. His neck was as wide as his flat hairless head and he leant on the haft of his double-bladed axe as he spoke.

'The softskin seems very sure of the enemy's strength,' he observed.

'She says the enemy troops number about four hundred. We have over twenty times as many.' Ashadzi eased back into the cushions with a tinkle of bracelets. 'I am grateful to her for her description of the enemy's factory. But I am unimpressed by her grasp of basic mathematics.'

'She's upsetting everybody. As usual,' whispered Splinter with a nod towards Chess. 'Probably arranging for someone else to try to slab us.'

Box's belly gurgled like a drain.

'The boy with the talking stomach,' said Splinter.

'We didn't get breakfast.'

'Lizards don't do breakfast.' Splinter sniffed in the direction of Ashadzi. 'They just lounge about, waiting to warm up.'

'But I'm starving.'

'Box,' complained Chess, glaring across at her brother. 'You're putting everyone off.'

'Yeah, fly head. They're planning a war and you keep spoiling it.'

'But I need fodder,' groaned Box. 'It's all right for you, Splinter. You could survive by licking stones. But I *need* juicy, greasy, gut-busting fodder.'

Firebras's eyes flashed across so suddenly that Box was startled into looking behind himself before he realized that the stonedrake was staring directly at him.

'Your breakfast is under your bed,' he heard Firebras

switch. 'Fresh biscuit and honey vine.' And then, in response to Box's next thought. 'Hunger focuses the mind, Box.' The stonedrake turned his attention back to the war council.

Box was astonished and his lower jaw hung dumbly.

'Eating air, fly head?'

'I can do it,' stammered Box.

'Do what?'

'The lizard thing; mind talking.'

Splinter pursed his lips and then snapped, 'Big deal. Maybe you'll grow a tail and start clicking next. You may be able to think like a lizard but that's nothing compared to what I can do. *Nothing.*'

Box hadn't forgotten what Splinter had said about being able to do special things on the day he'd gone missing, but he was too distracted by what his mind was catching to continue arguing. Now that he had clicked into switching with Firebras, he discovered he could fix onto the voice-thoughts of the others in the chamber. He moved closer to Chess.

The rugs had been pulled away from the foot of the queen's couch to reveal a map, carved in the rock floor and coloured. It showed the coast and the lands along it. Box could see the stonedrakes' volcano and the volcano that housed the factory.

Javoz was explaining the plan. 'Tomorrow dawn we sail across the bay. The culverins guard us as we disembark down the coast, here,' he indicated a gap in the mountains beyond the factory volcano with the end of his tail. 'We camp there and the following day we move up the pass to the volcano.

Although the pass is narrow we can spread out in front of the wall at the top. We have to attack by the pass because the siege engines cannot be brought into action by any other route.'

'Will they not be vulnerable in the pass?' asked Akrish calmly. However, his long thin tail described a little flourish in the air beside his head which showed how concerned he really was.

'We have seen no sign of weapons at the wall nor, for that matter, have we seen any guards. The wall is high and thick but it does not appear to be well defended. We shall storm it using the siege towers supported by catapults. At the same time we shall concentrate our attack on the one potential weak point in the wall.'

'The gates at the end of the strange track?' confirmed Ashadzi.

'Yes, queen, the gates. They will give entry to this factory. The female softskin has been most helpful, identifying where to go from there. We shall smash the place to pieces.' He paused. 'Once we have broken down the gates.'

'I can do that. I can do the gates,' interrupted Box, clumsily switching his way into the conversation. All eyes except Splinter's turned on him.

'The bush-headed softskin has woken up!' switched Ashadzi, clicking musically.

'How've you done it?' asked Chess.

'By being hungry.' Box patted his stomach which was flatter than it had once been. He spoke aloud, realizing that he could only switch with the stonedrakes.

'And how will you work this miracle?' Ashadzi's voice was

in his head but her eyes locked with his and were bright, twinkling.

Box blushed again. 'I can blow them up.' He searched for a way of conveying exactly what he meant. 'Break them to pieces like a marine culverin, but better: if I can get into the boiler room. I left something there when we escaped that could do the job; a bag full of stuff that blasts things.'

'A bag full of stuff that blasts things? You must be a magician!' Ashadzi's tail was curled up neatly so that its tip was close to the side of her face. She stroked it thoughtfully and turned her eyes to Chess, unblinking. 'You wish to go to this factory?'

'Yes.' Chess was resolute. 'I *have* to go back, to help the children who are being kept prisoner.'

'And you will enter by the way you escaped? Through the tunnel on the seaward side of the volcano?'

Chess nodded.

'That thing you do with your head means yes?'

Chess nodded and then said, 'Yes.'

'It may be in our interest to help the softskins get inside the volcano,' suggested Javoz.

'Akrish?' asked the queen, turning her head to look at the vizier.

'Unusually,' he said, 'I find I am in agreement with the Commander. If the enemy are as strong as the female softskin tells us, we will need the gateway to be opened as soon as possible.'

'This meeting is like listening to paint dry,' grumbled Splinter. The stonedrakes couldn't hear him. Chess and Box could, but neither of them said anything back.

'There is no advantage in sending a troop to support the softskins,' considered Ashadzi. 'That would be noisy and the soldiers will all be needed in the assault.' The queen closed her eyes and clicked erratically as if she was undecided about something. When she opened her eyes she said, 'You are my champion, Firebras. In all things I have you by my side. But you are worth many soldiers and whilst I hesitate to face the enemy without you ...'

'Firebras will be needed at the front, queen,' interrupted Javoz.

'I know it would be desirable for him to be at the front, Commander, but the softskins need our help and they may be crucial for the success of our attack. Firebras will stay with them. When the fleet crosses the bay tomorrow we shall send out a rowing boat to take them to the shore. Whilst the army deploys, Firebras and the softskins shall do what they can to open the gates.'

'I'm going to release the children,' said Chess.

'As long as the gateway is opened, you may do as you wish,' replied Ashadzi.

When the Tuesdays were back in their room, Chess told Splinter exactly what had been said.

'I can't believe you're taking orders from a lizard,' was Splinter's judgement.

'She's a queen,' protested Box.

'Right, and I'm Napoleon Bonaparte.'

Box swallowed the last of the biscuits and belched splendidly.

Chess was standing in the stone porch, looking out of the windows at the spiral sprawl of the city.

'Not satisfied with near-death at the hands, claws, guns and teeth of everything we've met since the hag first kidnapped us, now you've managed to plank us into a deranged stonedrake's slash-dot battle plan.' He was directing his comments at Chess. 'Why did you tell them we had to go back into the factory? Why not just wait until the fighting was over, let them get battered and then see what we can do?'

Chess wasn't going to waste energy arguing with Splinter. Instead she patiently outlined her own plan. 'I can find the way through the tunnels because I learnt it with the skulk rack. It's pretty much a straight line.'

'I know,' commented Splinter. 'I did it without a skulk rack, remember?'

'Once we get to the boiler room, I'm going to head for the top level,' continued Chess. 'That's where the control room is. I can open the cells from there, so at least the children will be freed. Hopefully the stonedrakes will have sorted out the Dog Troopers.'

'Somehow, I doubt it,' muttered Splinter.

'Anyway, once the children have been released we can use the VAP. Ethel will know what to do then.' She hesitated. 'Probably.'

'She hasn't so far,' observed Splinter. 'That's why we're here.'

'I can tell you how to get from the boiler room to the entrance gates, Box.' Chess was speaking to him because it was plain that Splinter didn't want to listen.

'We'll come up for you after we've done the gates,' promised Box. 'Or you come and look for us. Either way, we'll meet up.'

Splinter slapped his forehead. 'It's like you're organizing a picnic,' he derided. 'The troopers will slab anyone who goes in there. And that's before the Inquisitor gets to work.'

'Really?' snapped Box. 'And what's the Inquisitor going to do when he "gets to work"?'

'We're going to find out, aren't we,' jeered Splinter and he pointed at Chess, 'thanks to her.'

Firebras entered the room. He stopped short when he saw the three occupants who were inches away from each other's red faces. 'Javoz would welcome your aggression on the front line,' he observed. Splinter sauntered away and dossed down on the nearest pallet.

Behind Firebras were two servants dressed in simple brown gowns. In their arms were garments which they placed neatly on the spare pallet. Chess saw that there were grey robes and shirts of light chain mail.

'I have brought you clothes.' Firebras indicated the vestments on the pallet with a sweep of his tail. 'They will keep you cool by day and warm by night and the armour will protect your bodies. Also, and please do not think me rude, but the clothes you wear are full of holes. Or maybe that is the style in the place you come from?'

Chess looked at Box whose woollen trousers were shredded to the knees, whose T-shirt was torn over the shoulders and whose braces were tied round his waist like a belt to hold his trousers up. Box looked at Chess whose jeans were frayed round her shins and non-existent over her knees and whose T-shirt hung like a limp cabbage leaf over her body.

Splinter guessed what they were switching about. 'I'm not wearing lizard clothes,' he stated.

Box was already investigating one of the piles of clothes. 'Nice one!' He pulled a long dagger from its sheath and admired the mirror-bright blade.

'You may need it,' Firebras said.

'It won't be the first time,' said Box in reply.

'We sail tomorrow, early.' He strode from the room, scimitar slapping against his thigh, servants following his tail.

Chess unfolded a pile of clothes and found that it contained grey trousers, a grey jerkin and a long, baggy jacket that was also grey and was fastened by a sash of brown cloth. A shirt of chain mail was wrapped around a sheathed dagger and belt.

'I'll keep this.' Splinter took the knife and belt from the third pile of clothes and fastened it around his waist, under his jacket. He showed no interest in anything else.

Chess stripped off and experimented with the clothing. It was loose but not as hot as she had expected. It fitted her comfortably and immediately she discovered that it was easier to move in than a pair of grime-stiff jeans. Whilst Splinter and Box admired their new knives, Chess knelt by the pallet under which she had stuffed her backpack. Using her body to shield what she was doing, she exchanged the stonedrake dagger for the crystal knife that Balthazar had given to her two nights ago. Then she pulled the long jacket shut and tied the sash tightly so that the crystal knife in its amarantium sheath was concealed. She stood up and turned round wearing the innocent face that she used to pick pockets.

'How do I look?' she asked, adjusting her jacket. Box had

finished arranging his new clothes and he positioned himself by her side.

'Like a pair of slapstick ninjas,' was Splinter's withering assessment.

'You're such a jerk, Splinter.' Box jabbed the air with his left fist, his right and then delivered a roundhouse kick to his invisible opponent. He rolled his shoulder blades before spinning round to throw a right hook that stopped a razor's width from Splinter's chin.

Splinter didn't flinch. 'You're such a moron, fly head. Any group of homicidal maniacs offers you a uniform and you'll sign up. First it was the COE, now it's the fighting lizards.'

'I just want to survive.' Box jumped on his toes before snapping out a side kick.

'You're a street rat: of course you'll survive. Your problem is you fancy a lizard who thinks she's a queen.'

Box exploded. 'Shut up, Splinter. I'm sick of living like a piece of dirt. Chess is right. I'm sick of always running, getting crashed, being treated like I don't exist. And all you ever say is, "Too bad, we're street rats." Well, if having to stand up and fight is what it takes *not* to be a street rat, that's what I'll do.'

Splinter snorted contemptuously. 'Nice speech.'

'And I'll tell you something else, you lanky prat. I like this. I like being on the right side. I like not acting like a kicked dog. You should try it. You might stop looking like someone's shoved a fish hook up your nose.'

Splinter smiled. He strolled to the porch, hands folded behind the back of his black, long-tailed jacket.

'These lizards are so sure of victory,' he pondered aloud,

looking down at the busy harbour. 'I like to imagine what will happen to them.'

The Tuesdays were woken just after dawn by Firebras who escorted them down to the harbour. Chess and Box were dressed in the new clothes which they had worn the night before. Splinter was still in his narrow black trousers and morning coat.

The jetties jostled with troops and animals, waiting to embark. It was hot and the smell of salt and sulphur and thronging animals was so pungent that it stung the back of Chess's throat.

The noise was all-encompassing: thudding boots, clattering armour and weapons, lowing creatures and the roars of the boatswains and harbour masters who were cracking their whips to control the livestock.

Chess saw that on one jetty a file of lumbering, grey beasts was shuffling towards a broad-hulled boat. The boat was built of the same russet-coloured metal as the culverins and had a similar steaming bulb at the rear. These animals had the sagging hides and bad-tempered expressions of rhinoceroses although they didn't have horns on their heavily-boned heads. If the beast behind came too close to the one in front it was swatted on the nose by a thin, irate tail. They grumbled to one another with listless grunts.

'They're as big as elephants,' marvelled Chess.

'Fifteen of them,' counted Box, 'not including any already on the ship.'

Although they were talking aloud in a language he did

not understand, Firebras heard their thoughts and said, 'Those are ganuks. They carry troops into battle and pull the siege engines. These are the last ones to be loaded. There are thirty-nine more ships already full of them and waiting to sail.'

Chess noticed that some of the ships packing the waters were equipped with masts, rigging and sails and others were not. Those which weren't were fitted with huge metal bulbs at their sterns which smoked steadily. Firebras explained that these vessels were the heavier ones and they were powered by steam produced from hot rock that was mined from deep in the volcano and mixed with water inside the metal bulbs.

'Our people are great miners,' boasted Firebras, as they forced their way through the crowds. 'Underneath these waters are the roots of the volcano where the rock is red and flows like blood. We take heat and metals for our ships and our smiths forge weapons and armour. This is our strength and it comes deep from the belly of Varish.'

'Who's Varish?' Box asked Chess.

'Why are you talking about varnish?' asked Splinter who was increasingly irritated by hearing only fragments of conversation.

'We sail on the queen's barge.' Firebras pointed over the heads of the white robed soldiers trooping in front of them to a great warship docked on its own at the furthest harbour.

It was a combination of sailing ship and steamer, as tall and broad as a galleon, with three masts and rigging although no sails had been raised yet. On each side of the ship there were three huge water wheels. Chess guessed that these were driven by power from the steaming metal ball that sat high above the water line at the rear of the vessel.

On either side of the ship, copper-brown metal platforms spread in tiers like cantilevers. The platforms were lined with cannons and Chess could see that black-robed gun crews were strapping themselves to posts which allowed them to move on the platforms but would stop them from plunging into the water if they fell.

Having reached the dock, Firebras took the Tuesdays up the gangplank to the main deck and from there up to the quarterdeck where Ashadzi stood, overlooking the final stage of the preparations. The lizard queen was no longer wearing her green silks. She was dressed for battle in white robes over gleaming plate armour, her black face beneath a white turban. She wore a pair of scimitars, one hanging over each hip. In the pommel of one there was set a diamond the size of a plum. A ruby of equal size was set in the pommel of the other.

The prow of the queen's ship looked towards the centre of the lagoon so Chess had a good view of the fleet. She saw that there were sailing ships filled with soldiers and low, wide ships that held ganuks, siege towers and catapults, and there were narrow barques piled with supplies of weapons, barrels of water, cannon shot and cages of mice and chickens.

Chess didn't hear a final signal but suddenly she was aware that there were no more ships being loaded. Everything was waiting. The queen's barge raised its gangplank, the crew took their positions and with a hiss of steam and creak of straining metal, the paddle wheels began to revolve. The vessel rotated in its dock until the prow faced the tall gateway at the end of the harbour. The water beneath the high arch was dappled silver with sunlight.

Silently, the ship eased forwards with Ashadzi, Firebras, Chess, Box and Splinter standing on the quarterdeck. The towering masts passed easily beneath the roof of the gateway, so smoothly that when Chess looked up it felt as if the arched roof was slipping backwards rather than the ship gliding forwards. She watched the shimmering patterns on the stone arches, made by the lapping seawater and repeated to herself what Firebras had said to her about carrying friends with you, but it was hard. The wharf seemed far away and in between there were Dog Troopers, skulk racks, scream rooms, Inquisitors, stonedrakes and a tall, thin man with no eyes who came for her out of the darkness. A Narrow Man.

She wished that she and Box were wearing their old clothes, that she was not carrying a crystal knife that belonged to the Inquisitors and she wished that she and Splinter could be friends again, even if that meant letting him boss her about. She moved close enough to him to let her shoulder brush against his.

'Don't lean on me like a dog,' he grumbled and stepped away from her. Then the stone roof slipped away altogether and they were dazzled by the glare of the sun and the glittering expanse of the ocean.

Around them, the stone quays of the outer harbours fanned out from the tunnel-gates of the volcano. Every harbour mouth was guarded by a marine culverin. The queen's barge increased its speed with a rumble and hiss of steam from the sphere at its stern. Then with a cranking of metal and slapping of canvas, the sails were raised and the ship plunged into the open waters of the bay.

Once the whole fleet was clear of the outer harbour it spread into an arrowhead formation. The warships with their cannons sailed at the front and on the flanks and the troop ships and supply ships sailed in the centre and the rear. Marine culverins stalked through the waters a little distance from the fleet which they ringed to provide protection.

The rainforest and the high lands beyond it looked very different to Chess from the open water. There was a thin white strip of beach fringed with black rocks and then a wall of trees that stretched from the stonedrakes' volcano to the smoke-clad mountains many miles across the bay. Behind the trees and far inland, the forested cliffs mounted up as if they were waiting to push their way down the wide valley towards the ocean.

Chess tried to see where Balthazar's house had been but the dense vegetation revealed nothing. Gulls squealed and circled above the masts of the ship and Chess turned her eyes towards the volcano whose louring hulk dominated the far side of the bay.

When they were not yet halfway across the bay, there was a gush of steam, the paddles cranked into reverse and the ship came to a standstill. Splinter was sitting on the deck, propped against the wall. Box sat near to him and had been trying to balance his knife on his finger tip which was impossible in the ocean swell. Chess had been standing and looking over the bows at the coast. Her hair flicked around her nut-brown face in the breeze.

Ashadzi and Firebras had been standing close to Chess and next to one another. She could sense that they were switching but she couldn't hear what passed between them and she had not tried to listen.

'This is where you leave us,' said Ashadzi, turning to Chess. 'A rowing boat will take you and your brothers to the shore.'

'It's still a long walk to the volcano,' said Chess.

'I know,' said the lizard queen. 'That is why you go from here. You are less likely to be seen. You can follow the edge of the forest which will hide you from view until you reach the mountain. By that time the fleet will have passed the volcano and all eyes will be on us.'

Box had joined them and Ashadzi turned to him and said, 'The front gate, remember. You must open it, tomorrow.'

'I know,' said Box, wondering how long it would take them to reach the gates even if they didn't run into troopers or traders.

Firebras led the way down the ladders to the main deck. A small wooden boat had already been lowered into the water. It bobbed and rocked with two hefty stonedrakes already aboard, waiting to row them ashore. First Box, then Splinter and finally, Chess, climbed over the gunwale and down the rope ladder to the rowing boat.

As Chess descended she saw Firebras place the side of his face against Ashadzi's and click gently before parting from her. Even as he lowered himself over the side of the ship, their tails entwined and his slipped through the coils of hers until only the tips were touching and then he was climbing down. Ashadzi turned from the rail and walked away.

The stonedrakes were waiting for them, stripped to their waists, and they gripped the oars in their big, clawed hands, waiting to row. When Firebras had made himself comfortable, the rope attaching the boat to the ship was unhitched and the stonedrakes began to pull. Once the little boat was clear of the queen's barge, there was a hiss of steam, and the bigger vessel began to sail forwards again.

The stonedrakes guided their boat through the fleet and into the calmer water near to the shore. Chess listened to the dip-splash of the oars and watched the trees at the edge of the forest draw closer.

'Last chance,' said Splinter, looking into her big brown eyes with his narrow blue eyes. 'We can go. Now. You don't have to push this any further, Chess. We can go home. You can use the VAP.'

His sharp instincts told him how frightened Chess was and he used his kind smile as the boat rocked in the shallow water. 'Come on, Chess. Dog Troopers? Pitched battles? The Twisted Symmetry? You don't want any of that. Suppose they get you? What'll happen then?' He pulled a face and shook his head. 'Very nasty, Chess. Very nasty indeed.'

She looked across at the shattered slopes they would have to climb to enter the volcano. He rested his hand on her arm. 'Come on, Chess,' he crooned, 'stop letting everybody use you. Ethel? The Committee? Do you think they're bothered about you? Really? Why send you here if they care about you? This is hopeless.'

Chess turned her gaze from the volcano to Splinter. He was smiling in a way that made her want to let him be in charge of everything; like he used to be. He was very clever. It would be easy to let him take over. It would be easy to go home. But it would not be easy to forget the cries of the children.

'I can't go, Splinter,' she said, slowly. 'You know that. Just help me. Please.'

Splinter's face went white and his hand withdrew from her arm. His mouth twisted, bitter and hard. 'Don't count on it, Chess. You want to fight the Symmetry? Go and fight them. You won't win. As far as I'm concerned, when the time comes, it's every man for himself.'

General Saxmun Vane had just bolted down a bowl of blood jelly when there was a rap on his door. He lifted his long thin snout out of the bowl.

'Yes,' he bellowed, smacking his lips and slapping his great tongue over a glob of crimson jelly that he had spilt on his collar. He turned from the table to see who had disturbed him. 'Colonel,' he said, without pleasure. 'I wasn't expecting you. Why are you here?' He poured himself a goblet of caramel-coloured liquid but not one for the colonel who stood to attention before him.

'General, the lizards have been seen. A fleet has sailed by the volcano, heading down the coast, away from their territory,' and in case the General had not appreciated what this meant he added, 'into ours.'

'Of course they have,' rumbled the General, holding the goblet between his gloved hands and eyeing the colonel coldly. He stretched out his legs and leant back on his high-backed chair. 'Do you know what they are going to do, Colonel?'

'No, sir.'

'Of course you don't. That is why you are only a colonel whilst I am a general. The lizards will sail down the coast until they come to a gap in the mountains, half a day from here. Then they will bring their matchbox machines and club brains up the pass to the perimeter wall. Once there they will attempt to break through the wall or to scale it. But the wall cannot be breached by them, it is too strong. As for scaling it, the lizards believe it is undefended. Therefore we let them take their battle positions. Once they are at the foot of the wall and in point blank range, we destroy them.'

'Do we use the decimator magma-cannons, General?'

General Vane belched, sighed and shook his head. 'Did I make you a colonel, Colonel?'

The colonel swallowed hard and shook his man-mouthed head.

'I thought not,' grunted the General. He explained, 'These lizards are stonedrakes, Colonel. They would enjoy nothing more than to be pounded by molten rock. The decimators are no good against them. Use the storm guns. All of them. Pulp the lizards, Colonel, carve them up. I want the perimeter wall ankle deep in stonedrake blood by this time tomorrow.'

The colonel hesitated before he next spoke.

'What now?' growled General Vane.

Cautiously, the colonel said, 'Maybe we underestimate the lizards, General? They were able to ambush one of our patrols.'

'And?'

'Well,' stuttered the colonel.

'Well, what?' roared General Vane. 'Do you think I don't know about that? Do you think I might be making a mistake? Do you think that we should wet our pants like a litter of mewling pups?'

He sprang to his feet and thrust his long snout down to the pale man-skin surrounding the colonel's mouth. 'The captain in charge of that patrol was careless, Colonel. So careless that if the lizards hadn't done the job with their crossbows, I'd have torn his throat out and fed it to the sea birds myself. Do you understand?'

'Of course, General,' croaked the colonel.

General Vane took a step back from him. 'The lizards cannot breach the wall, Colonel. Now go back to the battalion you command and command it.'

When he reached the door, the colonel turned and asked, 'What about the girl?'

General Vane paused, goblet in hand. 'The girl will not be with the lizard army. She will return by the way that she sneaked out. We have orders not to interfere with her. A pity. I would like to deal with her myself.' He drained the goblet, his tongue chasing after a strand of drool that spilt from the corner of his muzzle. 'But even I have my orders, Colonel. The girl is to pass, freely. Somebody is waiting for her.'

CHAPTER 16

Plan B was still where Box had hidden it. He pulled the suitcase from beneath the boiler and clicked open the catches. He was kneeling on the floor and peering over his shoulders were Splinter, Firebras and Chess. Not far from them was the huge cylinder that was flushed with swirling bands of fire. It threw out heat and a glow that painted faces, arms and machines orange.

It had taken a day to reach the boiler room. They had gone more quickly than Chess had expected; she guessed this was because they were fitter and stronger than before and because they knew where they were going. But she noticed that now, Splinter walked with a slight limp. He blamed this on the stonedrakes. He insisted that although the Dog Troopers had kidnapped him first, they would have looked after him properly.

'They have the technology,' Splinter had said. 'All the stonedrakes have is a red-eyed god.'

Box opened the suitcase. Four orange faces looked inside. There were neat bundles of short sticks that looked like candles which had been strapped together tightly, small clocks that were wrapped in wire, polythene bags packed with something that Chess thought looked like putty, plastic strips with more wire wrapped around them, a pair of consoles with antennae and switches and a leaflet with large letters on the front cover.

'Nice,' whispered Box and then he laughed grimly and said, 'Nobody smoke.' He picked up the leaflet. They were close enough to the glow of the cylinder for him to be able to read it. 'Instructions,' he said. 'This is very easy: an idiot's guide.'

'Must have been written just for you,' observed Splinter.

After flicking through the pages, Box said, 'If we can get to the front gates I can use the remote control to blow them open with dynamite. But I have to get close enough to plant it,' and he patted one of the bundles of sticks. 'That means going down to the processing bay and getting right up to the inside of the entrance gates; where the track comes into the factory.'

'I have to go the other way to get to the top of the factory,' said Chess. 'That's where the control room is.'

Firebras clicked abruptly and his nostrils flared. 'We must move swiftly. The army will be waiting to attack by now.'

'I'll go now, on my own, like we planned,' resolved Chess. 'I've seen the control room through the skulk rack. Once I'm in there it will be easy to release the children. And on my own I'm less likely to get caught.'

'OK,' agreed Box. 'We'll do the gate. After that we'll come up for you. If we can.'

They were trying to sound as positive as they could but when Box said, 'If we can,' Chess knew he meant, 'If we're still alive.'

Her hand dropped to Box's shoulder. Still kneeling, he squeezed it. 'Just keep going,' he reassured her. 'That's what we've been doing so far.'

'Well, let's get going then,' interrupted Splinter, 'and stop the heart-breaking farewells. You two have gone soft.'

Box ignored Splinter. He gave Chess a bright smile. 'Orange suits you,' he laughed.

'I've heard voices, Box. Children's voices,' Chess began to say but Box cut her short before she could become upset.

'You're special, Chess.' He smiled, still holding her hand. 'You're different from us two. You feel things and do things differently. You're different from everyone. You always have been only now it's obvious. You can do this, Chess.'

She nodded and took her hand from his shoulder. She could do this. All she had to do was get to the control room without being caught. 'Look after them, Firebras.'

Firebras bowed. 'With my life,' he promised.

Then Chess was gone.

Commander Javoz surveyed his battle lines. Left and right his army stretched across the head of the pass, facing the tall black wall at the foot of the volcano. Smog hid them from the sun and veiled the land in twilight. Smoke drifted across the face of the mountain with its alien lights and pipework. The slopes that enclosed the pass to their rear loomed out of the shifting mists before vanishing again so that the landscape seemed to change with the wind. Somewhere a ganuk snorted and stamped its foot. There was a clatter of falling rocks. Then there was silence.

Eight thousand infantry armed with pike and cutlass waited for the order to advance. Their white robes flapped in the wind but they stood still. Amongst the ranks of infantry were the siege towers. Each tower was roped to two ganuks, their mounted drivers also awaiting the command to advance. When the command was given there would be a creak of wood and the ropes would strain as the siege towers rolled forwards. Once they reached the walls, ladders would be dropped and grapples fixed to enable the infantry to breach the defences.

Behind the infantry and filling the pass were cavalry, mounted on ganuks and ready for the order to charge. Even in the gloom their ornate, plate armour was brilliant. Their spears were raised, fluttering with pennants.

The crossbowmen had taken positions in the mist-draped slopes flanking the pass, looking down onto the wall. They would be able to strike down any enemy troops who tried to defend it.

The catapults had been left at the ships. A final reconnaissance before the army had advanced that morning had convinced Ashadzi and Javoz that they would not be needed. A swift action over the walls with cavalry entering once a breach had been made would be best. The marine culverins had been manoeuvred up the pass and they flanked the cavalry, ready to fire once the walls had been taken and the infantry had moved clear.

Mounted on his ganuk, with Queen Ashadzi on her ganuk next to him, Javoz was at the centre of the front rank. They were seated in hard, leather saddles that were strapped between the beasts' shoulders and necks. Immediately behind them rode two standard bearers, one carrying a tall banner displaying a white sun against a blue background, the other carrying a tall banner displaying a red sun against black. The banners slapped in the wind. A short distance in front of the commander was the gateway. This was the only break in the smooth face of the wall. His mount shuffled its feet, irritated by a piece of the track that it was standing on.

The army had come into position swiftly and Javoz had seen no sign of defence. He closed his eyes and savoured the moment. The wind might blow and stones might fall but his great army stood strong and still, waiting on his command.

He tilted back his helmeted head and roared long and loud. He was answered by the roar of ten thousand stonedrakes. Then, at the cries of the ganuk drivers and the crack of their whips, the siege towers jolted forwards and advanced on the high wall that ran the breadth of the volcano.

Javoz and Ashadzi followed the infantry a short distance before halting and watching them move to the foot of the wall. That way, they were close enough to the attack to give commands but far enough back to see what was happening along the line.

As the infantry halted, an unusual noise surprised Javoz; a smooth humming that seemed to come from inside the wall but was loud enough to resonate throughout the air around them. Suddenly, sections at regular intervals along its top slid to one side and out of the gaps there rose narrow metal frames, vertical and almost as tall as the wall itself. There were as many as thirty of these crane-like structures and mounted on each was a black, metallic sphere the size of a ganuk's body. On the front of each sphere were four, short, steel-grey barrels.

In silence, everyone watched the strange machines.

The wall hummed and the metallic spheres rotated and spun on the tops of their frames like eyeballs until the clusters of barrels were aiming in a variety of directions; at the ganuks pulling the siege towers, into the infantry, at the crossbow squads, at the culverins.

In that moment, Ashadzi realized that they had underestimated their enemy, fatally.

With a grating whirr, the barrel clusters spun and a wave of explosive-tipped bullets raked the stonedrake army. The infantry were scythed down, ganuks bellowed and reared and crashed into the dust as shells ripped them, the siege towers splintered and burst into flame and the cliff-sides along the pass evaporated in a storm of flying stone and tumbling troops.

There was no break in the onslaught. The storm guns blazed at the stonedrakes, acquiring and destroying one target before switching immediately to the next. The air was a roar of wounded lizards, screaming ganuks and the buzz-rip of the guns.

Ashadzi struggled to control her mount. The cavalry had withdrawn at her order to the ravines in the pass but not all of them had been able to control the ganuks in the mayhem. Those that had stampeded forwards charged into the all-destroying fire of the storm guns.

Javoz was steering his ganuk from the wall when the earth erupted in a streak to his left. The streak rushed towards him, stone and dust kicking into the air and he knew that he would never see the bright sun again.

Ashadzi watched her commander fall in a blaze from one of the storm guns. Her infantry had been cut down before her eyes and were heaped amongst the remains of the siege towers at the foot of the black wall. A culverin fired but the solitary boom seemed feeble against the relentless buzz of the guns. They turned on the culverin which was torn to pieces in seconds.

Ashadzi whipped her ganuk towards the pass. It had taken less than two minutes for her infantry to be destroyed. The remaining cavalry were pinned down in the ravines and even now the tireless guns were shattering rocks and stone to get to them. She knew that unless the softskins opened the gate and gave them the chance to charge the wall, she and her soldiers would die in the pass.

Box led the way from the boiler room to the processing bay: he had memorized the directions that Chess had given. To his relief and his surprise, the corridors were empty and they sneaked along them undetected. Slipping through a pair of double doors, he saw that they had come to the corridor behind the cells that lined the processing bay, the corridor that he and Chess and Splinter had first escaped into when they had been brought to the factory many weeks ago.

It looked different now because all the cell doors were open, so the wall was lined by a series of gaping portals that ran left and right until the ends of the corridor curved out of sight. The cells were empty and the bars that led from them onto the platform were open also. Box could see the platforms and the dark gap between them where the track lay. The lights were dim. The place was still and thick with shadow.

As Splinter and Firebras joined him in the corridor, he heard a vibrating hum that resounded in a steady pulse through the murk. Combined with the constant rhythm of the hum were the distant echoes of dull crumps, like explosions but a long way off.

'We'll follow the corridor round as far as it goes,' said Box to Splinter quietly, and pointing left. 'Keep the cells on our right. That should take us towards the gates.'

They slunk through the gloom, staying close to the wall on the left with the open cells to their right, hugging the shadows and listening for the least noise. Box held the suitcase against his chest with both arms.

After they had left the double doors so far behind that he could no longer see them when he looked back, Box noticed a ruddy glow out on the platform. It flickered back and forth and grew brighter as they crept forwards. The spars of light streaked the platforms and the rock wall on their far side, dancing like spindly fingers.

They drew close to the source of the rippling light and smelt wood smoke. Then the corridor turned sharp left and into darkness.

'Now we'll have to follow the platform to get to the gates,' whispered Box. He pointed to the final opening on their right. 'The track must carry on out there, even if we've come to a dead end in here.'

Splinter and Firebras leant flat against the wall they had

been following: Splinter a white-faced slash of black, Firebras black-faced but white gown and bright armour catching the flickering light. Box poked his head round the edge of the opening to see the platform. He pulled it back, very quickly.

'Traders,' he mouthed to Splinter. Even though Firebras could detect what he was thinking, 'traders' meant nothing to him so Box told him silently, 'Enemy. Armed with spears.'

'How many?' asked Firebras.

Box held up two fingers.

He had seen a brazier on the platform, just beyond the cell. It was heaped with burning wood. Near to the brazier were two traders, one leaning on his spear and the other sitting on the edge of the concrete, legs hanging in the channel where the train track ran. Although the smouldering glow diluted the gloom unevenly, there was enough light for Box to see that the platform ended only yards from where the traders were lounging. Where the platform ended, the track reached the foot of the tall gates. Box hadn't seen any mechanism for opening them but that didn't matter. He possessed his own.

He could hear the traders talking in lazy grunts. It wasn't much of a conversation but Box's knowledge of Chat was sufficient to enable him to overhear snatches: 'The food is rubbish', 'I haven't been to the toilet in a week' and 'The dogs are smashing up the lizards.'

It was as he translated this last comment to himself that Box realized the significance of the explosions he had heard.

'We can't waste any more time,' he dared to whisper and then to Firebras he added, 'I think your soldiers are getting battered.'

'We must take the platform. Then you must open the gates,' switched Firebras.

Firebras inched his head round the opening to size up the traders for himself. His hand slid the scimitar from its sheath with only a whispering hiss of steel and he crouched back with his tail coiled behind him as if preparing to spring out. Then he was gone. But he didn't charge across the cell and onto the platform. Box was amazed to see him dart round the wall and up, onto the bars of the cage which he scaled in a flash until he was hanging upside down from the bars at the top. He clung to them by his clawed feet, his free arm and his tail. Then he scurried forwards, still upside down.

Box peered with one eye round the edge of the cell. The traders hadn't seen what was happening.

Firebras sprang from the cell bars and through the air. He removed the shaggy head from the shoulders of the standing trader with one swing of his scimitar even as he dived over him. He landed on his free hand which he used to vault onto his feet. As the second trader scrambled up, Firebras swept his feet away with a lash of his tail. The scimitar flashed again and another trader toppled, his decapitated head thudding to the concrete floor and rolling across it before vanishing over the edge of the platform.

Box ran towards Firebras and saw a third trader who had been out of view until now, creeping towards the stonedrake, spear in hand. He had an instant to think. As the spear was thrust forwards, he dropped the suitcase and charged into the trader, driving his shoulder into the trader's lower ribs. The spear thrust missed Firebras. Box and the trader tumbled over the lip of the platform and down to the track.

The trader had lost his grip on the spear which had clattered to the platform but he whipped a bone-handled knife from his boot as soon as he had regained his footing. The knife blade was long and curved like the fang of a sabre-toothed tiger and he held it in a stabbing grip and advanced on Box, thick shoulders hunched.

'Kill you, boy,' he grunted in Chat. 'Cut you up.'

Box did not panic and he did not lose his temper. He did what he had been taught. He assessed his opponent. He observed how the trader was tensed with legs bent, waiting to spring forwards and how his knife grip would commit him to one downward thrust. He calculated how best to invite the trader's attack and then launch his own counter-attack. And he did all of this in the time it took him to blink.

Splinter was watching from the shadows of the cell. He was shocked to see Box lurch forwards as if he hoped to rugby tackle the trader. It was a stupid attack because it was bound to leave his back exposed to the down-thrust of the trader's knife. The trader thought the same thing and charging towards Box, he committed himself to a savage blow, down between Box's shoulders.

With inches to go, Box pivoted on his left foot and jumped up, spinning backwards and bringing his right leg round and driving it into the back of the trader's head. The trader staggered forwards under the momentum of his own attack and Box's spinning hook kick. He tripped on the track and crashed to the floor. When he swayed to his feet, he was met by a jab to his nose from Box's right fist, a cross to his jaw from Box's left fist and a jumping roundhouse kick from Box's right foot to the side of his head.

The trader's knees buckled and he fell like a wooden post. As soon as Box stepped back, Firebras leapt from the platform onto the prone body and used his bare hands to twist the trader's head until his neck made a sound like crunching cabbage.

'You fight well,' switched Firebras.

'I've been taught well,' replied Box.

A lump of wood cracked in the fire, spitting sparks high into the air. The smoke curled to the ceiling. Box rolled onto the platform.

'Now for the gates,' he said to Splinter who was standing by the brazier, tall and spiky like a white-headed thistle. Splinter said nothing as Box retrieved the suitcase.

'What's up with you now?' Box asked.

'Just watching and thinking,' replied Splinter.

'You've become really weird,' said Box, dropping back down to the track. Then he paid his brother no more attention because he had work to do.

He ran with the suitcase to the place where the track ended at the inside of the factory gates. They were tall and solid and they joined flush and firm. Box pushed them, just to check, but it was like pushing the mountain itself.

The air still reverberated with the humming noise and the crash of explosions but much more loudly now. The noise came from the other side of the gateway.

'Hurry,' urged Firebras, who stood beside him.

'I know, I know,' repeated Box, flustered. He rested the suitcase on the rails and breathed slow and deep. Then he opened it.

'OK,' he said, 'time for the fireworks.'

CHAPTER 17

A crag of rock disintegrated as the cavalry captain slid down the slope to where Ashadzi had taken cover. The rounds from the storm guns continued to smack into the boulders that screened him, showering the hiding troops with splinters of stone. The bottom of the pass was strewn with the bodies of those who had been picked off.

'We lose more troops every minute,' the captain told Ashadzi. He had been sheltering down the pass from the queen and had reached her by negotiating a chasm in the rocks above her position, rather than attempting to run up the deadly valley bottom.

'The enemy's sky cannons are cutting away the rock at our position. The ganuks are panicking. If we do not escape my troop will be dead before the hour is out.' Although he switched, he was panting from his dash to the queen's position.

Ashadzi sensed the fear and the weariness in his thoughts. She was kneeling behind a jutting curtain of rock, hands resting on the jewelled pommels of her scimitars. Her ganuk lay with its legs tucked under its belly by her side. Behind her, more cavalry waited, lying low, backed into the ravine as far as they could go. The rest of the cavalry were squeezed into other ravines along the pass. The situation was desperate but she could not say that to her soldiers.

'Have your troops ready to charge, Captain,' said Ashadzi. 'The doors will soon be open. Then we attack. We will be able to cover the pass before their weapons can fire on us.'

The captain scrambled back to his troops, spreading the queen's orders as he went. Ashadzi leant back against the rock. She did not believe that the softskins would succeed in opening the gateway but that was the only thing that could save them now. She listened to the rattle of the storm guns and prayed.

It was as Box began to pile the bundles of dynamite against the bottom of the doors that they were spotted. A lone trader had appeared out of the murk of the dark corridor and seen the headless bodies of two of his comrades on the floor of the platform and a stranger standing by the brazier. He turned and ran back into the darkness.

'We've been seen,' hissed Splinter from where he stood by the burning wood. 'There'll be more of them coming. We'd better go.'

'But it isn't ready yet,' protested Box, leaning another bundle of dynamite against the place where the two tall doors of the gate met.

'They're coming,' warned Splinter and as if to show that he was right, stark electric light flooded the processing bay. Box blinked in the glare and heard shouts and the sound of boots thumping towards them from the corridor that had been in darkness.

Splinter shifted from the brazier and began to move back up the platform and away from the gate. 'Come on, Box,' he persisted. 'I'm going. If you don't they'll get you.'

'*Jander*,' muttered Box and he yanked the suitcase upside down so that everything fell out of it in a heap at the foot of the gateway. He stuffed a radio detonator into the small mound of explosive and kept hold of the remote control. Looking left he saw a gang of traders running up the corridor that was now clearly lit, towards him. They had spears ready to throw or stab and their long legs carried them swiftly. From behind them came barking shouts and growls and Box saw the black uniforms of Dog Troopers.

He nodded at Firebras. 'Come on, let's go.'

'What about the gate?' The stonedrake looked as if he was prepared to stay and fight every trader and every trooper who was heading their way.

Box held up the remote control. 'This will do it. When I press the switch it triggers the detonator inside that lot and the whole load will blow. But we have to get a safe distance away. This is going to be one hell of a bang.'

Firebras dropped to all fours and roared at the advancing traders. They stopped short, but only for a moment. Then they hollered and charged. Box started to run up the track. Splinter was on the platform a little way ahead; his limp slowed him down.

Running up the tracks was difficult so Box stopped to clamber onto the platform, looking back down the tunnel as he did so. The area close to the gate was thronging with traders and troopers but nobody was coming after them.

'They're going to shift the explosive,' observed Splinter. 'If you don't blow it now it'll be too late.'

'We're too close,' said Box. They were about seventy metres from the gate. 'At this range the blast will be dangerous.'

Splinter shrugged his narrow shoulders. 'Only trying to be helpful,' he said.

But Box realized that he didn't have a choice. If he didn't fire the detonator now, the busy figures at the far end of the platform would move the small heap of explosives.

He switched on the control and pressed the button. Nothing happened. He pressed it again. Nothing. He kept pressing, jabbing the button harder each time as if that would make a difference.

'Did you activate the detonator at the other end?' enquired Splinter.

Box clapped his hand over his forehead. In the rush to get away from the gate he had forgotten to prime the detonator. That meant it would never pick up the signal from the control he was pressing. Which meant that the explosives in front of the gate were useless.

'Typical,' sneered Splinter.

And then something happened that Box had not expected. In the press of activity at the far end of the platform a clumsy trader reversed into the brazier. The iron bucket tottered and crashed over, spilling flaming brands of wood across the platform. They rebounded on the concrete and kicked out a shower of sparks like a Roman candle. Some of the sparks landed on the pile of dynamite.

The hullabaloo of the traders stopped dead. All eyes turned to the foot of the gate as first one bundle of dynamite and then the next fizzed into life. There was a pause. Box wondered whether the explosive would really work and if it did, whether it would be powerful enough.

Then he was face down on the concrete floor and his ears were pinging and rubble was raining down on his back and all around him. He didn't dare to move until the last chunk of stone had finished bouncing down the platform. Then he rolled over and sat up, hardly daring to look at his arms and legs for fear of what injuries he may have.

He saw no wounds and apart from the ringing in his ears he felt all right. Next to him, rock and plaster stirred and first Splinter and then Firebras rose from the debris. Splinter had a cut above his right eyebrow. The thin, dark laceration was crusted with grit and dust but not bleeding heavily. Firebras was uninjured.

'We're OK,' sighed Box with relief, 'unlike everything else. What a bang!'

The tunnel had been transformed. Not far from where they had been thrown by the explosion, the concrete and iron had been ripped apart by the blast and the damage grew steadily worse until the place where the gate had been. Now, instead of the high doors, there was a gaping arch fringed with jagged stone and twisted metal. Daylight poured into the tunnel, bright despite the pall of smoke that filled the sky above the volcano. The platforms were either lost beneath shattered chunks of rock and concrete or they were cracked and uneven like a broken ice floe. The iron bars of the cells were mangled and the train track was buried under rubble. There was no sign of the traders or troopers because none had survived.

As his hearing returned, Box became aware of the shouts of fresh troopers who were emerging from the openings of the wrecked cells near to the breach in the wall at the end of the tunnel. They scrambled over rock and metal, unslinging their blaze carbines and taking up defensive positions down what remained of the platforms and in the rubble that had collected over the track. Some of them worked quickly in pairs, setting up long muzzled, double-barrelled machine guns that were mounted on low-spread tripods. The gunners climbed into bucket seats at the rear, taking hold of the twin pistol grips in both hands. All weapons were trained on the opening at the end of the tunnel.

'What are they doing now?' asked Splinter who could not see why the Dog Troopers were getting ready to fight.

The tunnel was full of dust that clogged mouth and eyes. Box tried to see what was happening through the open gateway; why so many troopers had come to defend the breach. All he could see was dust. But he heard a rumbling that grew louder and louder.

Firebras rammed his fists to the floor, knotted his shoulders and thrust forwards his head as he roared. 'My people are coming.'

Ashadzi and her cavalry had been ready. When the pass echoed with a thunderous boom and a pillar of rock and smoke erupted high into the air from the place where the gates had been, they charged. The storm guns that covered the approach had been demolished. The flanking guns turned on the juggernaut-column of ganuks but they galloped so fast and there was such confusion that the head of the column was plunging into the gaping breach before the guns could start their work.

Leading the charge was Ashadzi. She leant forwards so that her body was shielded by the mighty head and neck of her mount. On either side of her rode a cavalry captain, heading his troop. The earth shuddered beneath the pounding feet of such a weight of fast-moving, heavy cavalry. As she charged through the broken gateway, she told her captains what they had to do.

The Dog Troopers had only just got into position when the first of the stonedrake cavalry hurtled through the wall. Fingers squeezed triggers and there was a crackle of gunfire. The queen's ganuk steamrollered over the rubble where the track had been, tree trunk legs crushing troopers. More fire from the blaze carbines and machine guns brought the beast down. But before it had fallen, Queen Ashadzi drew both her scimitars and, freeing her feet from the stirrups, she sprang from the charging ganuk and landed on the tunnel wall. As the falling ganuk smashed into the Dog Troopers, Ashadzi sprinted, zig-zagging along the blast-scarred rock and up onto the ceiling.

Close behind her came hundreds more lizards, ploughing into the tunnel, leaping from their mounts as soon as they crossed the threshold and star-bursting over the walls and roof. The Dog Troopers were unable to hold back the assault. Blaze carbines and machine guns pumped out rounds but the ricocheting bullets were as lethal to the troopers as they were to the stonedrakes.

Now the walls and roof of the tunnel were covered in a swiftly crawling mass of stonedrakes. Then, as one, they dived into the Dog Troopers and the fighting was desperate and bloody. It was too close for gunfire so it was scimitar and cutlass against mace-blade. The tunnel walls rang with the clash of steel against steel and leading the way was Ashadzi, scimitars flashing like sickles as she made the Dog Troopers pay for what they had done to her people.

'If the enemy didn't know we were here before, they will now,' said Box as more troopers ran onto the platform and the stonedrakes fought their way up the tunnel. 'We have to find Chess.'

Firebras read Box's thoughts. 'I'll stay with you.' He clicked with satisfaction at the battle that was rolling towards them like a train.

'We're all right,' Box told him. 'The fighting's all here. Chess is right at the top.'

'No. My duty is to protect you until this is over.'

There was no more time to debate the matter. They would be in the thick of the fighting if they didn't move now.

'We're going to find Chess,' Box explained to Splinter.

'She says she'll be OK,' said Splinter.

'Well, I hope she's right,' Box replied and he hurried through the nearest cell and into the corridor beyond. Firebras ran with him. Splinter was the last to leave the platform. Before he did so he cast about and his eyes settled on a short length of iron that had been torn from one of the cells and now was jutting out of the debris. He pulled it free and took it with him.

'What's that for?' Box asked him when he emerged into the flickering electric light of the corridor.

'A weapon,' replied Splinter.

'You've already got two knives,' observed Box, 'how many weapons do you need?'

Splinter responded with the knowing smile that he had cultivated.

'When all of this is over,' growled Box, 'I'm going to sort you out.' Then he led the way up to the double doors.

He had spent enough time talking with Chess to know where to go. The control room was right at the top of the factory and could be reached by a central stairwell. However, there were also stairwells at the ends of the main corridors that ran across the centre of the factory on each level. Box decided that it would be safest to find the nearest main corridor and then take the stairs at the opposite side of the factory from where the Dog Troopers and the stonedrakes were fighting.

The lights had been flickering since the explosion and now the corridors were webbed with shadow. It was difficult to see what lay ahead.

Box traced the way back to the main corridor and then took Firebras and Splinter to the stairwell at the far end. It climbed into darkness.

'Can you make it to the top, peg leg?' Box asked Splinter.

'Only if the stairs don't collapse under the weight of your fat head,' replied Splinter, tossing the iron bar in his hand.

'Your brother is very odd,' Firebras switched with Box. 'If he were not your brother I would not trust him. I would watch him more closely.'

'He's all right,' Box answered, but Firebras could tell that Box was not as sure about Splinter as he tried to sound.

They ascended the stairs in silence even though they seemed to be alone. When they reached the top the light was very dim and Box could not see back down to the bottom. He stopped to catch his breath. Next to him was a door that should open into a corridor which would take them to the final staircase; the stairs to the control room. Chess would be waiting there. Hopefully, she would have released the captive children. Then she would press the VAP and they would go home.

The thought of going back sent a spark of excitement through Box; not because there was anything good about going back but because there was plenty bad about where he was. All they had to do was find Chess.

They crept through the door and into a passage that was deep in shadow. Wan, yellow lights flickered and buzzed inside metal cages on the ceiling. They emitted a feeble light that seemed only to make the darkness darker. Box's hand dropped to the handle of the knife at his waist and he stooped slightly as he led the way. He scried the gloom for the final staircase and after what felt like a mile of slinking beside the stone wall a flight of stairs loomed out of the murk like the stern of a ship seen in a foggy harbour. He let out a tight, shallow breath. They had made it.

But then he heard something that turned his guts to water; the thud of a pair of heavy boots on stone and the clink of chains. It came from the dark space under the stairs and it was approaching them. Box stopped dead in his tracks with Splinter and Firebras right behind him. They waited.

From out of the shadows came the tall, cloaked figure of General Saxmun Vane. He walked towards them slowly, a deep growl grating from the back of his throat, black lips thin on his jackal snout. His gloved hand drew the baton from his belt and he released the long steel spike as he advanced.

Box stood still, not because he was brave but because he didn't know what to do. His thoughts scrambled and then fell into place. The General had been waiting for them as if he was guarding something. Guarding the stairs. He was there to stop anyone from going up the stairs, to stop them from going up to Chess. He was there to make sure that Chess was on her own in the control room. If it was just a control room. What was up there? What had been waiting for Chess?

Where was the Inquisitor?

'What's in that room, Splinter?' whispered Box. 'What's happening to Chess?'

Silence, apart from the crack of the General's boots, the clunk of his armour and his raw growl.

'They've got her, Splinter. We've let them get Chess.'

His shoulder was gripped hard and he was pulled backwards. Firebras stepped in front of him and drew his scimitar in a smooth sweep.

'Go to your sister,' Firebras told him. 'Help her. I will stand and fight.' Then he leant forwards, the knuckles of one hand against the floor and he filled the corridor with his searing battle-cry.

There was no time for Box to switch in reply because General Vane was upon them. With a snarl he swung his mace-blade hard at Firebras's face. Firebras blocked with his sword but the spike clanged the scimitar aside with an elbow-cracking jolt. Firebras retreated under the weight of the blow and parried another that speared at his chest.

No matter how quickly Firebras moved, even when he backed up and onto the wall, the mace-blade was ahead of him, the General coolly anticipating every move he made, every attack he tried to launch.

'Go,' switched Firebras. Box read the thought that for the first time in his life, the lizard champion was facing an opponent whom he would not defeat. But still Firebras confronted General Vane, fending off the powerful blows from the mace-blade. The passageway resounded with clashing steel.

Firebras dropped from the wall to the floor and swung the scimitar high at the General's head. The General parried with the mace-blade, and with unexpected speed spun away from the stonedrake whilst driving the long spike backwards. Box saw the metal tip disappear into the gap above Firebras's chest plate. Firebras stepped back and blocked the General's next blow, but now Box could see blood pumping from the lizard's neck even as he fought. It was a mortal wound.

'Come on,' Box urged Splinter who was watching the duel with delight. 'This is all going wrong. We have to find Chess.'

'Sure,' said Splinter. 'You lead the way. I'll follow.'

Box ran towards the stairs. Splinter followed him, iron bar in hand. But just before they mounted the steps, he struck Box hard across the back of the head with the bar. Box folded and dropped to the floor like a log, senseless.

'Idiot,' sneered Splinter.

Then Splinter worked quickly.

He darted to the space under the stairs and then followed the wall of the passage until he found what he wanted. There was a door in the wall and behind the door there was a shallow closet stacked with buckets, tools and rope. In the half-light, Splinter knelt and found a space at the back of the alcove. Then, out of habit, he looked about to check that nobody was watching.

If anybody had been there to watch, they would have seen something very curious. They would have seen Splinter dip his hand into one of the inside pockets of his long-tailed morning coat and pull out a small wooden box. They would have seen him place the box on the floor in the back corner of the closet and open the lid.

A finger of smoke curled out. There was a silver glow. Splinter hurried back to where his brother lay on the floor at the foot of the steps. He hoisted Box's body over his shoulder.

Hump-backed, like a crane fly carrying a sack of loot, Splinter sneaked through the shadows to the closet and stepped inside. He slipped one foot into the opening of the box. It accommodated the foot and the rest of the leg easily, despite its apparent size. Then he pulled his other long, black-trousered leg behind him and onto the glowing, swirling vapours.

If anybody had been there to watch, they would have seen Splinter's body slip into the box with his brother still slung over his shoulder. They would have seen the lid of the box flip shut behind him. Then they would have seen nothing but a signature of mist and a little wooden casket in the shadows at the back of the closet.

CHAPTER 18

Chess put her hand against the control room door and pushed gently. It opened smoothly. She walked inside. The door slammed behind her.

This was not what she had been expecting. There were no banks of television screens showing children in cells and there was no desk with controls to open them.

The room was almost empty and was lit by a light so bright that it made her feel as if she was under a microscope. The walls and ceiling were domed and made entirely of glass. Through the glass she could see a churning grey smog that seemed to press in on all sides. Around the edge of the room the floor was made of steel. In the centre of the room the floor was glass and it was circular. This glass was a luminous kaleidoscope of reds and yellows and oranges like a disc of fire.

At the centre of this disc stood a desk, wide and glass-topped with a tubular steel frame. On the desk there was an angle-poise lamp, a sheaf of papers and a computer. Behind the desk there was a swivel chair and in the chair there was a man.

The man had black hair that was slicked back. He wore a crisp white shirt, open at the neck with the cuffs rolled up to his elbows, a pair of blue braces and slate-grey trousers. His face was pallid and lean and his lips were thin and mauve.

'I've been waiting for you, kid. What kept you?' the man said as soon as the door had shut. He stood up and held out his right hand. 'My name is Behrens. Pleased to meet you, at last.'

'Behrens!' gasped Chess. Her heart lurched against her ribs. Balthazar had said that there were five Inquisitors and their names were Azgor, Malbane, Veer, Snargis, and Behrens.

What have I done? thought Chess. Shock clenched every muscle in her body, draining the strength from it. She ignored the proffered hand and stayed where she had halted on the steel ring of floor.

'Where are the television screens? Where are the children?' was all she could say.

'Come on kid, you're smarter than that.' Behrens smiled and walked round from behind the desk. He wore brilliantly shiny patent leather shoes and they clicked on the glass as he walked. 'What do you *think* has happened to the children?'

Chess shook her head. 'I saw them, on the screens, in here.'

'You saw them through the skulk rack,' Behrens corrected her. 'You should never trust what you see through a skulk rack. Surely Balthazar told you that? When you've been in this game as long as I have, kid, you learn a few tricks; bluff, counter-bluff, double counter-bluff, that sort of thing. Trust no one. And trust your dreams least of all: you never know who might be listening in. The truth is, you were so hard to catch I decided you'd have to come to us. Which you have done. Thanks,' and he flashed her a perfect set of teeth by way of a smile.

'But the children . . .' Chess began to say. Her heart was thumping.

'There are no children. Not now. What's left of them is here,' and Behrens tapped the flaming disc with the toe of his shoe. 'All their suffering, all their pain.'

The inside of the disc swirled with flame and Chess realized that it was not a disc at all. It was the top of the cylinder that they had seen in the boiler room. So the cylinder must have run like a core through the middle of the factory, from the bottom all the way to the top.

'What have you done?' asked Chess, her voice cracking.

'Hey!' Behrens held up his hands. 'Take it easy, kid. You're called Chess, right? Funny, you're smaller than I expected. And prettier. Listen, Chess, I'm going to be straight with you. Really straight. I guess you've been told a lot of stuff about me, about my brethren, about the Twisted Symmetry.' He said 'Twisted Symmetry' in a mock-spooky voice and he smiled reassuringly. 'But I bet there are plenty of things you haven't been told; things you want to know but no one will tell you.'

Chess tried not to let Behrens see he was right. She looked down at the steel floor.

'Well, unlike everyone else who's been giving you half the story, I'm going to tell it straight. OK?'

Chess kept her head down. 'You're evil,' she muttered.

'Yeah,' replied Behrens, 'I'm evil. What we do is wrong. How's that for honesty, kid? But who's calling me evil? Who's sent you here and nearly got you killed? Who's hidden the truth from you and who's talking straight now? Look at me, Chess.'

Chess lifted her chin even though she didn't want to. Behrens walked towards her and stuffed his hands into his trouser pockets. He stopped at the edge of the glass floor, facing her.

'We need the children for their essence, Chess, their energy. We have to extract it from them; we do that in the scream rooms. Sorry about the name, but why lie? But the raw energy is useless. We need it in a form that can be used *everywhere*.' As he said 'everywhere' he spread open one hand and Chess was hurtling forwards and backwards and inside and out at once. Behrens snapped his hand shut and she rushed back to the point where she'd been standing. 'We're talking *all* time, *all* space. Like the way I did that?'

Chess shook her head and kept her mouth clamped shut. She had felt the same nausea when Ethel had first met them and reversed time.

'It's geometry, kid: strictly non-Euclidean. The raw energy has to be fused with this stuff called amarantium.'

'Crystal,' mouthed Chess.

'Hey! Are you working for us already?' Behrens flashed another easy smile. 'This factory is packed with atom smashers, particle accelerators, colliders, the lot. We ship the crystal in and fuse it with the raw energy. You know what that means? Energy plus crystal means BOOM! Everywhere. All time. This is big science, Chess.'

-[293]-

He pointed downwards. 'Our stockpile of these cylinders could fill a small planet. But this is a three-stage process; extraction, fusion and delivery. The problem is, we're still working on delivery. But once we get there, like I said; BOOM!'

'That's why the Committee have to fight you and beat you.' Chess tried to keep her voice steady, tried not to show fear.

'The Committee?' chuckled Behrens. 'That's one of Mevrad's ideas, I bet. She's always inventing names. Yeah, we fight them, whatever they call themselves. They fight us. There are two sides to every story, Chess.'

'What you do is evil,' Chess accused him.

Behrens shrugged. 'Sure, it's evil, if that's what you call evil. But we need this evil to survive, just like you guys need to kill plants or animals for food. We can't help that: neither can you. So where's the evil?'

Chess wanted to reply, to tell him he was wrong, but she couldn't think quickly enough. And what he said sounded honest and logical, even if it wasn't right.

'The universe is broken, Chess. All we want to do is fix it; take it back to the original moment with all its beauty, all its balance, and keep it there. That's why we need the energy and that's why we need to deliver it *everywhere*.'

'So *you* can live forever?' Chess wanted Behrens to know that she understood this much.

'Do you blame us? No one wants to die, kid. Or are you the exception?'

Chess didn't want to agree but Behrens's words snared her in their logic. 'No,' she said, louder than she needed to.

'Then you're no different from us. Let me get to the point, Chess. We want you. We want you on our side. Do you know why? Have any of your new friends cared to tell you, to let you in on the secret?'

Chess shook her head.

'Typical,' said Behrens, as if Chess had been wickedly betrayed by everybody. He ran his hand through his brilliantined hair.

Chess hazarded a guess. 'The Eternal. You need me to help you find the Eternal.'

Behrens nodded. 'Good, Chess. Yes. Exactly. You're smart, see, like I expected. We do need the Eternal. We need you to help us get it. Now, answer me this; what is Mevrad doing for you? She sent you, right? What's she going to give you?' When Chess raised her eyebrows, Behrens said, 'A big fat nothing, baby. Zero. You risk everything; you get nothing. Not much of a deal is it? Not for you, anyway.

'Now, straight up, what can I offer you? How about some proper clothes? A leather jacket and a pair of trainers maybe? After all, life's not a fancy dress party and you're not a stonedrake. What about somewhere nice to live? Family? You need family, Chess. You *deserve* family. We can do that for you, and more. You know I'm telling you the truth. I'm only offering you what you should have.'

Chess told herself that something horrible was hiding behind Behrens's tender smile, that his taut lips were still as cruel as when she had first seen them, that she didn't want anything from him. But she wasn't sure. This was not what she had expected. What was right and what was wrong had been clear before Behrens had started talking. She could feel herself sliding from certainty to a place where the only certainties lay in what Behrens said. A place where she would let him take control. She forced herself to look away from his searching eyes.

'Can you remember your mother, Chess? How she held you, what she felt like? It's not there is it? I bet you've even forgotten her face?'

But with that, Behrens had said too much. Chess looked up into his flint-hard eyes and saw a creature that dealt in death and destruction, a creature that tore the spirit from children to satisfy its own craving for life. Steady as granite, she said, 'I remember her voice.'

'You want more than a voice, Chess. We can give you a life that is more than a memory.'

'No,' said Chess. A steel corridor; terror; screams. 'You can't give me anything.'

Behrens changed. His gaunt cheekbones seemed to knuckle more densely under his eyes, his face looked longer and his mauve lips darkened and drew downwards, revealing his lower teeth.

He stepped from the glass circle onto the metal floor, towards Chess. Chess backed away. He spat words at her like they were poison.

'You think you have a choice? You think you can withstand me? You think you can withstand the Symmetry?'

His voice had changed too. It kept slipping into a much louder, much deeper voice; a voice that sounded like earth cracking at the bottom of the ocean. A voice that had been trying to stay hidden, until now.

Chess shook her head, retreating all the time. 'No, no,

I just don't want ...' but a blow from the back of the Inquisitor's hand sent her sprawling to the floor. She scrambled to her feet. Her right cheek was stinging and she could taste blood in her mouth. The Inquisitor reached towards her. His fingers stretched and kept stretching, wriggling and slithering through the air. Chess turned to run but the tentacle-fingers gripped her hair tight.

The Inquisitor pulled and Chess was dragged backwards, legs kicking. He drew her up by her hair until the back of her head was against his chest and her face was next to his mouth.

'I don't care if I have to let the mind feelers dissect your brain. You will help us.' He threw her across the floor and into the front of the desk as if he were tossing a doll. Chess crashed to the floor. The Inquisitor loomed over her. 'You don't know what you are dealing with,' he said. 'And I have been too patient.'

A crash of metal slammed him out of unconsciousness and Box opened his eyes. His head felt as if Plan B had exploded inside it; it pulsed painfully and he felt sick. He seemed to be suspended in mid-air and it was only when he looked to his side and saw the metal grille of the mortice-gate rotating slowly like a never-ending wheel that he realized where he was.

'What have you done, Splinter?' He sat up, blinking in the vast nothingness of the vortex.

Splinter sat beside him, his arms clasped around his skinny legs which were drawn up to his chin. 'It isn't easy, being in charge.' His voice rose and fell tremulously. 'All the time, I have to decide what to do. I had to bring us here, Box. I'm sorry about your head but it was an emergency. It was no longer safe to be in the factory so I've hidden us both in the vortex.'

Box gawped. 'Are you mad?'

Splinter's voice hardened. 'Not mad, Box. Clever. Very, very clever. And as usual, where would you be without me?'

'Not stuck in the middle of nowhere.'

'It's natural that you should be frightened,' acknowledged Splinter with a note of lofty disdain in his voice now. 'You don't understand these things and probably you never will.' Then his eyes flashed and he began to gabble. 'You see, Box, I'm special. I can do special things. I took the old hag's casket and kept it with me because I knew I would find out how to use it. All those hours I spent in Broom the loon's library have been put to very good use. I learnt the password for the mortice-gate. It wasn't easy. I had to practically squeeze it from the Omnicon, but I did it. Do you remember the day you were all looking for me?'

Splinter laughed in a way that made Box want to edge away. 'What a bunch of cretins. You'd never have found me. I was inside the vortex and exploring. My first time.'

'Take me back, Splinter. Now,' demanded Box.

But Splinter was listening only to himself. 'From here you can travel to anywhere in the universe, Box, even to different times. You just have to know where to go. I'd only just started to explore properly when those stupid reptiles kidnapped us. That's when I lost the tesseract; it fell out of my pocket. But if we're very, very careful, we can still use the reachings.'

Box stretched out an arm and dipped his hand into the colourless vapours which surrounded them. As soon as his fingers began to dissolve into space, he pulled them back and pressed them against his chest to reassure himself that they were whole.

'And I learnt more from the Omnicon,' Splinter was saying. 'I learnt about the Symmetry, Box. All kinds of things. Things that the old lady never told us, things that Broom never told us. The Symmetry are very powerful, Box. Much too powerful for anyone to beat. But the thing is, the more I found out, the more I realized that they may be right about a lot of things.'

'You *are* mad,' said Box, quietly.

'No, listen, Box. I've been thinking. The Symmetry could do things for us. I bet that anything you wanted, you could have. But if you stand against them you're dead.' Splinter's voice changed again. Now it was hard and aggressive. 'I'm telling you, Box, we have a choice to make. I think we've been tricked into joining the wrong side. The Symmetry could help us. They could be good for us.'

'Listen, you maniac,' shouted Box. 'There's nothing good about the Twisted Symmetry. And the only person who needs help right now is Chess. Remember? She's stuck in that room with whatever was waiting for her. I'd strangle you for hitting me with that bar but I need you to take me back. So take me back. Now.'

'Chess, Chess, Chess,' wheedled Splinter. 'Everybody's so obsessed with Chess. If she's so special she can look after herself.'

'She's your sister,' shouted Box.

'So?' sneered Splinter. 'So?'

'So help her.'

Splinter smiled his superior, knowing smile. 'No, Box. She wanted to be so important; she can face the consequences. She may be my sister but she's selfish and weak and she deserves everything she gets. Only people who are strong and clever deserve to survive. People like me.'

Then Splinter felt something sharp dig into the skin under his ribs. Box spoke calmly into his ear. 'Take me back, Splinter, or this knife goes all the way. I'm not joking. I don't care if I have to slab you and stay here for eternity. We're not sitting here and leaving Chess. Take me back. Now.'

As soon as Chess landed on the glass she heard the voices. They rushed through her like a wind, screaming in a raw blast. She needed to think and she tried to push them out of her mind. When she lifted her face from the glass and looked up she saw that the Inquisitor was staring down.

One of his hands rested on the desk and looked perfectly normal to the ends of its neatly manicured nails. The other hung by his side and the fingers stretched to the luminous floor where they trailed across the glass like eels. His head was longer than it had been at first and his eyes were bigger and rounder and absolutely black like the eyes of a shark. He breathed heavily and watched her without blinking.

Chess sensed that she was looking at something hard and cold and empty; something that was mercilessly void of sympathy. She closed her eyes because looking into Behrens's was like falling, fast and forever.

Putting a hand on the desk, she pulled herself to her feet. All the time the children's voices were coming at her, filling her head. But when she stood up on the glass she felt a bolt of energy crack through both her feet and out of the back of her skull. Her bones crunched and she was in the scream room, watching the shapes in the green light that were coming for her, reaching her hand towards a little round window, screaming herself. The vision left her as quickly as it had burst in her mind and she was back in the domed room. Her legs buckled from the blast of energy and she dropped to her knees in front of the Inquisitor, her ears full of voices.

Without lifting the long hand from his side, the Inquisitor gripped her round the neck by snaking fingers that had grown even longer. The fingers extended further and Chess was lifted up until her feet were clear of the floor and her face was level with the his. She gulped for air.

She thought that she was passing out because it looked as if Behrens's bottom jaw had come unhinged from the rest of his head and was floating down to his chest, leaving a black space in-between. But she wasn't hallucinating. The detached jaw was drifting lower and the rest of his head started to tip back. It kept tipping backwards until all Chess could see was an open black gullet topped by an arc of white teeth.

Then, with a hiss, darkness poured from the gaping head. It was a billowing, inky blackness that blotted everything it touched. With the darkness came fear, cold, despair, loneliness. Chess knew these feelings, her life had been full of them but they had never been as crushing as this onslaught. The room was vanishing around her and the darkness ate deeper, making her weaker.

'Not this,' gasped Chess. 'Please, not this.'

Behrens squeezed her throat. She could hear blood pumping in her ears and the torrent of children's voices. The long fingers tightened. She reached inside herself to find something, anything that could give her the strength to fight back. She raced through thoughts and memories but her mind was slipping away.

Then she heard the singing. It was far off at first but when she called, it came to her, bold and loud. She clung to the voice and it wrapped itself around her spirit. But it was singing to the slowing beat of her heart. Her last thoughts flickered like jumbled snap shots; a green room; Box hanging; Gemma crying out; their pain and her rage; a gift handed to her beneath a storm-split sky and Balthazar's words: 'Sometimes the darkness destroys itself.'

Behrens squeezed: windpipe closing, the final, sinking thud in her chest, consciousness blotting out. But the voice sang and suddenly it all connected; the pain, the energy, the darkness that destroyed itself. There was a way to fight.

The time had come for the children to be set free.

Chess let go of the memory: the song stopped. As Behrens choked the last of the light from her, her fingers crawled drunkenly inside her jacket. They closed on the cold handle of the crystal knife. Then, falling under its own weight, her arm plunged down.

She thought she had missed because the dagger moved so smoothly but then she felt her own hand thump onto cold flesh. The amarantium blade had pierced the back of the

Inquisitor's hand and driven through the glass top of the table, pinning it there.

The reaction was instantaneous. The fingers uncoiled from Chess's throat and she was dropped to the glass floor. The Inquisitor's body whip-cracked away from the table but the blade held him firm. His open head snapped shut crookedly and he roared through a face that was stretched and twisted. The tentacle-fingers lashed themselves around his pinioned wrist to wrench it from the table but no amount of pulling could tear it free.

He began to transform into human, animal, rock, gas, spirit, fire, noise, the changes coming more and more rapidly as he sought a form that could release him from the knife. But there was no escape from the crystal blade. The Inquisitor returned to his part-human form. Two of the snaking fingers encircled the hilt of the knife and tugged it up. The blade moved slightly. He howled with agony as the pain seared his body but he kept tugging at the knife, easing it up from the table and out of the back of his hand.

Chess did not see what he was doing; she was not looking. When the Inquisitor had dropped her to the floor her legs had crumpled and her body thudded onto the glass. Immediately the voices broke upon her but this time she did not resist them. She let them fill her mind as she crawled to her feet, flames swirling beneath her, flaring bright.

Shocks of power surged up and through her, jerking her spine to breaking point. And now she was there, inside the scream rooms; she saw what happened to the children and it was happening to her, over and over again. The glass floor cracked, her mind reeled and her body was bursting as the column of energy rushed into her, but she absorbed it all.

With a gasp, the Inquisitor pulled the knife free. He swung round to face Chess. Knife in hand, squid-like fingers writhing, he opened wide a cavern of a mouth and came for her.

Chess focused all the energy that filled her and concentrated it at him. As Behrens closed on her she released the children.

For a moment a wave of darkness rose to break upon her but then her arms flung apart and the power burst from her. The Inquisitor was engulfed in a blinding-white whirlpool. Within the brilliant cyclone he fought back, spinning darkness. Now a pillar of light and dark twisted high into the air and the energy roared from the cylinder and through Chess.

Chess was showered with glass as the disc beneath her feet and the dome above her head shattered simultaneously. Her body was wracked as the spirit of every child who had vanished in the scream rooms hurtled through her and streamed into the pillar where light and dark battled into the sky.

I am going to die, she thought.

It felt as if she was being crushed and torn apart at the same time, so that every bone in her body was snapping and her brain was being shaken from her head. Then she felt her body go limp, as if she were a marionette whose strings had just been cut. She was suspended in the energy that poured from the cylinder. She looked up and saw the column of light and dark twisting high and out of sight, into the churning clouds, like a tornado.

Suddenly the column collapsed, as if it had been sucked inwards. All that remained was a speck of bright light that was no bigger than a pea. It hovered in the air a couple of inches in front of Chess's face.

There was total silence.

Then a shrill scream tore through the world and the tiny ball of light burst wide in a flat ring, crushing glass, ripping metal, levelling rock and hurling Chess across the space that had once been the room.

Somebody was shaking her shoulder.

'Chess, Chess.' It was Box.

She opened her eyes. She was lying in the sky on a narrow strip of buckled metal that was the only remaining piece of the floor. Nothing more of the room was left. The metal was connected to the girders below by a mangled set of stairs. Beneath her was a battered shell of what had been walls and corridors and below that was rock that the blast had not destroyed, still containing the lower levels of the factory. To have moved two feet in any direction would have been to roll into oblivion.

Patches of charcoal-grey smoke drifted in the wind. The ragged swathes of smoke no longer masked the violet of evening. Night began to fall and the factory smog vanished like a whisper, leaving a red sun that was swollen and heavy and hanging low over the jagged-backed mountains.

Box was kneeling on the top step. Behind him stood Splinter, arms folded, face like a stab of ice.

'You're all right?' asked Chess. They were easy words to

think, but she slurred them when she spoke: it was an effort to talk. She felt very weak.

'We were sheltering, in a way,' explained Box. Splinter said nothing. 'When we came out we found all of this. Anyway, forget that; are *you* all right? You've cut your face and your hand is a real mess, Chess. Don't look.'

'Firebras?' asked Chess. She swallowed hard because her throat was so dry it felt like she was talking through hot sand.

Box shook his head. 'General Vane was waiting for us. Firebras fought him so that we could get to you. Down there.' Box motioned down the mangled remains of the stairs. 'He was really brave Chess. There's nothing else I can say.'

Chess bit her lip and felt her eyes sting. Now that Box had told her about her hand she could feel a fiery sensation at the end of her right wrist. She turned her head away so that she wouldn't see what was there.

'What about the Inquisitor?' asked Box.

'Gone,' was all that Chess said and Box asked no more.

Splinter cleared his throat as if he was going to speak but then said nothing.

'We can go home now,' said Chess.

Box nodded and he spoke to Splinter. 'You, up here, where I can see you.'

Splinter squeezed round Box and knelt by Chess. He placed his hand on her shoulder. Box, who was kneeling slightly behind Splinter, rested his hand on the back of Splinter's neck.

'OK,' said Box, 'Everybody touching each other? Good. Take us home, Chess.'

She felt for the VAP. It was on her right wrist where Ethel had fastened it. It was slippery to touch. Blood. Box had said her hand was a real mess and it hurt. She didn't look at it. She felt for the two small buttons, one on either side of the slim, circular face of the device.

'Ready?' she asked.

'Ready,' replied Box. Splinter nodded and he stared into Chess's eyes with a look she had not seen before; a sad, searching kind of look. She returned his gaze, suddenly confused although she didn't know why. Then she pressed the buttons.

Instantly the factory and its surroundings shifted out of focus and she was surrounded by figures in battle dress who bristled with rocket launchers, machine guns and communication equipment, just as Ethel had said they would. There was a time when Chess would have been astounded at how they came to be in the air around her, but now she knew that they were crossing from their dimension into hers. There were more than a dozen of them but Chess could see only two clearly.

In front of her stood a boulder of a man in black body armour that encased him up to his neck. He was as tall as a trader and his timber-thick shoulders were as wide as Chess was long. Each of his battering ram forearms was buried in the mechanism of a plasma punch the size of a motorbike engine with a trumpet-shaped barrel like a blunderbuss. His neck was buttressed with ribbed muscle and his head was broad across his nose and brow like a bull's. The bone of his skull swept blade-smooth up from his nose and over to the back of his head where it knuckled in segments down his neck and into his armour. He surveyed the territory, swinging the plasma punches right and left as if they were as light as handguns.

Next to him stood a thin woman in grey combat fatigues. She had long, yellow hair and crimson eyes with no pupils. Her skin was chalk-white and her face was sunken beneath high, sharp cheekbones. She was holding a monitor with a screen that displayed data in fluorescent green lines and dots and which spoke in a language that Chess didn't understand. She studied the monitor and paid no attention to Chess.

Beneath her there hovered a metal tube the size of a tank. It had neither wings nor rotor blades but it stayed level in mid-air. Two more of these armoured pods hovered overhead.

Chess saw all of this in the time it took for her to fill her lungs with air so that she could scream.

As the ruins of the factory and the file of mountains and the low, red sun blinked out of existence, Chess yelled, 'Stop.' But it was too late. The snatch squad had done their job. They were taking her away. But only her. Box and Splinter weren't with her because when she had pressed the VAP, Splinter's hand was no longer touching her shoulder.

CHAPTER 19

Voices in the darkness.

Chess could hear two people talking. The sound was muffled as if she was listening through water. It was a woman and a man and they were arguing. The first voice she heard clearly was the man's.

'It has started to go wrong. We were meant to hide her from them.'

Then the woman spoke. 'You don't understand. They would have found her anyway. But they never expected this. Nothing like this has ever happened to them before.'

The man said, 'Had you seen this? Did you send her, knowing this would happen?'

They are talking about me, thought Chess. It felt as if she was swimming up to the voices now. They were louder and seemed closer and she recognized them.

'The fifth node is approaching,' said Ethel. 'Time is running out. They nearly had her, Joachim, but we outmanoeuvred them. What has happened, what will happen, is part of a sequence of moves. They have planned it very carefully. So have I. They never expected this. She is already much stronger than they thought.'

'She is not some gambit pawn,' warned Joachim in his thick, guttural voice. 'And do not think that you are so clever, Mevrad, that the enemy cannot be thinking ahead of you.'

'I know that, Joachim, and I know how precious she is but I see how this ends.' Ethel spoke in a way that meant the argument was settled, as far as she was concerned.

Now Chess became aware of a prickling sensation in her right hand, as if it was being jabbed gently by hundreds of pins. It didn't hurt but it felt unusual. It made her want to know what was happening. Surfacing from semi-consciousness, she opened her eyes.

She was lying under thin sheets on a metal-framed bed and she was wearing a short-sleeved hospital night dress. Above her a bright lamp with a conical shade hung from the ceiling. All around the bed were tall monitors and computer units flashing with data. Figures in long white lab coats moved within the darkness beyond the monitors, like ghosts.

Chess's right arm was strapped to an iron bar that held it out of the bed, perpendicular to her body. The bar was supported by wires strung from a frame that was bolted to the ceiling above the bed. At intervals plastic tubes ran from the iron and into her arm where they were fixed in place by surgical tape. At the end of the bar and standing on a table was a white box. Her right hand was inside this. The box was slightly bigger than a shoe box and was made of metal. It fastened around her wrist firmly with a rubber cuff.

Ethel was standing close to the head end of the bed. Her

grey hair was dishevelled and it clustered in greasy tufts that stuck out from the sides of her head and around her face. The light from the lamp overhead glinted on her spectacle lenses where they were not smudged with oily streaks. She was wearing a tatty frock that was patterned with flowers.

At the foot of the bed, Joachim Breslaw sat in his wheelchair, face florid, ginger moustache sprouting over his mouth, hands folded over his barrel of a belly, one good eye looking straight at Chess.

'Where's Box? Where's Splinter?' asked Chess.

Ethel sat on a chair that was by the left side of the bed. 'Well dear, I was beginning to wonder whether you'd left us for good. You've been very busy, I must say.'

'Box? Splinter?' repeated Chess, trying to sit up but discovering that there was no strength in her shoulders. The iron bar attached to her right arm made it difficult to move. She flopped back onto the flat pillow.

'You tell me, dear? They weren't with you when the snatch squad recovered you.'

Chess thought that Ethel did not look pleased about this. 'I don't know,' Chess explained. 'They were meant to be with me. Splinter had hold of me and Box had hold of Splinter and then the moment I pressed the VAP, Splinter wasn't touching me any more. He must have slipped or something,'

'Do you really think so, dear?'

Chess didn't reply at first. She was remembering the way that Splinter had looked at her just before she pressed the VAP. Then she said, 'Well, he's lost now.'

'Splinter was lost a long time ago.' Ethel sighed.

'Both of them are lost. I don't know what's happened to them.' Suddenly, Chess felt very tired and very alone. 'I don't know what's happened at all.' Her voice choked.

Joachim Breslaw leant forwards and placed a big pink hand on the sheets that covered her ankles. 'You must be very tired still,' he said in a gentle voice. 'She is upset, Mevrad,' and he patted Chess's feet and struggled a smile.

'Of course she's upset,' replied Ethel. 'I can see that.' Then, to Chess, 'I don't know what's happened to your brothers. We sent a snatch squad back to look for them, but they weren't there.' She squeezed Chess's shoulder. 'I'm sorry, dear.'

'He's got them,' groaned Chess.

'Who's got them?' enquired Ethel.

'The General. I know he has.'

Ethel looked over to Joachim who raised his eyebrows and hunched his shoulders. 'You met General Vane did you, dear?'

Chess nodded. 'In a way.'

'Goodness,' remarked Ethel. 'You really have been busy, haven't you? Quite the little socialite.'

'The General will have taken them prisoner. He'll have taken them to the Twisted Symmetry.' Chess felt dizzy. She imagined what the Symmetry could do; the sort of punishments they might inflict on her brothers. 'We have to help them, Ethel. We've got to look for them. Please.' She tried to sit up again but when she lifted her head it ached and she felt sick. She pushed her head back into the pillow and closed her eyes.

'The girl must rest, Mevrad,' urged Joachim. 'She is recovering from shift-sickness and her body has to adapt to all the changes. She does not require interrogation by you.'

Chess did feel tired; too tired to ask where she was or what was happening to her hand inside the white metal box or what was going to happen to her now.

Ethel stroked Chess's hair and pushed it away from her forehead. 'Of course you're tired. Joachim's right, he usually is, he is a professor after all, dear. You must be exhausted.' She spoke tenderly. 'I'm sorry your brothers aren't here, Chess; sorry for you. It's been very worrying, for all of us. There has been so much at stake and you have had to do more than anyone expected.'

She placed the flat of her hand on Chess's forehead. Groggy heat flowed from Ethel's palm into Chess's skin and through her body. It eased her muscles and stilled her mind.

'Sleep,' said Ethel.

The room was suffused with an ash-grey light when next she opened her eyes. She was still lying on the bed but the machines had gone. Chess recognized the room now; the low ceiling, the concrete floor and the windows covered with iron mesh. It was where she and her brothers had met Joachim and Julius, the first time that Ethel had brought them to the Committee HQ, at the old city bus depot.

Beside the bed was the table with the white box that contained her right hand. Her arm was no longer attached to the iron bar but hung limp between her body and the box. It was dappled with purple-brown bruises from shoulder to wrist and at the centre of each big bruise was a patch of sticking plaster.

Next to the bed there was a hard wooden chair. Ethel was sitting in the chair and she was knitting. Beneath the clacking of the needles was the soft cooing and churring of the three pigeons which were roosting on top of the iron window mesh, pink feet bright against their tarmac bodies.

Leaning with his back against the wall next to the window was the bull-faced figure Chess had seen in the snatch squad. Now, he was wearing a pair of trousers that were so thick they seemed to be quilted. Save for these he was naked. His torso was immense, with fins of muscle flanking his ribs and curving slabs of chest that were partly exposed bone and partly flesh. The more that Chess looked at him, the more he reminded her of a picture she had seen in a museum window in which the bones and muscles of a human body were displayed without their covering of skin. His body was a combination of grey bone and heavy, brown, fibrous muscle. He looked incredibly ugly and incredibly strong.

One of his feet was drawn up against the wall so that his thigh and knee jutted out and over the top of this thigh rested a plasma punch. With the cooling tubes which ridged its broad mechanism it was as thick as a tree trunk but he was strong enough to rest it over his leg with ease. He caught her eye and winked.

Beyond the foot of the bed, at the far end of the room, was the door that she and her brothers had hidden behind, to listen to the Committee's plans when they had first come here, months ago. The door was shut now and standing in front of it was the woman with the long yellow hair and glassy red eyes who had also been part of the snatch squad.

Her slender body was absolutely still. She didn't even blink. She just kept staring in Chess's direction.

'Don't mind her, dear,' said Ethel, head still bent over her knitting, 'she's on our side. She and Lats have been on watch every since you were brought here. We can't be too careful now. The enemy may strike at any time.'

But the enemy already had her brothers; Chess knew it. 'What are you going to do about Box and Splinter?'

'We shall discuss that later.' Ethel was equally blunt.

Chess huffed and slumped noisily into the bedding. It didn't seem right that Ethel was so guarded when Chess had done so much for the Committee; for her.

'How long have I been here?' she muttered. There couldn't be any objection to that question.

'A bit more than a week,' replied Ethel, needles clicking. 'Before that you spent a week at the orbital rescue station the snatch squad recovered you to.' Ethel placed her needles on top of the ball of wool that rested on her lap and she looked at Chess over the rim of her spectacles. 'You were in a bad way, dear. Your hand was severely damaged and you had lost a lot of blood, your energy level was dangerously low and you had an acute attack of shift sickness.'

'What's shift sickness?' Apart from the prickling sensation in her right hand and an ache in her right shoulder from where her arm had been held rigid, out of the bed, Chess felt good. As she moved beneath the sheets, her body felt bigger. Stronger. Her concern was for her brothers.

'There can be side effects when you move from one place to another or from one time to another. It's rare but it can happen, particularly when the movement is extremely fast and particularly when you don't come back the way you went. You have been badly affected. Then again,' added Ethel, 'the snatch squad have to do their snatching quickly, and you could hardly have come back via the Fat Gobster, could you?'

'Well, I feel all right now.'

'Yes, dear,' said Ethel, who didn't sound convinced, 'you probably do. There has been a lot of medical intervention and the sickness has been treated, but there have been ... how can I put this? There have been changes.'

Before Chess could say any more, a man in a white coat walked round from behind the bed. He had been out of sight until now although when she thought about it, she had been aware, vaguely, of a presence at the back of the room. The man was carrying a polythene tub the size of a wastepaper bin.

'It's ready, Ethel,' he said. He didn't look at Chess but she looked at him. His face was long and thin with expressionless eyes. The sort of face you get after doing too many experiments, thought Chess.

'Good. The timing is perfect, Mr Stillson. Our patient is wide awake and feeling well.' Then, turning to Chess, Ethel said, 'Now dear, about your hand.'

Chess looked to where her wrist ended at the rubber mouth of the box. 'What about my hand?'

'I'm afraid that we've had to change it.'

'Change it? Because of the shift sickness?'

'No dear. The shift sickness brought about other changes. Your hand was damaged by shrapnel. Lucky it was only the hand that was hit. But hit it was. By the time you had been recovered to the rescue station your hand wasn't much of a hand.' Ethel took hold of Chess's left hand and gave it a squeeze. 'Best to remove it altogether and give you a new one.'

Chess looked from Ethel to the white box on the other side of the bed and back to Ethel again.

'Well, let's see it then.'

Ethel beamed at her. 'That's the spirit. Full of surprises.' Then, smile vanishing she said, 'Not what I'd expected at all. You're quite unpredictable, even by my standards. It's strange; does time repeat itself because we make it do so or would it repeat itself even if we weren't here?' Ethel sighed. 'So much of this has happened before.'

Mr Stillson coughed loudly.

'What's the matter, Mr Stillson?' enquired Ethel. 'Bored by an old woman's ramblings?'

'Sorry, Ethel,' apologized the man in the white coat, 'but this has to be fitted now.' He indicated the cylindrical tub that he was holding with a jerk of his head.

'I know, I know,' agreed Ethel. 'I was merely contemplating matters of universal and timeless magnitude. But science and Mr Stillson wait for no man, or woman.' She stuffed her knitting under the chair and slapped her thighs with her hands. 'Do they, Mr Stillson?'

Mr Stillson shrugged.

Ethel stood up and walked round the bed to the table. She fiddled with something at the back of the box. 'What you've got now is state of the art, my love.' She fiddled some more before complaining, 'Why can't they make release mechanisms that are easier to open? This needs a drop of oil, Mr Stillson.'

'Just whack it, Ethel,' said the technician.

Ethel regarded him severely, her spectacles balanced on the end of her nose. 'Thank you for that piece of advice. Very helpful. I'm glad you're not a dentist. Aha!' she exclaimed as Chess heard a catch snap open. 'Bingo!'

There was the sound of metal moving inside the box, like bolts being drawn, and Chess gasped as what had been a gentle prickling sensation over her right hand changed to one of intense pressure. Then there was a hiss of air escaping and Ethel lifted off the top half of the box.

Chess wriggled her fingers and then squeezed them tight into a fist before stretching her hand wide open and raising it from the bottom half of the box. Her arm was stiff and the elbow ached as she bent it and drew her new hand towards her face.

Where the flesh of her wrist ended there was a hand that was bright and shiny and silver. Chess turned it to see the back and front. It was contoured just like a normal hand with a pad of muscle at the base of the thumb and with wrinkles across the palm and whorls of fingerprints on the tip of each finger. Silver cords of tendon flexed on the back of the metallic hand, just as they would have done on her own hand. Except that this *was* her own hand now. When she straightened her new fingers, small folds rutted the knuckles just like they did on her old hand.

Chess touched her face with the hand and was surprised to discover that the hand was not cold like metal but as warm as it used to be.

'I like it,' Chess said, holding her arm above her head and drumming the fingers in the air. 'It looks like Julius's hand.

Except he's got two like this and a silver head.'

'Those who resist the Twisted Symmetry lose parts of their bodies, dear. But those who surrender to the Twisted Symmetry lose parts of their soul.' Then Ethel added, 'Julius's hands are not quite the same as yours. His are specially modified.'

'It feels exactly like a real hand,' reported Chess, still wiggling the fingers.

'Good. That's exactly as it should be, my love. This has been designed so that it feels and functions just like your old hand. Of course, there are differences. It won't bleed if you cut it, the fingerprints aren't the same as they were and it can't be damaged by cold. Intense heat will damage it but normal fire won't.'

'It does look different,' observed Chess and then, so as not to appear ungrateful she added, 'being silver, I mean.'

'Not for much longer, dear,' announced Ethel. 'Mr Stillson?'

Mr Stillson rested the polythene tub on the bed and unscrewed the lid. When he removed it, Chess could see an ultra-violet glow which emanated from inside.

'Sit up dear,' requested Ethel, politely.

Chess shuffled her bottom up the mattress and pushed with her legs so that she was leaning against the iron framed head of the bedstead. As she did so she had a feeling that something was out of place. There was an awkwardness about her body but she couldn't decide what it was.

When she was comfortable and the bed had stopped shaking, Mr Stillson pulled a wire hoop out of the tub. Drooping from the hoop was a pale-pink membrane, as fine as a cast-off snake-skin but slimy and dripping with viscous liquid.

'Hand out,' commanded Ethel.

Chess eyed the gooey membrane with suspicion but did as she was told. Mr Stillson took hold of her forearm to keep the silver hand steady. His fingers were cold and his grip was hard. He positioned the hoop so that its centre was directly in front of the tips of her fingers. Then he drew the hoop over her hand so that her hand went through the middle and into the membrane. He took the hoop up to just above her wrist. The substance that was hanging from it coated her fingers and thumb and the front and back of her hand until it was covering the skin of her wrist.

'It's freezing,' gasped Chess.

'It's liquid skin,' explained Ethel. 'You'll warm it up quickly. Just keep your hand out like that whilst it sets. It only takes a couple of minutes, doesn't it, Mr Stillson?'

Mr Stillson grunted in agreement. He was concentrating on holding the hoop still as the last drops of the liquid skin drained onto Chess's wrist.

'It will look like your own skin when it's dry and it will work the same although it won't bleed if it's cut. But it will repair itself if it gets torn so don't worry about that.'

'Thanks,' said Chess, quietly, watching the skin drying. Where it had been glistening like fresh mucus it was darkening and moulding itself to the contours and wrinkles of her new hand. Mr Stillson removed the hoop from her arm, put it back inside the glowing tub and replaced the lid. Then he marched behind the bed. Chess could hear him shuffling at the back of the room.

'Now, dear, whilst we wait for that to dry, I want you to answer some questions for me.'

Ethel proceeded to ask Chess questions about everything that had happened to her and her brothers. The questioning went on long after the liquid skin had dried and night had draped the iron-meshed windows. All the time, Lats and the woman with the red eyes remained in their positions.

Chess realized that Ethel knew already or had guessed a lot of what had happened.

'If I had my way, I'd smash their child-stealing operation,' announced Chess, after she had told Ethel about what the Twisted Symmetry did in the factory. 'I'd make sure they don't hurt any more children.'

Ethel adjusted her spectacles. 'You've become very bullish, dear. And I'm sure you *could* do a good deal more to inconvenience the enemy. But you're not going to be having your way.'

'But if we stop them getting children, they won't have the energy they need.'

'It's not as simple as that.'

'I think it is,' said Chess. It seemed obvious.

But Ethel was more interested to hear about General Vane and the thing that looked like a face with long black legs. 'Aha! A messenger. The General has secret business of his own,' she said mysteriously.

She was less impressed by Balthazar Broom. 'The man is a fool, and clever, which makes him a dangerous fool.'

Chess couldn't bring herself to disagree so she explained how kind he had been. But when she complained that it didn't seem fair for him to have been exiled for a thousand years Ethel said, 'Fairness doesn't come into it. It was just. Justice is not the same thing as fairness, dear.' And when Chess told Ethel about the skulk rack and how it had made her look at the Narrow Man who had no eyes, Ethel stamped her sandalled foot and snapped, 'That is bad. That is very bad,' as if nothing else had been bad at all. 'His interest in this is not what I had expected; not yet, anyway. Broom is a bigger fool that I thought.'

'Did you plan for me to find Balthazar?' Chess was not going to let all the blame lie with Balthazar.

'I have planned so much,' replied Ethel, wearily. 'There are millions of possibilities and I have considered them all. The possibility that you might meet Broom was one of them. But I had bargained on five hundred years having taught him something.'

'He helped us.'

'I don't think he did, dear,' said Ethel, patiently, 'but that is my fault.' Then she patted Chess's hand. 'But you are very powerful, my love. Stronger than anyone realized.'

Chess took a sip of a tooth-grindingly sweet drink that had been handed to her by Mr Stillson. 'I don't feel it,' she said and then asked, 'Why am I like this? Why am I able to do what I did?'

'Because that is how you have been made,' replied Ethel.

'That's not much of an answer,' grunted Chess. Behrens had been right about one thing; she wasn't going to get the full picture from Ethel. But she wanted the full picture. Chess had had enough of Ethel's secrets.

Ethel was watching her over the rim of the glass from

which she was drinking. 'Was there anybody else you met, dear?'

Chess hesitated. There was someone else, someone who had shown her kindness, someone who had been brave. But someone whom she was not sure about. She sensed that Ethel wanted to know about this person.

'No,' said Chess, cool as a market-day pickpocket. 'There was no one else.' We can both play secrets, she thought. Saul was going to stay her secret.

'Hmm,' mused Ethel, eyes still searching Chess's face. 'Funny. I thought there might have been.'

'Well there wasn't,' lied Chess and then she said, 'Are we allowed to talk about my brothers now? What are you going to do about them?'

'Mr Stillson?' called Ethel, standing back from Chess. 'Pistol, please,' and then to Chess, 'Don't be alarmed, I don't want it for you, dear.'

Mr Stillson opened his coat to reveal a shoulder holster that contained a black, semi-automatic pistol. Ethel drew the weapon and placed it on the sheets at the foot of the bed, near to where she was standing.

'We cannot find your brothers. Not yet.'

'We have to,' insisted Chess.

'We can't,' repeated Ethel, raising her voice. 'Do you realize how much danger you are in? What you did to Behrens has never happened before. But as a result, the Twisted Symmetry know exactly who you are and they will do everything they can to find out where you are. There is not one rock anywhere in the universes that they will leave unturned. And now, it seems, a very troublesome player has emerged; this Narrow Man as you call him. They are all working together.

'But time is running out. Behrens's loss will destabilize the Symmetry. And they must find you before the fifth node passes or it will be too late. So the Committee have decided that you must be hidden. After the fifth node has passed it will be safe to find your brothers.'

'But I can't just forget about Box and Splinter.'

'If the Symmetry catch you, all of this is over,' fired Ethel, angrily. Chess felt the hairs on the back of her neck tingle. 'Everything. Not just Box and Splinter but everyone. Your world is gone, including you and your brothers. Stop the Symmetry from finding you and we might save your brothers. But if they get you ...'

Chess remembered that she was not arguing with an old bag lady called Ethel: she was arguing with the Baroness Mevrad Styx whose power spanned time and the universes. This was not an argument that she was going to win. But she had had enough of the truth being hidden from her; enough of being used. She would do this her way; she would find out who she really was, she would find her brothers, and she would stop the Twisted Symmetry from stealing children; she would stop whatever happened in the scream rooms. She knew she could do this. She was going to fight the Twisted Symmetry even if the Committee wouldn't. But she knew better than to say any of this to Ethel.

'OK. I'll do what you want,' lied Chess, again. 'What happens next?'

'We have to keep you out of the way, for the time being.'

'How long's that?'

'By our calculations, rounding up, thirteen months and twelve days. Then this will be over. Jones will stay with you.'

'Jones?'

Ethel pointed to the woman in front of the door. 'It's not her real name, dear. She doesn't have what you would call a name. She isn't like you; she's not human although she looks a bit like one. She comes from a plane that you would think was an equation. Her sense of the world is entirely mathematical. She experiences data, not sounds or smells or things that you see. She calculates, she doesn't think. Her real name is a mathematical proposition that has no sound at all but translated it would be something like "Many Numbers Beautifully Returning". I think "Jones" suits her very well, don't you? She will be on Close Protection Duties. We will try to keep you hidden but wherever you go, Jones will be there to protect you.'

To guard me, more like, thought Chess. To make sure I stay where the Committee want me.

'She is trained in close-quarter battle and because she is a preactive, she is always one step ahead of the game.'

'A preactive?'

'Normal people have reactions,' explained Ethel, 'but because Jones processes data from the world around her extremely rapidly, she can react to events moments before they happen. She has preactions.'

'Like reading the future?'

'Not like that dear, no. She doesn't know what will happen next week or tomorrow or even in one minute's time. But she can react just before someone decides to do something.'

Ethel snatched the pistol from the foot of the bed and

spun round to fire two rounds at the place where Jones was standing. The abrupt bangs reverberated through the room and sent the pigeons flapping round the low ceiling before they returned to their perch on the wire mesh. A chunk of ceiling crumbled over Ethel's head, the plaster-dust sprinkling her hair and her floral dress. She used her free hand to pat it off the faded fabric.

Chess saw that Jones had stepped aside even as Ethel was pulling the trigger. Two bullet holes marked the spot on the door in front of which she had been standing. Now she stood in front of the adjacent piece of wall, her glassy, red eyes unblinking, her lithe body absolutely still.

Getting away from you is going to be difficult, thought Chess.

'That was a preaction, dear,' explained Ethel, offering the pistol to Mr Stillson who retrieved it from her, handing her a fresh cup of tea at the same time. 'You could say that it is a reaction before something has actually happened. Very handy. Whatever the situation, Jones will be ahead of everyone else.'

Chess sneezed. Dust had got up her nose. It was a shrieking-loud volley of a sneeze and it echoed round the room. Jones's head jerked to one side as the sneeze erupted.

'She didn't know I was going to do that,' snorted Chess, rubbing the water from her eyes.

'She's there to help you, dear,' said Ethel with a stern look.

'Thanks,' muttered Chess.

'Do you think you're strong enough to walk, my love?'

'I feel stronger than ever,' said Chess who was surprised at how fit she felt. She flexed her legs and stretched her arms.

'You've been at HQ for too long. We have to move *now*. The Committee have made all the necessary arrangements: we need to get you out of here whilst we still can. The enemy are coming.'

'But everything's quiet,' observed Chess.

'It usually is, before they arrive. The noise starts once they get here. Mr Stillson, would you bring the clothes?' Ethel patted Chess's bare arm. 'We can't have you walking the streets in a hospital night dress, can we dear? So, I've splashed out; a new pair of jeans and a T-shirt. Well, new for you, that is. I bought them from a charity shop. Real bargains. Amazing what you can find. It's all a question of knowing where to look,' and she tapped the side of her small nose confidentially.

Mr Stillson approached the bed bearing the clothes which he placed next to Chess.

'Up you get then,' said Ethel. She paused, pursed her lips and then said, 'We'll look away whilst you put them on.'

'Were you going to say something else?' asked Chess as she began to slide her legs out of the bed.

'Nothing in particular, dear,' replied Ethel, airily, and she turned her back towards Chess.

Chess could see behind the bed-head now. Mr Stillson was occupied with packing cables and small monitors with glass dials into stout cardboard boxes that were stacked on a table against the rear wall of the long room. Also on the table was the polythene tub, a kettle, a tray with glasses, mugs, a bag of sugar and a bottle of milk and a small, automatic machine gun.

Lats was inspecting the ends of his fingers. Jones was watching Chess, red eyes never closing.

Chess pulled the night dress over her head and let it fall onto the pillow behind her. The room felt cold now, but she didn't pull on the T-shirt straightaway. She didn't do anything apart from stare at her body.

'I'm different,' she said, bluntly. She had known that something had happened but with all the talking and with everything that had been going on she had not realized what it was. Now she could see it. 'I'm ... I'm ...'

'Older, dear,' said Ethel, helpfully. 'You're older. About two years older. I said that there had been changes. It does happen, sometimes, when you don't come back the way you went and when you don't take precautions. It's my fault. I didn't think of this, dear. I never expected it.'

Chess was silent. Then she said, 'Neither did I.'

'You were away for about four weeks, by our time. But travelling can do strange things to a body. By our measurements you are nearly thirteen and a half now. It's only two years but that makes quite a difference to a body at your time of life. I am sorry, dear.'

Chess moved her arms and legs and felt how much bigger and stronger they were. She looked at her new shape and then at her clothes.

'I've missed two birthdays,' she observed.

'I'm sorry about that as well,' apologized Ethel.

'Don't be,' said Chess. 'I hate birthdays. I don't get presents, I don't get cards and I don't have parents.'

'Well,' said Ethel cheerily, 'you've got new clothes today, so maybe we can call this you birthday. Happy birthday!'

'Happy birthday,' echoed Mr Stillson from the back of the room, his white-coated back towards Chess.

'Thanks,' said Chess. So what if she was two years older? She was bigger and stronger and she liked the way she had changed. She shook open the T-shirt with her new right hand and pulled it over her head, tugging her long brown hair out from where it was trapped under the neck. Then she pulled on the jeans.

'They fit me,' she said, standing up. Then she had to lean forwards, with the palms of her hands on the mattress because her head swam and her thigh muscles felt weak.

'Easy does it,' Ethel encouraged her, walking round the bed to rub her back. 'Your body's been through a lot.'

'You're telling me,' said Chess, breathing slowly before standing upright again. Then she sat on the edge of the bed and looked up at Ethel. 'These aren't new clothes really, are they?' she said quietly.

'Well, no, not if you're being technical about it,' admitted Ethel, suspiciously.

'And I have missed two birthdays, haven't I?' continued Chess.

'You have,' admitted Ethel, 'although I'd have thought that for someone who doesn't like birthdays, that wouldn't matter.'

And I've lost my brothers and I'm going to find them whether you want me to or not, thought Chess, still smiling sweetly at Ethel. But what she said was, 'You could buy me a leather jacket and a pair of trainers; as special presents. Then you could take me to wherever you're going to take me.'

'Could I now?' replied Ethel.

'Yes,' said Chess, definitely. She thought about what Splinter had said to her in the jungle; that she was a street rat and that would never change. 'I'm not going to steal them. They're going to be presents, from you to me.'

'They would be very expensive presents,' observed Ethel, 'and I am a very poor and elderly lady.'

'Ethel,' said Chess, 'you are not poor and you are not elderly. You are one of the most powerful people in the universe.'

'In the universes,' Ethel corrected her. 'Anyway, that's not the point.'

'Well, I think it is,' insisted Chess. 'After everything that's happened it's not wrong to ask for a present.'

Ethel had taken the small tartan purse out of a hip pocket in her frock and she held it in front of her nose as she looked inside it.

'It's not wrong, is it?' repeated Chess.

'Right and wrong,' Ethel muttered to herself, 'everything comes down to right and wrong.' Then she looked over the brass clasp of the purse and frowned at Chess. 'A leather jacket *and* a pair of trainers?' she asked. But a smile played at the corner of her mouth.

Chess nodded.

'I'll see what I can do,' said Ethel.

N'APPARTIENT PLUS
À LA BIBLIOTHÈQUE
MUNICIPALE DE GATINEAU